"I would never settle for a marriage of convenience, which is what you are suggesting," Missy said.

Wade lifted one shoulder. He hadn't suggested it at all. He simply wanted her to stop hammering on her opinion that he should find a way to keep the children. "It's what you're suggesting on my behalf."

"That's different."

"How?"

She didn't get the opportunity to answer as in the distance, the house door banged shut.

She jerked her gaze away. "The children... Are you coming back in?"

When he didn't answer, she met his look again, her eyes full of hopes and wishes and, as he looked deeper, a hint of a challenge. He averted his eyes before she could see his doubt, the depth of his failure, his sorrow, the emptiness of his heart.

If only he could allow himself to think of marrying again. It would enable him to keep the children.

But both were out of the question.

D0051991

Linda Ford lives on a ranch in Alberta, Canada, near enough to the Rocky Mountains that she can enjoy them on a daily basis. She and her husband raised fourteen children—four homemade, ten adopted. She currently shares her home and life with her husband, a grown son, a live-in paraplegic client and a continual (and welcome) stream of kids, kids-in-law, grandkids, and assorted friends and relatives.

Books by Linda Ford

Love Inspired Historical

Christmas in Eden Valley

A Daddy for Christmas
A Baby for Christmas
A Home for Christmas

Journey West

Wagon Train Reunion

Montana Marriages

Big Sky Cowboy
Big Sky Daddy
Big Sky Homecoming

Cowboys of Eden Valley

The Cowboy's Surprise Bride
The Cowboy's Unexpected Family
The Cowboy's Convenient Proposal
Claiming the Cowboy's Heart
Winning Over the Wrangler
Falling for the Rancher Father

Visit the Author Profile page at Harlequin.com for more titles.

LINDA FORD

A Home for Christmas

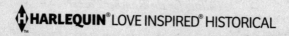

HARLEQUIN® LOVE INSPIRED® HISTORICAL

If you purchased this book without a cover you should be aware that this book is stolen property. It was reported as "unsold and destroyed" to the publisher, and neither the author nor the publisher has received any payment for this "stripped book."

LOVE INSPIRED BOOKS

Recycling programs
for this product may
not exist in your area.

ISBN-13: 978-0-373-28338-5

A Home for Christmas

Copyright © 2015 by Linda Ford

All rights reserved. Except for use in any review, the reproduction or utilization of this work in whole or in part in any form by any electronic, mechanical or other means, now known or hereinafter invented, including xerography, photocopying and recording, or in any information storage or retrieval system, is forbidden without the written permission of the editorial office, Love Inspired Books, 233 Broadway, New York, NY 10279 U.S.A.

This is a work of fiction. Names, characters, places and incidents are either the product of the author's imagination or are used fictitiously, and any resemblance to actual persons, living or dead, business establishments, events or locales is entirely coincidental.

This edition published by arrangement with Love Inspired Books.

® and TM are trademarks of Love Inspired Books, used under license. Trademarks indicated with ® are registered in the United States Patent and Trademark Office, the Canadian Intellectual Property Office and in other countries.

www.Harlequin.com

Printed in U.S.A.

We may even call each other friend again someday. But until then, it'd probably be for the best if you live your life and I live mine." She backed away. "Speaking of that, I need to go and console Mandy." Taking one step, she halted. "*Danki* for letting her name the cow. That made her happier than I've seen her since…"

She didn't finish. She didn't have to. His heart cramped as he thought of the sorrow haunting both Leah and Mandy. They had both lost someone very dear to them, the person Leah had once described to him as "the other half of myself."

The very least he could do was agree to her request that was to everyone's benefit. Even though he knew she was right, he also knew there was no way he could ignore Leah Beiler.

Yet, somehow, he needed to figure out how to do exactly that.

Don't miss
AMISH HOMECOMING by Jo Ann Brown,
available January 2016 wherever
Love Inspired® books and ebooks are sold.

Copyright © 2016 by Harlequin Books, S.A.

LIEXP1215R

SPECIAL EXCERPT FROM

Love Inspired

*Desperate for help in raising her niece, Leah Beiler
goes back to her Amish roots in Paradise Springs,
Pennsylvania—and the boy next door who she's never
forgotten. Could this be their second chance at forever?*

*Read on for a sneak preview of
AMISH HOMECOMING by Jo Ann Brown,
available in January 2016 from Love Inspired!*

"In spite of what she said, my niece knows I love her, and she's already beginning to love her family here. Mandy will adjust soon to the Amish way of life."

"And what about you?"

Leah frowned at Ezra. "What do you mean? I'm happy to be back home, and I don't have much to adjust to other than the quiet at night. Philadelphia was noisy."

"I wasn't talking about that." He hesitated, not sure how to say what he wanted without hurting her feelings.

"Oh." Her smile returned, but it was unsteady. "You're talking about us. We aren't *kinder* any longer, Ezra. I'm sure we can be reasonable about this strange situation we find ourselves in," she said in a tone that suggested she wasn't as certain as she sounded. Uncertain of him or of herself?

"I agree."

"We are neighbors again. We're going to see each other regularly, but it'd be better if we keep any encounters to a minimum." She faltered before hurrying on. "Who knows?

Sing to God, sing in praise of His name, extol Him
who rides on the clouds; rejoice before Him—
His name is the Lord. A father to the fatherless,
a defender of widows, is God in His holy dwelling.
God sets the lonely in families.
—*Psalms* 68:4–6

To my readers:
may you find the real joy that Christmas brings.

Chapter One

❧

Christmas 1882
Eden Valley Ranch, Edendale, Alberta

"We aren't having Christmas this year, are we, Uncle Wade?" Joey asked the question, but his sister, Annie, regarded Wade with both anxiety and accusation in her big brown eyes.

"Joey, I'm doing the best I can." It was Christmas Day and Wade Snyder had failed to give the young children a home and a family. His failure hung about his shoulders like a water-soaked blanket.

Joey hung his head and mumbled under his breath, but Wade heard him. "That means no and we aren't supposed to be upset."

Wade had done everything he could to see that his recently orphaned niece and nephew were settled someplace for Christmas, but all his attempts of the past three months had met with failure. The Bauers, a couple from Fort Macleod who expressed an interest in adopting the pair, had failed to appear on the latest stagecoach. Instead, they'd sent a letter saying

they would be there at a later date. One they failed to give him.

With that plan scuttled, he'd thought to spend the day with his friend Lane, a single man like himself, but Lane had other plans. He'd been invited to spend Christmas with a family that had recently moved in south of Lane and had a beautiful, marriageable-aged daughter.

As if those disappointments weren't enough to contend with, Wade had encountered a young lady in Edendale who had overheard him explaining to the children that he would be leaving and they couldn't go with him.

A pretty young thing with blue-green eyes and a halo of golden hair. Not that he'd given her more than a passing glance. She'd confronted him, her eyes flashing with a whole lot of emotions that he pretended not to notice.

"You need to give these children the assurance they aren't a nuisance," she'd said. "They've lost their parents. Shouldn't that be reason enough to make a few sacrifices on their behalf?"

He'd edged past her before she could say more. How had she learned so much about the children in the few minutes he'd been in the store? And what did she know about what he should or shouldn't do? Or what he could or could not do, for that matter? He hadn't even been able to look after his wife, a full-grown woman. How could he hope to take care of two children? Besides, one would only have to take a look at his cowboy way of life to know he couldn't give his niece and nephew a home.

He turned the wagon toward the west. For several

turns of the wheels on the frozen ground he allowed himself to wish things could be different and he could keep Joey and little Annie. They were all the family he had left. But the plain and simple truth was he couldn't care for them.

No, he'd do what was best for the kids.

Once the two were taken care of, he would ride up into the hills where his friend Stuart ran a ranch. Every year, after a few weeks visiting his sister and enjoying Christmas with her and her family, Wade took over for Stuart while he went south to visit his mother.

Every year, Stuart made him the same offer. "Throw in with me. We'll be partners. It's time you settled down."

Every year, Wade refused. He'd once had a home of his own, a wife and dreams of a family. All his hopes had come crashing to an end when he discovered his wife dead in their bed. She'd taken her own life. He hadn't even noticed how unhappy she was, had put down her frequent dark moods to the fact she'd failed to get pregnant. He'd done his best to console her and assure her she was all that mattered to him.

Her death taught him a valuable lesson. One he didn't care to repeat. He couldn't look after those he loved. Couldn't judge what they needed. Wasn't enough for them. So he rode all summer for some ranch outfit, spent Christmas with his sister and family, then took Stuart's place on his ranch until spring, when Wade repeated the process. It was what he'd done for the past six of his twenty-six years.

Annie edged forward from the back of the wagon box where the pair had been sitting and perched her elbows on the bench. "Uncle Wade, do you like us?"

A groan tore from his heart but he swallowed back the sound. "Come here." He pulled her to his lap. "You, too, Joey." The boy climbed to the bench and crowded to Wade's side.

Wade hugged them both. "I love you more than you'll ever know."

Annie nestled her head under his chin and sighed. "I miss Mama and Papa." A sob stole the last of her words.

He tightened his arms around the pair. He missed his sister with an unending ache. "I know you do. I do, too." Though his loss was but a fraction of theirs. "I tell you what. I'll spend Christmas with you and we'll have a real good time."

He had purchased popping corn, ribbon candy and some gifts at Macpherson's store. Wade pulled the wagon to a halt and, not knowing what the day might hold, handed them the gifts he'd purchased. Nothing much. A picture book for Annie and a pair of leather mittens with fringes for Joey.

The two smiled and thanked him, though their smiles seemed a little forced. Even a piece of the candy for each didn't give them their usual joy. Presents and games wouldn't replace a mama and a papa, but he'd do his best to help them have a good time. Handing out gifts in a wagon wasn't a great start.

"I was afraid we wouldn't have Christmas," Annie whispered.

"We wouldn't forget to celebrate the birth of baby Jesus." He hadn't told the pair what lay ahead for them except to say they couldn't go with him. He was certain they'd welcome a new mama and papa, but he figured it was too soon after losing their own for them

to see the wisdom of his decision. But hadn't Susan's last words been to demand a promise that he'd see they got a good home?

He turned off at the Eden Valley Ranch trail. Lane had said the people there welcomed strangers and people needing help. Well, he surely needed help if he was to give these kids the Christmas they deserved.

They approached the big house. Several wagons were drawn up to the door.

"Who lives here?" Joey asked as Annie clutched Wade's arm.

"Nice people." He figured they must be nice if they welcomed strangers.

"Do you know them?" Joey persisted.

"Only by reputation."

The boy pressed into Wade's side as if he meant to disappear. Wade's heart squeezed out drops of sorrow and regret. He'd lost his sister and her husband to pneumonia. Susan had been his anchor since his wife died. Four years his senior, she was the only person in the world who made him believe in love and happiness. All that was left of her were her children. He loved them to the very depths of his soul and it about killed him to think of giving them up, but he must do what he'd promised. At that moment, Wade made himself another promise. He would do everything in his power to see that these kids had an extra-special Christmas before they got adopted by a new family.

He pulled the wagon to a halt and jumped down. As soon as the horses were tended to, he lifted the children from the wagon and, with one clutching each hand, crossed the few feet to the house. He stood there staring at the fine wooden door.

"Uncle Wade, aren't you going to knock?" Annie asked.

Wade nodded. He had to do it. Had to have this one last Christmas with them, then let them go. He dropped Joey's hand and rapped on the thick wood.

In a matter of seconds, the door opened. "Howdy, stranger, what can I do for you?" The man there looked and sounded friendly enough.

"I hear you help people."

"We do if we can."

"Then perhaps you'd let us spend Christmas with you. Me and these two children."

"You're more than welcome. Come right in." He threw the door wide and ushered them inside.

Wade felt the eyes of a dozen people upon him but he noticed only one person.

The young lady from town who had scolded him royally. The flash in her eyes informed him she hadn't changed her opinion of him. No doubt she'd see his visit as an opportunity to further chastise him.

His hopes for a pleasant Christmas lay whimpering at his feet.

Missy Porter's mouth dropped open and she stared in a way that was most rude. At eighteen she knew better but she couldn't help herself. It was *that* man. The one she'd spoken to in Edendale after overhearing a conversation between him and his niece and nephew. She'd paid his appearance scant attention then, but now gave it a thorough visual examination. He was tall and lean like an old piece of hickory. He wore a dusty cowboy hat and a denim winter coat, faded almost white where the sleeves folded when he bent his arms. She

noticed a flash of blue as the light hit his eyes. When he took off his hat as soon as he stepped inside, his brown hair looked surprisingly well trimmed as if he'd recently visited a barber. But it was the determination in the set of his jaw that made her clamp her mouth shut and swallow loudly.

He was a hard man. One who would not understand the tender hearts of little children.

She shifted her attention to the two sweet children at his side. With dark brown eyes and dark brown hair, they were almost Spanish looking. The little boy did his best to look brave, while the girl blinked back tears.

Linette Gardiner, hostess and wife of the ranch owner, Eddie, rushed to the trio, her baby cradled in one arm. "Come in. Come in. Let me take your coats." She waited while they shed their outerwear and hung it on the nearby hooks. "Now, whom do we have the pleasure of meeting?"

"Wade Snyder, ma'am, and this is my niece, Annie Lopez, and my nephew, Joey."

"So pleased to meet you." Linette squatted to eye level with the children. "Merry Christmas. I hope you like toys and food because that's what's in store for the day."

"Oh, yes." Little Annie's eyes shone with joy.

Joey grinned widely, then his smile flattened. He leaned back. "Our mama and papa died and we thought we wouldn't have Christmas this year." He shot Wade an accusing look that echoed in Missy's mind. From what she'd overheard, she knew he hadn't planned on spending Christmas with them. It had sounded as if he planned to leave them and ride away. What kind of man would do that?

"I'm sorry to hear about your mama and papa." Linette met Wade's eyes.

"My sister and her husband," he explained.

Linette paused, her hand pressed to her chest as if feeling a sympathetic pain, then turned back to the children. "How old are you two?"

"I'm seven," said the boy. "My sister is five."

"Then you'll fit right in with the other children. Grady is almost six." She indicated the crowd of children playing in one corner.

Joey and Annie clung to Wade's leg.

Linette straightened and stepped back. "When you feel like it, you can join them. In the meantime, come and meet everyone." She introduced Eddie first, then started around the large circle. There were so many young couples—Roper Jones and his wife, Cassie, who had arrived in Linette's company a little over a year ago. Grace and Ward Walker, who lived on a little ranch nearby. Eddie's sister, Jayne, and her new husband, Seth Collins.

As they continued around the circle, introducing yet more newlyweds—Sybil and Brand Duggan, Mercy and Abel Borgard, Blue and Clara Lyons—Missy began to wonder how it was that so many had met and fallen in love on the ranch. She began to suspect there had been active matchmaking going on.

Her own sister-in-law, Louise, had married Nate Hawkins back in Montana, but it wasn't until they reached the ranch that their love became real, which half confirmed the suspicions about the ranch's role in romance. As for herself, Missy had no intention of joining the couples in matrimony.

An older pair was likewise introduced. Cookie and her husband, Bertie, ran the cookhouse.

As they were introduced, each one murmured condolences to Wade and the children, until Missy wondered how the children could stand to hear it one more time.

Missy sat at the far corner. She'd be the last to be introduced and she could hardly draw in a breath as they drew closer to her. All too soon they stood before her.

"And this is Missy Porter," Linette said.

Wade's eyes grew icy and she knew he recognized her. She'd spoken out of turn when she saw him in town. But when she'd heard him inform the children that he'd make sure they were in a safe place before he left, and when she'd heard their voices break as they confessed how they missed the mama and papa they'd so recently lost, an avalanche of unwanted memories had slammed into her. She'd been thirteen when she encountered the same emotion. She would never forget the shock of listening to the preacher explain that her parents had died in an accident.

"The horses bolted and the wagon flipped." The preacher had said more, but Missy stopped listening. The details were too dreadful to hear.

Her brother, Gordie, was not yet eighteen and he'd not been pleased at being saddled with a younger sister to care for. He never let her forget that she was the reason he couldn't live the life he wanted. Not that he did much caring. She took over the cooking and cleaning. He took over earning money to keep them, but soon he hooked up with Vic Hector, a very unlikable man in Missy's opinion, who convinced Gordie there were

easier ways to make money. By "easier," he meant on the shady side of the law.

When Gordie married Louise and she moved in, Missy had truly gained a sister. They shared the household duties and became friends. But now Gordie was dead by a gunshot wound during one of his and Vic's escapades. Louise had remarried and Missy was about to be on her own. She meant to face the future without depending on anyone else.

Except God, she added quickly, lest He think she was being prideful. She certainly didn't mean to be. No, she wasn't going anyplace without God.

There wasn't a doubt in her mind that He had carried them safely on the journey from Rocky Creek, Montana, through a snowstorm and bitter cold. God had protected Louise and baby Chloe from Vic, who'd thought he owned them and Missy. She shivered at the memory of how Vic had treated her, trying to get her alone, and when he did, pressing against her in corners. Then he'd moved into the Porter house and both Missy and Louise knew he'd be taking advantage of the situation. So they'd fled to Eden Valley Ranch.

Never again would Missy allow herself to be made to feel she was an unwelcome burden. No more having others tell her what to do and what not to do, where to go and when and how. No, she had plans that would prevent that.

Before her, the newcomer named Wade tipped his head, breaking into her thoughts. "Nice to make your acquaintance, miss."

She knew she wasn't mistaken in hearing a mocking tone in his words. Hopefully, the others didn't notice. She tipped her head in response. "Likewise, I'm sure."

A flicker of his eyelids informed her he understood her silent message that she was as thrilled as he to be forced to spend Christmas together. Which was not at all.

She turned her attention to the children, wanting to let them know she understood how alone and afraid they were at the moment. "I, too, lost my mama and papa when I was a child."

"What happened to them?" Annie asked, her eyes big with curiosity.

"There was an accident."

The children nodded solemnly.

Joey released a long sigh that ended in a shudder. "Our mama and papa got sick and died." He studied her. "When did yours die?"

"Four years ago." Four and a half and a bit. She used to count the months and weeks and days, but had stopped doing that. Nothing would make her forget them but she had to face the future.

Missy rested her hand over the pocket that contained a piece of paper. She did not need to see it to know what it said.

Miss Evans offers young ladies the opportunity to become self-sufficient and earn twice the salary of a public schoolteacher. You'll learn how to operate a typewriter. Become a secretary and you will be able to get a job anywhere.

Missy had sent in a deposit from the coins she'd been saving for her future. The next class was to begin in March in Toronto, which left her three months to earn the rest of the cost of tuition.

She allowed the tiniest smile to curve her mouth. She'd soon be independent. Her future would be in

her hands, not in the hands of others. A shiver trickled down her spine. Like these children, she knew how
it felt to lose important people in her life. It was best
to be on her own. That way she wouldn't have to deal
with the pain of losing anyone else.

"Ours died a little time ago." Tears rushed to
Joey's eyes.

These children needed so much care and tenderness
at the moment. Turning her gaze back to Wade, Missy
felt her smile flatten, her lips curl downward. He had
made it clear he didn't want these children. Perhaps
he was sending them to relatives—kinder, more loving people. She certainly hoped so.

Annie rocked forward, seeking her attention.

"What is it, child?" Missy asked.

"Did you have Christmas without your mama and
papa?"

Missy knew what the child meant. "I missed them
terribly. I still do. But I know they would want me to
be happy, especially at Christmas."

Annie nodded, satisfied with the answer. "I think
so, too."

Wade took his niece's hand. "Come along, Annie.
You shouldn't bother the lady."

Missy's insides curled at the way Wade made it
sound as if she didn't welcome Annie's questions. Ignoring his warning glance, she brushed her hand over
the girl's shoulder. "You're not a bother to me."

Right then and there, she promised herself she would
do everything in her power to make this a Christmas
Day these children would remember with joy.

The only place left for Wade to sit was next to
Missy. He almost refused Linette's invitation to be

seated, but he had asked to be included in their Christmas. Seemed it meant enduring Missy's narrow-eyed looks. He plunked onto the chair and pulled Annie to his lap. Joey sat on the floor in front of him, watching the other children playing.

Annie turned to regard Missy. "You live here?"

"I'm only visiting. Louise is my sister-in-law." She pointed out a young woman with a tiny baby in her arms and a man hovering adoringly at her side. "She and Nate are going to live at his ranch as soon as he fixes the cabin."

Wade fleetingly wondered if Missy would be living with them.

Annie reached out and fingered the fabric of Missy's dress. "I like your gown. It feels nice."

"It's satin. Royal blue was my mama's favorite color. I like to wear it and remember her."

Annie leaned forward. "Mama's favorite color was pink. I like pink, too. Maybe I'll get a pink dress when I get big. I gots a pink sweater she knitted me. It's my favorite thing."

It was the most Annie had talked since her parents died. Before that she had been a regular chatterbox.

She turned to Wade. "Where's my pink sweater?"

He had no idea. The neighboring women had helped him pack up the children's things. "I expect it's in one of your bags."

"In the wagon?"

"Yes. Everything is under a tarp." He wanted to reassure her that her belongings were safe.

"Oh." The one syllable was both a question and a demand.

"We'll find it later."

"Oh." Disappointment and reluctant patience colored her voice. How could a little girl pack so much meaning into one small word? But Annie had always been good at letting her feelings be known.

She turned back to Missy. "If you don't live here, where do you live?"

Even though they didn't touch and he didn't look directly at her, Wade felt the young woman stiffen. Why did such an ordinary question cause such a reaction?

"I'm staying here for now. And then...well, I'll find something else." Beneath the cheerful words ran a river of uncertainty that made Wade tighten his arms around Annie lest she feel it, too.

But he couldn't prevent the child's understanding. "That's like us. We're going someplace but I don't know where. Only that Uncle Wade is leaving us and going..." She lifted her hands in a dramatic show of I-don't-know.

The gesture made him ache. As did her words. If only he could give them specifics as to their future, but at this point, he had none to give. *Please, God. Make their adoption work out. Sooner would be better than later.*

Missy shifted slightly so she could give him an accusing look. He ignored her, gazing down at the floor. She needn't think he acted selfishly. He had to do what was best.

Linette broke the tension as she announced her departure. "I need to go finish the meal preparations." She put baby Jonathan in his cradle and headed for the kitchen. Immediately, the other ladies, including Missy, exited the room. Wade drew in a deep breath. The delicious aromas that had assaulted him as he entered the house now drew saliva from his mouth and

growls from his stomach. The smells made it difficult to focus on anything else, until he felt Annie get up and start to follow Missy. Wade roped in his attention. "Stay here," he said.

Missy turned, favored him with another of her accusing looks and continued on her way. Wade let her go without comment, deeming this a battle not worth fighting. Right or wrong, the woman was entitled to her opinion.

For the first time since he'd seen Missy in the room he sat back and tried to relax. But the smells of turkey and stuffing, ham and mincemeat made him miss Susan so badly he felt a sting of tears. Thankfully, all the other men had their attention on Eddie as he regaled them with a story about finding stranded cows in a snowstorm.

Wade's stomach was kissing his backbone by the time Linette invited them into the dining room. "Children, you have a table in the kitchen. Daisy's in charge. Be sure you mind her."

The older girl, Daisy, who looked to be about thirteen, had a toddler perched on one hip and reached out her free hand to Annie. "Come on. It's fun to sit at the children's table."

"Daisy is very good at minding the younger ones," Linette assured Wade. "She's Cassie and Roper's oldest. With two brothers and a sister, she gets a lot of practice."

The little boy named Grady signaled to Joey. "You wanna sit with me?"

And as easy as that, the two clinging children left Wade.

He wanted to call them back, but Linette waved everyone to chairs.

Somehow Wade ended up beside Missy. A glance around the table revealed they were the only single adults present, so he supposed it made sense to his hostess.

He forced himself to sit calmly as Eddie said grace, even though having Missy so close made his nerves tingle. He tried to cover it up by squirming about in an attempt to see or at least hear the children.

"Relax," Missy said. "If Linette says it's okay it's okay."

He nodded, though he wasn't sure he agreed.

Linette spoke from the end of the table. "You couldn't know it, but Daisy and her brothers and sister were orphans. Roper and Cassie adopted them. In fact—" she glanced about the table "—all these people have children who lost at least one parent." She guided the passing of the food as she spoke.

Louise sat on the other side of Missy and leaned around her to speak to Wade. "Even little Chloe. Her father never had a chance to meet her. Now Nate is her father."

The couples around the table smiled lovingly at each other, obviously content with their new relationships.

Wade filled his plate with turkey and stuffing, ham and green tomato chutney, mashed potatoes and gravy, carrots and turnips. He realized all eyes were on him. Had he taken too much food? But a glance about the table revealed every plate held a generous amount.

"Did I miss something?" he asked, silently acknowledging he had been interested only in the food.

Everyone slid their gaze to Missy and back to him.

"It seems like marriage would be the perfect solution for you, as well," Linette said. "Both of you."

He shook his head. "Oh, no. Marriage isn't for me."

Missy held up her hands. "Nor me."

"Why not?" Louise demanded of her sister-in-law. "What's wrong with marriage?"

"I didn't say there was anything wrong with it. It's fine if that's what you want. I have other plans." She dug into the pocket of her blue satin gown and pulled out a piece of paper. She unfolded it and showed it to Louise, who read it aloud, then stared at her.

"A secretary?"

"Using a typewriter." Missy made it sound as if that made a world of difference.

"Where will you get the money to take this class?"

"I'll earn it." Her voice rang with determination.

"But—"

Before Louise could finish, Missy returned the paper to her pocket. "That's what I'm going to do."

Wade released pent-up air. Thankfully, there'd be no more matchmaking.

Every pair of eyes returned to him.

"I'm sure there are other prospects," Linette began. "I heard a family moved in this fall with an almost grown daughter. I haven't met her yet but by all accounts she is pleasant and hardworking."

This must be the family Lane had gone to visit. Wade rolled his head back and forth. Even if he had any interest in marriage, the last thing he needed was a young woman barely old enough to leave her parents. Besides, Lane had his sights set on the young lady and Wade had no intention of being competition. "Marriage isn't for everyone. And to provide for a family, a man needs a home. I have none. I'm a cowboy."

"Look around the table," Eddie said. "These fel-

lows were homeless cowboys, too, until they found a reason to settle down."

The conversation was thankfully dropped as people turned their attention to the bountiful food. Wade savored every mouthful even though the meal carried sorrowful memories of similar occasions spent with Susan and her family. But as Missy had said to Annie, his sister would want him to enjoy the day.

Beneath the rumble of a discussion about the new church, Missy murmured, "One would think two orphaned children would be enough reason to settle down."

So much for thinking the topic had been abandoned. Wade's enjoyment of the meal turned sour.

Linette lowered her fork to the table. "Tell me, Wade, what are your plans for the children?"

He, too, lowered his fork, knowing his answer would bring more criticism from Missy. Not that it was any of her business. "Ma'am, I've been in contact with a Mr. and Mrs. Bauer from Fort Macleod regarding adoption."

A collective gasp came from others at the table.

"I had hoped to hear from them by now because I have to leave almost immediately. I've agreed to look after a friend's ranch while he takes a trip."

A beat of silence passed before anyone responded.

It was Missy who spoke. "I guess you'll have to take the children with you." Obviously she knew that wasn't his plan, but she meant to force him to reconsider.

"That's not possible. I can't take care of them and the ranch, too." Before Missy could voice any more disapproval, before any of them could, he spoke again.

"I need someplace safe to leave them until the couple comes. I hope...hoped they could stay here."

Linette and Eddie looked at each other for a moment. Eddie answered Wade's request. "We'll discuss it later."

With those words, he had to be content, though he could not relax with Missy's heavy disapproval coming off her like a wave.

The main part of the meal ended, the dishes were cleared away and mincemeat pie served. Wade hoped the children were enjoying the dessert more than he was. Every mouthful was full of regret from his own heart and silent accusations from Missy.

Finally the meal was over.

"Everyone return to the sitting room. There are gifts for all the children," Linette said.

Wade had begun to rise, but at that he sank back in his chair. He must find a way to draw Joey and Annie away so they wouldn't be disappointed when they received no gifts.

Linette waved a hand to indicate he should join them. "There's something for Annie and Joey, too."

Missy waited at her chair as if to make certain he didn't skip out.

He had no such intention and rose to follow her back to the other room. In a flash he saw that everyone had resumed their previous positions, which left him sitting at Missy's side. He would have avoided the seat, but the room was crowded and he had no other option.

The children raced in and sat in a circle before the decorated evergreen tree next to the window.

One by one, Eddie handed gifts to the young ones. When it was his turn, Joey opened his package. "A ball

for playing catch. Papa taught me to throw and catch."
He gazed at it, his lips quivering.

Wade would have gone to him, but wondered if the
boy would find it embarrassing to be needing comfort.

Annie opened her gift, a sock doll with black button
eyes, brown yarn hair and a pink cotton dress.

She stared at it and burst into tears.

Wade sat motionless, his heart shredding with
shared sorrow. Before he could move, Missy sprang
forward, sat beside the child and pulled her to her lap.
"Shh, shh." She rocked Annie in a tight embrace.

Finally the tears stopped. Missy returned to her
chair, with Annie clinging to her like a sweater.

"I'll take her." Wade reached for his niece, but
Missy shook her head.

"She's fine here on my lap." Missy's eyes, too, were
awash with tears.

Wade closed his eyes against a rush of wild emotions—a burning desire to comfort them both, a burst
of fresh pain at his own sorrow and beneath it all, his
unending sense of failure in not being able to give these
children what they needed. And in not having seen
how sad and desperate his late wife had been. The accusations hurled at him by Tomasina's parents that it
was his duty to see to her needs were no stronger than
those from his own heart.

He never again wanted to experience such failure.

Missy held Annie as tightly as Annie held her.
How well she remembered the first Christmas after
her parents had died. The aching feeling that nothing
would ever be the same, that no one would ever understand and love her the way Mama and Papa had. She

and Gordie had gotten presents for each other—she'd bought him a new pocketknife she'd seen him admire in the store and he'd bought her a set of ivory hair combs. She hadn't noticed them in any of the stores and wondered where he'd gotten them. It was much later that she realized he'd probably stolen them, and she'd never again used them.

She shook off the memories and flicked her gaze to the man beside her. She noted that his hands were curled so tightly the knuckles were white. From under her lashes Missy studied him. His expression revealed a mixture of emotions—uncertainty and sorrow.

He'd lost his sister. Of course he felt sorrow.

In her judgment of him she'd forgotten to take that into account. At the first opportunity she would correct the matter.

Annie cuddled close as the other children played with their new toys. After a bit, Joey left the others and scooted over to sit with his back against Wade's legs. Wade rested his hands on the boy's shoulders.

Missy smiled as uncle and nephew released tiny sighs and sank toward each other, giving comfort and consolation.

One by one the guests rose, gathered up their children and bade Linette and Eddie and the others goodbye. Louise and Nate excused themselves and took baby Chloe to their room. Only Missy remained beside Wade, with Annie on her lap and Joey at Wade's knees.

Eddie and Linette approached Wade. "We need to talk."

Knowing they meant to address Wade's request to leave the children at the ranch, Missy struggled to

her feet. "I'll take the children into the kitchen. Come along, Joey."

The child was too tired to argue and shuffled after her, but by the time they sat down at the table, his curiosity kicked in.

"They're talking about us, aren't they? Is Uncle Wade leaving us here?" The boy's voice cracked, not only from fatigue. The poor child dreaded being abandoned.

Annie sobbed and tightened her arms about Missy's neck.

She forced herself to take two slow breaths. How could Wade think of leaving these children? Yes, she understood he had a job to go to, that someone was counting on him to take care of their ranch. Yes, she understood he was an unmarried cowboy with no home. But the facts did not change her feelings. She knew what it was like to have people she cared about snatched out of her life, and to feel as if she was only an inconvenience to those who were left. She even harbored a suspicion that Louise had married her brother, Gordie, simply to protect Missy from Vic. The thought twisted through her gut. A nuisance and a burden.

Praying her voice would be firm and reassuring, she pulled Joey to her side. "Listen to me, both of you. Wherever you go, whatever happens to you, you are not alone. You have each other. And you have your mama and papa inside you." She didn't know how else to say that their memories of their parents would always be with them and always guide them. "And God is with you. He will never leave you nor forsake you. He is as close as your next breath. He sees what you need and He will provide it."

Two pairs of dark eyes watched her, practically drank her in, taking the encouragement and assurance she offered.

"You can trust God no matter what. Can you remember that?"

Annie and Joey nodded.

The kitchen door swung wide. Wade stood in the opening, his eyes on her. "Missy, would you please join us?" He turned to the children. "You two wait here."

Missy set Annie on a chair next to her brother, caressed both heads and smiled. "Remember what I told you." She reminded herself of the same thing—God was with her—and followed Wade into the sitting room.

She felt the heaviness in the air around her as she sat down opposite Wade.

"What's this all about?" she asked.

Linette answered. "You heard Wade say he was trying to find an adoptive family for the children."

Missy nodded, her lips pressed together to keep her opinion to herself.

"We've asked him to stay until he makes those arrangements. For the children's sake."

"Quite so. They've had enough loss to deal with already." Missy released the words in a rush and blinked hard to keep from piercing Wade with her challenging look.

Linette continued. "However, he doesn't feel he can take care of them on his own."

Eddie spoke at that point. "I won't let Linette be responsible for them. Not when Jonathan is only a few days old." The baby boy slept in her arms.

Wade cleared his throat and Missy's gaze jerked to-

ward him. So many feelings rushed through her—fear that he meant to give these children away, hope that it would give them a loving home and... Oh, yes, she meant to express her sympathy at his loss. Before she could say a word, he spoke.

"I would like to hire you to look after Annie and Joey until I can make other arrangements."

She opened her mouth, but again he cut her off. "You can put the money toward paying for the secretarial course you want to take."

She'd meant to say she'd gladly take care of the children free of charge, but his words reminded her that she needed funds to fulfill her plans. Still she did not answer him. Somehow to say yes felt as if she'd be giving approval to his plan, aligning herself with him rather than the children.

But if she said yes, she could spend time with them, help prepare them for their future and help them find enjoyment in their current situation.

"Yes, I'll do it. On one condition." She hesitated. Was she asking the right thing? "You—" she nodded to Wade "—spend time with them, as well."

Their gazes held as they measured each other. Likely he wondered at her reason even as she wondered at his.

"I'm amenable to that."

Eddie slapped his knees. "Then it's settled. Things have a way of working out for the good of everyone."

Missy wondered what he meant. She couldn't see how things would work out for the good for Joey and Annie. They'd lost their parents and would soon lose their uncle and go to live with strangers.

None of them had any control over the future. But

as she'd told the children, God would never leave them. If she could do one thing in the few days she'd have with them, it would be to make sure they believed that.

In so doing, she'd make certain they enjoyed their time at Eden Valley Ranch—even if it meant she'd have to interact with Wade Snyder to make that happen.

Chapter Two

Eddie got to his feet, took the baby and helped Linette to stand. "I think my wife should have a little rest. It's been a long day." He led her up the stairs.

Missy watched them go, then glanced about the room. Not long ago this space had been crowded with guests. Now there was only Wade and her. Not that they were really alone. The children were in the next room; Linette and Eddie, Nate and Louise were upstairs. Nevertheless, Missy's nerves twanged with tension. Would Wade use the quiet to inform her that she had stepped into his business too many times? She knew she had but didn't regret it.

There was only one thing she meant to change. "I have never expressed my condolences over the loss of your sister and brother-in-law. I'm very sorry. I recently lost my brother, so I share a little knowledge of how you feel."

"Thank you. I didn't know you'd lost your brother, though I suppose I should have realized it when Louise said her husband had never met baby Chloe. I didn't make the connection. I'm sorry for your loss, as well."

Missy let her gaze find his as she offered her sympathy. It was nothing but a cool, impersonal meeting of the eyes, but at his kind words, something shifted between them. Their circumstances might be different, but the pain and loss were similar and they silently acknowledged it. She felt his sorrow in the depth of her heart, even as her own sense of loss tightened her chest.

Her breath stuttered in and she broke their visual connection. "Do you intend to tell the children of your plans?" she asked, bringing her gaze back to his.

He looked away, his eyes full of uncertainty. "I don't know how much I should tell them." He turned back to her. "I don't want to take away from their enjoyment of Christmas."

She nodded. "Nor do I. In fact, I'll do everything in my power to make their stay here enjoyable. Too bad Christmas is over." In the ensuing silence, she heard a distressing sound. "Is that Annie crying?"

They were both on their feet in an instant and rushed for the kitchen door.

Joey sat with his arm about his little sister. Her sock doll lay on her knees as tears dripped to its face.

Missy knelt before the child. "Honey, what's wrong?"

Annie sobbed an answer.

Missy could not make out what she said and was about to sit down and pull the child to her lap when Wade beat her to it. He held Annie so tenderly, his face so full of sorrow and concern, that Missy blinked back a few tears of her own. How she wished to help this hurting trio. *God, I told the children You would help them and guide them. Let me assist if that's possible.*

She sat beside Wade and rubbed Annie's back. After a moment the little girl quieted and was able to speak.

"Mama made me a doll. I don't know where it is." Her crying intensified again.

Missy's heart twisted and she gave Wade a look of despair. "She's lost so much."

"She hasn't lost her doll." He shifted Annie to Missy's arms and strode from the room.

"Where's he going?" Joey clutched her hand. "Is he leaving?"

"I don't think so." Missy was as uncertain as Joey until she reminded herself that Wade had agreed to stay until the children were placed.

He returned in quick order carrying two bulky boxes and two valises. "Your doll is in this stuff. We just have to find it." He dropped his burdens to the floor.

The children sprang forward and fell upon the baggage as if they'd been returned home from being lost. In a sense, Missy supposed it felt that way. Everything they owned and were familiar with was before them.

Wade pried open the first box and let the children dive into the contents. Blankets, clothing, a pair of woolen mittens were all pulled out. Annie pressed her face into each article and breathed deeply. Joey fingered the fabric and then slipped his hands into the mittens, a look of joy and pain twisting his features.

They emptied the box and sat back. No doll.

Missy carefully repacked the contents while Wade opened the next box. Again he stepped back as the children examined the contents. With a squeal, Annie pulled out a pink sweater and slipped it on. She rubbed her sleeves and smiled through a sheen of tears. "My sweater Mama made me."

Joey dug further. He didn't say anything, but it was obvious he was hunting for something. When the box was empty he sat back on his heels. "It's not there."

"What are you looking for?" Wade asked.

"Something." Joey would say no more.

Missy repacked the box, with the children following every move of her hands, as if saying goodbye to each item. As if saying goodbye to their life. A tear dropped to the back of her hand but she wiped it off and continued until everything was back and Wade closed the top on the box.

The two valises sat untouched and the four of them stared at the bags. Would they contain something to comfort the children or would there be only disappointment? Missy didn't want to face the possibility of the latter. It seemed the children didn't, either. But Wade pulled one valise closer and folded back the top. "We might as well see what's here."

With less enthusiasm than they'd shown previously, the children pulled out items. This bag held boy's clothing. Missy realized it contained the things Joey needed for the present. Annie sat back and let him remove the contents. He carefully lifted each shirt and each pair of trousers, almost reverently setting them aside. At the bottom of the bag he felt something and grew still, his eyes wide. Slowly, he lifted out a photograph and stared at it. "Mama and Papa." The words came out in a whisper.

He turned the picture so Annie could see it. She sucked in a sigh and then released it.

No one moved. Missy wondered if anyone breathed as the children drank in the likeness of their parents.

Joey kept the photograph on his lap and searched the corners of the bag for something more.

Missy knew the moment he'd found it. He froze, one hand in the valise, his eyes wide, his mouth open. Then he swallowed twice and slowly withdrew his hand. "My ball." He burst into tears.

Wade and Missy reached for him at the same time. Their arms crossed as they comforted Joey, but neither of them withdrew. The weight of Wade's arm across Missy's sent a rush of warmth straight to her heart. She was instantly thirteen years old again, longing to be comforted. She'd gone to Gordie in tears, overwrought about their parents' death, but her brother had pushed her away. Told her it was time to grow up. Wade, to his credit, simply held Joey now and let him shed as many tears as he needed to.

Annie scrambled over the valise, lifted the photograph from Joey's knees, crawled into his lap and wrapped her arms about him.

Missy wiped the back of her hand across her eyes. She could not bring herself to look at Wade, fearing her emotions would riot out of control and she would become a teary mess.

When Joey's sobs subsided he shared a memory. "Papa played catch with me every time he could." He darted a glance to his uncle.

Missy almost chuckled at the boy's subtle hint.

Wade nodded. "Tell you what. We'll play catch, too."

Joey grinned. "I'd like that."

Annie slipped from her brother's lap and squatted in front of the last valise. Wade opened it and the others sat back as Annie slowly lifted out little-girl garments and set them aside. After each she looked from

Missy to Joey to Wade. Not until her uncle said, "Go ahead," did she take out the next item.

She looked into the bag and squealed in delight, but kept her hands on her knees and stared at the object.

"What is it?" Missy asked softly.

Gently, Annie lifted out a soiled and worn cloth doll. "My dolly, Mary." She hugged the doll to her neck and rocked back and forth, humming a lullaby.

Missy heart overflowed at this child's pleasure. But her joy was intermingled with unshed tears. She shared a glance with Wade. From his trembling smile she guessed he struggled with the same emotions she did.

Their gaze remained locked. His smile fled and then returned with warmth and understanding, finding an answering smile in her heart. They might not have much in common. They had plans that didn't involve the other. Certainly they were at odds about what his plans for the children were. But unmistakably they shared tender affection for these children.

Annie looked about the room as if searching for something else, saw her new doll on the kitchen table and trotted over to get it. "Mary, you have a sister now. This is Martha." With one arm clutching each doll, she hugged them both to her neck.

Joey shifted to face Wade. "Are you leaving us here?"

Still on the floor, Wade sat back and crossed his legs with an ease that said he often sat this way. Missy could imagine him on the ground before a campfire, a tin cup of steaming coffee in his hand. The picture made her smile and, at the same time, filled her with an unfamiliar restlessness.

Her smile fled as she waited for Wade to explain his plans to the children.

He caught Annie and pulled her to his lap. "I'm not leaving for a little while. You both know I don't want to ever leave you but…" He shrugged, then brightened. "But Missy is going to help take care of you while we're here. How do you like that?"

Joey grinned. "I like that."

Annie reached for Missy's hand and pulled her closer. "Me, too."

The children looked at each other, sharing a secret. Then Joey nodded. "I'll ask." He considered Wade a moment as if gathering up the nerve.

"What is it?" Wade prompted.

"Annie and I want to have our own Christmas. Not one with so many strangers."

Wade turned to Missy. "What do you think?"

"Sounds good to me." She turned to Joey. "Did you have something in mind?"

Joey wriggled with excitement. "Tomorrow is the day after Christmas. Boxing Day, Mama called it. She said it used to be when people gave their servants money and gifts back in England. We don't have servants, but she said Grandma considered the animals her servants, so they would go to the barn and decorate it to celebrate Jesus being born in a manger. Can we do that tomorrow?"

Missy's throat clogged. The children didn't want gifts for themselves; they wanted only to make Christmas memorable.

She turned toward Wade, intending to tell him she'd help him decorate the barn if Eddie approved.

But Wade looked as if he'd been stabbed through the heart.

He shifted Annie to Missy's lap and strode from the room.

Wade stumbled out the back door into the clear evening. Trying to calm himself, he sucked in the cold air and commanded his thoughts to fall into order.

The door behind him opened, threw out a patch of golden lamplight before him, then closed softly. He felt Missy at his side but did not look her way nor acknowledge her.

Her hand touched his arm and rested there. "Wade, what's wrong?"

He shook his head. "Nothin'."

"'Nothin'' doesn't send a man rushing out into the night."

She had a point. His thoughts untangled and dashed to his tongue. "It was my mother who began the tradition of decorating a manger for Christmas. Born and raised a proper English miss, she couldn't dismiss Boxing Day as just another day. I remember how eagerly Susan and I looked forward to our trip to the barn the day after Christmas."

"Susan was your sister? The children's mother?"

He nodded. "My parents are gone. My sister is gone. My wife is gone."

Missy's fingers trembled on his arm. "You were married?"

"A long time ago. I tried to get her to decorate the manger with me but she didn't see the value of doing so." To Tomasina it was a silly, childish practice. After

her death, he'd been glad to join Susan and her family in carrying on the tradition.

"It will be good for the children to continue their customary way of celebrating the day."

Enough light came from the window for him to watch Missy's hand run along his arm. Was she even aware she did it?

He shifted away, forcing her to drop her arm to her side. He didn't need or want comfort. Not for himself. She could save it for the children. He lived the life he wanted and deserved.

"It's getting cold." He opened the door and held it for her to enter. When they stepped inside, Joey and Annie watched them with wide, fearful eyes. He understood life was uncertain for them at the moment, the future unknown. The best he could do was get them settled as soon as possible. Only then could they begin to adjust to the facts of their life.

They were young enough to adapt.

He knew he never would. He'd learned his past went with him, bleeding into his present and staining his future. One simply did not forget finding one's wife dead of her own choice. At least Susan and her husband had died of natural causes. One could put that down to God's timing. Then all one had to do was believe God had a good and perfect plan in mind. Though, truth be told, there were times Wade found it hard to see the good in things. But then wasn't that what trust was— believing when he couldn't see?

To reassure the children he pasted a smile on his face. "I'll ask Eddie about decorating a manger."

"What is it you want to ask Eddie?" The man in question entered the room.

Wade explained the Snyder tradition and Eddie wasted no time consenting. "It sounds great."

Grady was at Eddie's heels. "Can I go with you to-morrow?" the boy asked Wade.

"Of course you may."

Grady grinned in pleasure and Eddie squeezed his shoulder, as happy as the child, then he turned to the others. "My wife has fallen asleep. I think Louise and Nate have, as well. That leaves us to fend for ourselves for something to eat." He set out leftover ham and tur-key and sliced a loaf of bread, while Wade put Annie's things back in the valise and pushed their boxes and bags to one side of the room.

When the three adults and three children gathered around the table, Eddie asked the blessing. Annie placed her two dolls on either side of her and patted each.

Mealtime was quiet, the children tired out from the long day and the adults somewhat subdued, as well. As soon as they were satisfied and the dishes quickly disposed of, Eddie led Wade and the children upstairs. Missy apparently had a room on the main floor and called good-night as the others climbed the steps.

Annie paused on the steps, looking over her shoulder. "Where are you going to sleep?" she asked Missy. "You aren't leaving, are you?"

"I have a room down here. I'll be here when you get up tomorrow."

Wade gathered his niece in his arms and carried her up the stairs. She was practically asleep on his shoulder by the time Eddie showed him a room for the chil-dren and an adjoining one for himself. He helped the

children prepare for bed, then withdrew to the next room, hoping the children wouldn't be upset by being separated from him.

He woke the next morning to two children bouncing on his bed.

"It's morning," Annie said with a bounce.

"You sure?" His voice was gravelly.

"We're doing something special today. 'Member?"

He cracked one eye open. "Not before breakfast."

"Aren't you getting up?" Joey bounced twice just for good measure.

"Where's Missy?" Annie added another bounce. "I want to wake her up." She jumped toward the side of the bed.

Wade lifted his head and eyed her. "You will not go downstairs until I say so." He cocked an ear and listened. "I don't think anyone else is awake. And you shouldn't be, either." He let his head fall to the pillow, closed his eyes and wished for the forgetfulness of sleep.

"They're awake, Uncle Wade. I heard baby Chloe and baby Jonathan crying when we came in here." Joey seemed to think that was reason enough to make sure everyone in the house was up.

Wade had jerked awake a couple times in the night, hearing the babies cry. Once, he'd thought he was out in the range and coyotes were nearby. He'd reached for his rifle, but found only bedding. By that time his heart raced and he was wide-awake.

Now as he lay there his thoughts harkened back to the previous day. His agreement with the Gardiners meant he would be days late getting to Stuart's place.

Stuart would wonder when he didn't show up, though he'd wait a few days before he gave it much mind. By then, Wade would be there.

There wasn't much traffic to and from Fort Macleod this time of year, but a man and woman anxious to adopt two children would find a way of making arrangements. Until then Wade and Missy Porter would entertain the children.

He tried to decide what he thought of that young lady.

Very pretty for sure.

Alone. Just as he was. Except he at least had the children for the next few days. He pushed aside the sorrow of knowing he would soon have to say goodbye to them. Perhaps never see them again, depending on the wishes of the new parents.

Missy was opinionated, as well. She certainly knew what she wanted, which was to his advantage. He could offer her a paying job.

Doubts crowded his mind. Had he done the right thing in asking for her help?

But she was kind and she'd be good to the children. They needed tons of kindness and affection at the moment.

He rubbed his arm where she had touched him. Warmth trickled into his heart like water from a block of ice under a warm spring sun.

The children, realizing they must wait before going downstairs, curled up beside him.

"Tell us a story," Annie begged.

"Yes, do," Joey added, trying not to sound as eager as his younger sister.

"Me?"

"Like Mama used to." Annie voice threatened tears.

"You're all we got." Joey had no idea how inadequate that made Wade feel.

"Okay, I'll try. Once upon a time there was a cowboy."

"Oh, I like that." Annie's eyes were wide with expectation. "A cowboy who loved a lady."

"Hey, whose story is this?"

"You have to have a lady." Annie nodded with absolute certainty.

"You're sure?" He looked to Joey for backing on this idea, but his nephew nodded. The boy offered no escape at all.

"Okay." Wade wasn't going to be able to avoid it. "There was a cowboy who had a lady."

"Loved a lady," Annie corrected.

He sighed. "How do you know he loved her?"

"He knew it here." She patted her chest.

"Is that what your mama said?" Susan had been such a romantic.

Annie shook her head. "I just know it. Right, Joey?"

Joey considered her question. "I don't know." At the fear and hope laced through his words, Wade's throat tightened. Joey was awfully young to be afraid of love, though perhaps he had as much reason as Wade did. But Wade didn't care to see such doubt in his nephew and decided he would tell a story about a cowboy who loved a lady.

"She was a beautiful lady," he said.

Annie sighed. "Like Missy."

Wade didn't argue the point. How could he when he pictured Missy in the role? Not that he saw himself

as the cowboy. Nope, that wasn't a part he intended to take.

"This young lady liked to cook and sing and play the piano. She liked children and hoped she could have dozens of them." He swallowed back a bitter taste in his mouth. How had his story gone from thinking of Missy to thinking of Tomasina?

"Did she?" Joey asked.

"What?" He'd gotten lost in his thoughts.

"Did she have lots of kids?"

"She did. Six little boys and six little girls." Might as well make the story big and give it a happier ending than his own.

"And the cowboy played games with them?" Joey leaned over him, his face so close Wade could smell his little-boy scent. Joey's eyes were intent. Wade realized play was very important to this child.

"He sure did. He played ball and chase and tag and taught all the children to ride and rope."

Joey flopped to the bed and stared up at the ceiling. "I wish…"

Wade waited and when Joey didn't finish he pulled him back to his chest so they stared into each other's eyes again. "What do you wish?"

Joey looked at Wade's chin. "It doesn't matter."

"Hey, it's Christmas. What better time to wish for something?"

Joey's eyes slowly came to Wade's. "I wish we had a home and…"

"Our mama and papa." Annie finished for him.

Joey flung himself from Wade's arms and lay stiffly on the bed. "See? I knew it was impossible."

"I'll make sure you have a nice home."

Both children sat up and looked at him. "Here? With you?"

"We're all going to stay here until I sort things out."

The pair looked at each other, their mouths in matching frowns. It was the best he could offer. Someday they would understand that.

"Miss Porter is going to help look after you." He hoped they would see it as a fair exchange for him not being able to fulfill their dreams.

"I like Missy Porter," Joey said, a goofy look on his face.

"You should address her as Miss Porter."

The boy's brow furrowed. "What's the difference between Miss and Missy?"

"One letter. *Y.*"

"Because I was wondering."

Wade grinned secretly at Joey's literal understanding of *why* and *y.* It would be fun to watch the kids grow and learn. He clamped down on the thought. He wouldn't be the one enjoying it.

Before the sadness could find lodging in his heart, he heard footsteps in the hall. The household was awake. Good. He could get up before the children delved any deeper into the mysteries of life. "Get dressed and then we'll go to the kitchen."

Both children hopped off the bed.

"Mind you be quiet in case the babies are asleep."

Annie's rushing footsteps stalled. "I wish we had a baby brother or sister." A ragged breath rushed from her lungs, then she sighed dramatically. "Guess Mary and Martha will have to be my babies." She trudged to the adjoining room as if she had lost something she valued.

Wade slipped into his shirt and trousers and began to follow, intending to comfort the child, but he made it as far as the doorway and saw she was dressed and singing to her dolls. He grinned. Drama should have been her middle name. "Are you two ready to go downstairs?"

They sprang to his side, as eager to go down as he was suddenly reluctant. He did not like uncertainty and at the moment everything about his life was a question. Would the Fort Macleod family continue with adoption plans? How long would it be before he could be on his way to Stuart's ranch? And most uncertain of all…was he asking for a continual dose of disapproval by enlisting Missy's help with the children?

He filled his lungs and squared his shoulders as they reached the bottom step. He was about to find out what he'd gotten himself into.

Missy had been up for some time. She'd made coffee, mixed up biscuits and put them to bake. She'd set the table, sliced bacon and put it to fry.

Linette had come downstairs several minutes ago, her eyes shadowed. "I think Jonathan has his days and nights mixed up," she'd said. "I hope we didn't keep you awake."

"Not at all. I had a good sleep." Apart from a few moments when Missy wondered what she'd gotten herself into by agreeing to care for the children, then insisting Wade be involved. Not that she regretted the first. Not in the least. In fact, her mind flooded with things she could do to make the time special and comforting for the children.

But with Wade at her side?

There was something about that man that put her nerves on edge. It was more than the fact she thought him too much like Gordie. Not that she thought him dishonest and living outside the law. No, that wasn't what bothered her. It was his attitude toward the children. He seemed to be doing his best to be rid of them, and yet he was so obviously fond of them. It was such a strange contrast that she couldn't decide what to think. But then what did it matter? He'd offered to pay her and she'd take his money, but more than that, she'd enjoy her time with the two children.

She'd fallen asleep with a smile on her face as she'd played over the scenes with them—opening gifts, going through their belongings, hugging each other, feeling little Annie's arms about her neck…

Missy heard a footstep in the hall and turned, a smile filling her face. It was only Eddie. She told herself she wasn't disappointed and returned to setting out preserves for the biscuits.

At the sound of more footsteps she looked up again, slowly this time. It was Louise and Nate with baby Chloe.

Louise looked as if she had gotten little sleep. "Chloe still won't sleep without being rocked."

"You two sit," Missy told the two new mothers. "I'll take care of breakfast." She tended the bacon and broke a dozen eggs into a fry pan.

"Good morning."

At Wade's greeting she almost dropped the next egg. With one hand pressed to the thudding pulse in her neck, she spun about. His hair was slicked back and his eyes bright. Obviously he'd slept well. A child clung to each hand.

Annie held her dolls. Joey swung back and forth as if clutching a school yard swing, making Wade sway slightly.

Missy grinned. "Good morning." Her gaze rested on each child, then came to Wade.

He grinned back as if realizing she found Joey's play amusing. "These two are raring to go."

Joey paused. "We're going to the barn, aren't we?"

"After breakfast and chores." The resigned note in Wade's voice gave Missy cause to think he might have had to explain it a few times already.

"Breakfast is about ready." She returned to the stove and a few minutes later put the food on the table.

"I surely do appreciate your help," Linette said.

"It's my pleasure." For some reason she wasn't ready to explore, Missy liked helping in this house. She did it not out of obligation or duty but because she wanted to, and perhaps that made all the difference. Not to mention it was appreciated.

Grady, Joey and Annie chattered freely at the table and the adults gave them attention, just as her mama and papa had done with her.

Reliving her memories of her parents through these children was better than any Christmas present Missy could have wished for, and she knew a sense of joy and rightness she had not known since her parents had died.

The meal over, the men excused themselves.

Eddie stood at Linette's side. "Is there anything you need before I tend to chores?"

She pressed her hand to her husband's arm. "I'm fine. You don't need to worry about us." She glanced

toward the cradle where little Jonathan slept peacefully.

"I'll give you a hand." Wade joined Eddie and Nate as they left the house.

Joey and Annie stared after their uncle. Annie's lips trembled.

Missy sprang into action before they could start crying or worrying. "I need help with the dishes."

Linette wanted to help, but Missy shooed her away. "Sit and rest while you can."

She assigned each child a chore and turned putting food away into a game of "what's next?" Laughter rang through the kitchen.

"You're very good with the children," Linette observed.

Missy chuckled. "It's because I'm not much more than a child myself."

Linette and Louise both snorted. Louise shook her head. "When was the last time you looked in a mirror?"

Missy grinned, purposely misunderstanding her. "Why, is my hair untidy?"

Louse chuckled. "You'd be beautiful whether your hair was tousled or tied back in a tight bun."

"Thank you." Missy hugged her sister-in-law.

Annie watched, her eyes studying Missy's hair. "You have awfully pretty hair." She yanked at her tangled locks. "Mine is ugly."

Missy grabbed the child and hugged her. "Not so. The first time I saw you, I thought what a pretty little girl. With those big dark eyes and thick curls, you could never be anything but beautiful." She eyed the

child's hair. It could do with a brushing and maybe some styling.

"As soon as the dishes are done, I will fix your hair so pretty you won't recognize yourself." She stuck her hands in the dishpan full of hot soapy water and a stack of plates.

Annie grabbed a drying towel and handed one to each of the boys. "Let's hurry."

The women chuckled at her eagerness, and in no time the kitchen was clean and the dishes done. Missy got her brush and sat behind Annie. Slowly, gently, she worked the tangles out of the curly hair. As she brushed she talked to the children about the stagecoach trip she and Louise had recently completed.

"Weren't you scared?" Joey asked, when she told about the snowstorm they had been forced to travel through.

"Maybe a little, but the men seemed to know what they were doing. I was awfully glad to get to the next stopping house, though." Equally glad when the storm ended and they could move on. The old man at the stopping house had done his best to get Missy interested in his advances. She stopped a shiver before it could race through her body.

She French braided Annie's hair into a thick rope, then showed the girl a mirror. "What do you think?"

Annie stared into the glass a long time and when she lifted her face to Missy, tears filled her eyes. "Mama braided my hair like this," she whispered.

Missy hugged the child. "I hope it's okay that I did it, too." Perhaps Annie preferred to remember her mama's hands on her hair.

"I like it being like Mama did it."

Joey had slipped away to the window overlooking the ranch, and Missy went to him.

He leaned on the ledge, peering at the scene down the hill. "I don't see him."

Missy knew he meant Wade. "He's there someplace helping with the chores."

Joey turned and fixed her with a demanding, yet sorrowful look. "What's going to happen to us?"

Missy's throat tightened. She'd agreed the children should enjoy some special days before they were faced with the truth, but oh, how she wished she could give them assurance that their future was secure, that they would stay with the one person they knew and loved.

But Wade had made his plans clear, as well as his reasons.

"What's going to happen? We are going to enjoy a special Boxing Day celebration."

Annie's eyes grew wide. She covered her mouth with her hand.

"What's wrong, honey?" Missy asked.

"We need a star." The child's voice trembled.

"What kind of star?"

"A paper star to take to the barn. We hang it over the manger."

"Don't you worry. We'll find a star."

Missy asked Linette for paper and scissors. She pointed her toward the cupboard. "There's brown paper and everything you need in there."

Missy led Joey and Annie to the cupboard, while Grady hung back at Linette's side, looking down at his sleeping baby brother.

"Will this do?" Missy asked.

Annie and Joey nodded in unison.

She spread the paper on the table. "How big?"

"Big," Annie said. "Real big so the wise men can see it."

Missy sketched a five-pointed star on the one-foot-square piece of paper. "Is this good?"

The children nodded, their gazes riveted to the sheet.

She cut the star out.

"I'll carry it," Joey said, and Annie didn't argue.

Joey returned to the window. "Uncle Wade won't forget, will he?" Worry darkened his voice.

Missy glanced past him. "Look. He's just leaving the barn."

The children rushed for their coats, except for Grady, who held back. "Mama, they said I could go, too."

Linette glanced at Missy, who nodded. "Wade said it was okay."

"Very well, you may join them."

There ensued a flurry of activity—struggling into coats and hurrying to do up the buttons, finding hats and scarves and boots. By the time Wade stepped inside, three children bundled up for winter waited at the door.

He gazed at the children, a puzzled expression on his face. "Looks like you're going out."

Three heads nodded.

"Got something planned, do you?" He kept his voice quizzical, but Missy saw the flash of teasing in his eyes and leaned back to watch how it would play out.

Annie nodded decisively, but the two boys looked at each other as if to check if they had misunderstood the plans.

"Anything I should know about?" Wade asked.

"Uncle Wade." Annie's voice dripped with impatience. "You know we're going to the barn for Boxing Day."

"Oh, that. I thought we had all day to do it. I didn't know you were so eager."

"We're ready *now*." Annie emphasized the last word.

Joey watched.

Missy sensed his uncertainty. The child half expected to be disappointed. She wanted to warn Wade not to tease too long, but before she could speak, Wade tugged his nephew's hat. "You ready, too?"

Joey nodded, his eyes filling with eagerness.

"How about you?" Wade tugged Grady's hat next. "I'm ready."

"Then let's go." He reached for Annie's hand.

Missy hadn't been included. She hoped her smile looked sincere, when inside she fought disappointment. Somehow she'd seen herself as part of this mysterious celebration.

Wade waited at the door. "Hurry and get your coat," he said to her.

Missy hurried.

Joey reached for her hand at the door and she offered her other one to Grady.

They trooped down the snow-crusted hill to the barn and stepped into the dim interior. The smells of horses and hay filled the air. Dust motes drifted past

the squares of light from the row of windows. The nearest horse turned and whinnied a greeting.

Eddie stood to one side, watching without intruding.

Wade led them toward an empty stall. "Here we are. A manger for us to prepare. Who wants to put in fresh hay?"

"That's my job." Joey handed the paper star to his sister and took the pitchfork that had been placed nearby. He lifted fresh hay from a little pile and spread it as carefully as a hand-knit blanket.

The door swung open and Daisy and her sister and brothers slipped in. They approached the group, each clutching something in their hands.

Again the door opened and closed as three cowboys stepped inside and came to stand by Eddie.

Wade grinned. "Seems word got around about the Boxing Day event."

"You don't mind?" Missy wasn't sure if this was a private family occasion.

"Everyone is welcome, right, kids?"

Annie and Joey murmured agreement, but their attention remained on smoothing the hay in the manger. Finally satisfied, they stepped back. "The manager is ready just like it would have been for baby Jesus."

"I have the star." Annie handed it to Wade. "Can you please hang it for me?"

Wade must have known about the star. Of course he would. This was a family tradition. He stuck it on a nail above the manger.

The children stepped back, forcing Wade to crowd to Missy's side. She thought of moving, but there was nowhere to go, so she stayed where she was, Wade's

arm brushing hers. She felt him in every pore, the scent of him, fresh hay and old leather, the size and strength and determination of him. And something more. Something that transcended the five senses. She didn't know what it was, but knew she wasn't mistaken in thinking there was more to him than what a person saw on the surface.

Her nerves twitched. Her cheeks burned. Why was she assuming to know his feelings? She knew practically nothing about the man, and what she did know she wanted to change. Her desire was to see the children stay with him, not go to strangers, despite his reasons for feeling he had to make this decision.

She stiffened, trying to pretend she was unaware that their arms touched. She was here only to encourage and support the children and to help take care of them. But she fully intended to use what little time she had to convince him not to send away two little ones who adored him.

Joey signaled to the waiting children and Daisy led them forward.

"I brought a blanket," she said, and spread a worn cloth over the hay.

Daisy lifted her youngest sibling, little Pansy, who dropped a bright button to the blanket. "I bring shiny."

Their brothers, Neil and Billy, stepped forward. Little Billy left a cookie, Neil a red feather.

Grady had disappeared into the tack room and emerged with a leather strap. "He'll need this to fix things."

The children crowded around the manger and the cowboys moved closer.

Missy turned to smile at Wade. "The first Christmas Day must have been like this."

He nodded, his eyes full of dark mystery as if he was caught somewhere between the past and the present, perhaps remembering other occasions when he'd taken part in this ceremony.

Joey caught Wade's hand, drawing his attention away from Missy.

"Mama taught Annie a song to sing when we did this."

"She did?" Wade squatted to face the children.

Missy watched emotions journey across his face. First surprise, then sadness and then love for the two children clutching his hands.

She didn't know what prompted her action, but she rested her hand on his shoulder, squeezing gently. All she wanted was to let him know she sympathized with the tangle of emotions he must be feeling—sorrow at the loss of his sister and brother-in-law, and sadness at facing the further loss of these children.

But something else happened when her palm touched him. She felt a yearning, as strong and undeniable as his muscles under her hand.

She jerked back. What was she thinking? Wade did not offer what she wanted and needed. He was a wandering cowboy who considered those he loved to be inconvenient to his way of life. Her mind said her judgment might be a little harsh but her heart felt the familiar pain of being a burden to someone.

The children should not feel that way.

And yet didn't they deserve to be with an uncle who loved them?

How could he love them and plan to give them away?

It was a question she meant to put to him. There had to be a way for him to keep the children, and she'd help him find it.

Chapter Three

Wade's heart had momentarily stalled when Missy's hand pressed his shoulder. Perhaps she had come to understand the wisdom of his decision regarding the children and, seeing how difficult it was to think of saying perhaps a final goodbye to them, offered her sympathy. It would be nice to have someone stand by him through a wrenching farewell.

Then she'd removed her hand, leaving a cold spot on his shoulder and an empty hole in his heart as reason returned. No sense hoping she would change her opinion of him.

He brought his thoughts back to the here and now. "Annie, I'd love to hear your song."

The child stood before the manger, her hands folded at her waist, and faced those gathered before her. She smiled widely, her eyes shone and she looked beyond them as if seeing something the rest couldn't.

Wade guessed she was seeing her mama, perhaps thinking of the times they'd spent learning this song and so much more. Susan had always been a good

teacher even when they were children together. His throat tightened with sweet memories.

Then Annie began to sing, her clear, sweet voice reaching to the rafters.

"O come, little children, come one and come all,
O come to the manger in Bethlehem's stall,
And see what our Father in heaven above,
Has sent to us all on this earth with his love."

Wade couldn't stop the tears that stung his eyes nor the lump that swelled in his throat. He would not weep. Not in front of all these people. Joey grabbed his hand and squeezed hard. He dared not look at the boy, who was likely assaulted by memories every bit as much as Wade himself.

On his other side, he reached for Missy's hand, not allowing himself time to consider his actions or forecast what her reaction would be. He only knew he needed to hang on to something—someone who wouldn't let him go. When she gripped his hand and rubbed his arm, he drank in her comfort. There'd be time enough later to tell himself she could save her sympathy for the children.

He didn't dare look at the other cowboys in the barn, but a muffled cough or two informed him there might be others struggling with sad memories and overwhelming emotions.

Annie finished and her audience clapped loudly. She curtsied, then hurried to Wade and pressed against his legs. He lifted her in his arms. She buried her face against his neck and he held on tight. He never wanted to let her or Joey go. But he'd promised to see they

got a good home and he meant to keep his promise. He had nothing to offer them. Even if he did, they deserved far better.

One by one the men left. Daisy led her brothers and sister away. Grady had gone with Eddie. Only Wade, Missy and the children remained.

"I'll leave you with the children," she murmured, and slipped away from his side.

For some strange, inexplicable reason he wanted to call her back, but he had no cause. Yes, she'd agreed to help with the children, but how much help did he need to stand with them in a barn stall? So he shrugged and said nothing.

"Where you going?" Annie's voice rose to a squeak.

Missy stopped and smiled at the child. "I think you and Joey need to be alone with your uncle."

Annie's bottom lip quivered and Joey, trying his best to be strong, squeezed Wade's hand hard enough to send a thread of admiration through his unsettled thoughts. The boy had a good grip for one so young.

"Please don't go," Annie begged, and reached out for Missy's hand.

She looked at Wade, seeking his decision. "No reason you have to run off," he said, not realizing how unwelcoming his words sounded until they were uttered. "We aren't staying much longer, anyway." That didn't sound much better. Best he just shut his mouth before he made things worse.

"Very well." Missy straightened and faced him squarely. The flash in her blue-green eyes made him blink. Was she silently trying to tell him something? What? He searched through his scrambled thoughts but could find no clue.

"Is that the end of the Boxing Day event?" Annie asked, about the time the silence between them grew heavy.

He jerked his attention back to the scene before him. The manager lay as if prepared for the baby Jesus. The children watched him, waiting for him to answer, perhaps even to suggest how the day was to proceed. The light from the barn windows formed a glow about Missy's head. Feathers of her blond hair captured the pale yellow light. Her bright eyes were like beacons in the sky.

"Uncle Wade?" Joey jerked on his arm. "Is that all there is?"

Faint expectation colored the boy's words. Joey, he'd come to realize, did not allow himself to hope for things, fearing disappointment, or worse, pain, sorrow, loss. How well Wade understood the boy's caution, but Joey was too young to let life's uncertainties keep him from enjoying life's joys.

"I'm sure there's lots of good things ahead. Let's go back to the house and see what's next." He led them down the alley and held the barn door for them to step out.

Annie grabbed Joey's hand. "Let's run."

Wade followed Missy from the barn. "Wanna run?"

She laughed—a sweet pure sound like a morning bird. "Not today, thanks."

They fell in step side by side. He matched his stride to hers, content to take his time reaching the house. The children ran and skipped and played tag with each other.

"It's good to see them enjoying the day," he offered, hoping she would see he gave them enough to

make them happy for the present. If only he could offer them the future. He slammed a door on such thoughts. A man must do what was right. Not necessarily what suited him.

"Children know how to make the most of the moment," she said, though he detected a hesitation in her voice, as if she didn't quite believe it. Then she continued, "But I suppose even children can't ignore the past or the future."

She stopped, and he did also. He faced her, knowing from the expression on her face he wouldn't care for what she had to say.

"Wade, why won't you make a home for these children? It's obvious they love you and you love them."

Her words ripped a bleeding path through his heart. She would never understand and he wouldn't try to explain his reasons, so he simply repeated the words he'd said to himself seconds before. "A man must do what is right. Not necessarily what suits him. I promised their mother I would see they got a good home and I intend to do just that." Wade turned to stare ahead, seeing nothing but the agony of his own regrets and failures. If only he was a better man, one who could take care of those who depended on him.

His heart hurt so bad he thought it might bleed out through his pores.

Missy caught his arm, sending a jolt through him. "You could give them a good home."

He shook his head and refused to look at her, instead focusing his attention on the spot where her hand touched his arm. He drew in a deep breath. "I can't." He would say no more. "But I promised them we'd celebrate Christmas." That gave him an idea. "You

must have done something special as a family the day after Christmas."

Her fingers pressed into his arm as if a spasm had passed through them. She blinked and then her eyes widened. "We did but I'd forgotten. How could I?" Her gaze bored into him as if searching for the reason. "I was thirteen when my parents died. Old enough to remember all the things we'd done, yet somehow, I've forgotten much of it." Her eyes fairly danced and pleasure filled her face. She laughed low in her throat. "Mama had us write down all the good things from the past and a prayer for the New Year." Her expression flattened. "I don't suppose that would be a good activity for Annie and Joey."

Wanting to bring the joy back to her eyes, Wade said, "Why not? Might be fun."

She nodded slowly. "I always enjoyed it. Sometimes we did a play, too."

"Did you write them?" He could almost picture her enthusiasm as she made up a story and acted it out with her siblings. Then he remembered. "Did you only have the one sibling?"

She nodded. "Just Gordie." Sorrow laced the words and somehow, without planning it, Wade had captured her hands and held them between his own, trying to warm them even though it was only moderately cold out.

"It hurts to lose a brother."

The smile she gave him trembled. "Or a sister."

Their gazes locked as they silently offered understanding and sympathy. And found comfort. At least he did. He could only wish he successfully gave it to

her as well, but had he? He'd thought he gave Toma-sina what she needed, but he'd failed.

He dropped Missy's hands. "How about we follow your suggestion after lunch?"

"Okay." She tucked her hands into her sleeves, hiding them completely.

They continued on their way up the hill, watching as the children scampered into the house. When they finally reached the threshold, Missy stepped across and Wade began to close the door.

"Aren't you coming in?" she asked, stopping him.

"I'm going to help with the chores." He shut the door between them and remained motionless as he tried to put his feelings into perspective.

He could deal with this upcoming goodbye better if Missy Porter didn't continually suggest with words and looks that he was somehow failing the children.

She had no idea how badly a man could fail.

Missy stared at the door. Then she shrugged. He had every right to leave her to care for the children while he did other things. She fully intended he would not regret one penny he paid her. In fact, if she managed things right, she might even make him see that he could give the children the home they deserved. He'd have to remarry or hire a housekeeper, but surely providing the children with a home was reason enough to choose a woman who would put the children's interests above her own.

I could marry him.

She snorted as the thought echoed in her mind. She had other plans. And even if she didn't, she had no desire to be seen as a necessary nuisance again. If she

ever married— She stopped before she could complete the thought. Knowing how fragile life was, how easily it could be snatched away, leaving the survivors floundering, she didn't plan to marry.

But if she ever changed her mind, she would marry for love. A great, consuming, overwhelming love that made it impossible to think of any option other than marriage, other than being bound together until death parted them.

She would do her utmost to help Wade find a suitable woman. Her shoulders sagged. She was hundreds of miles from where she knew all the maiden ladies. The only women she knew at Eden Valley Ranch were happily married. Where would she find someone willing to marry Wade and become a parent to Joey and Annie? It was impossible.

With God, all things are possible.

Please, Father God, send someone to love the children and be willing to marry Wade to give them the home they deserve.

Dismissing her hesitation at uttering the prayer, she went to the kitchen to help prepare dinner. The children played nearby, their gazes often darting to her as she worked.

"There's more butter in the pantry," Linette said, as Missy set out the meal.

Missy went to get it. When she returned, Annie and Joey stood at the end of the table, eyes wide, expressions drawn tight. Oh, no, had they thought she'd dropped out of their lives just because she'd disappeared for a moment? Her heart twisted within her chest, making her head feel light from lack of air. She set the butter aside and pulled them both to her side.

"I promised I would take care of you as long as you are here, and I will." And lest they thought it was only because she felt she had to, she knelt to face them. "I cannot think of anything in the world I would sooner do than spend time with you two."

Annie threw her arms about Missy's neck and hung on, her breath rushing out in a hot gust.

Joey would have hung back, but Missy pulled him against her other shoulder and pressed his head close. She smiled with a heart full of joy that she could help this pair. She knew the pain she would feel when they were wrenched away to their new home, but this was one pain she would not regret.

The outer door opened and Wade stepped inside. He took in the two children cradled in Missy's arms and his eyes narrowed. She had no way of knowing what he thought of the scene and at the moment she did not care. She was only following her heart.

A few minutes later, the others joined them around the dinner table. As soon as the meal ended, Missy jumped up before either Louise or Linette could get to their weary feet. "You two take your babies and have a rest while I clean up."

With grateful nods, the new mothers left the room.

"Thank you," Eddie said.

"Yes, thank you." Nate gave her a sideways hug.

The three men lingered over coffee as Missy did the dishes and the children played nearby.

"Are you done?" She indicated the empty coffee cups.

"Done." Eddie pushed back his chair as she scooped them up and washed them. "Nate, why don't I take a look at that broken wheel on your wagon?"

"I'll help." Wade followed the men, reaching for his coat on the hook by the door.

Missy planted herself in front of him. "What about our plans?" Had he already forgotten? She could live with being so easily dismissed, but wouldn't allow it for the children.

His eyebrows headed upward. "We have plans?"

Heat rushed up her neck and pooled in her cheeks. He'd misunderstood, thought she mean the two of them. "An activity for the children?" she managed to choke out.

"Oh, that." He let out a gust of air.

She narrowed her eyes as she looked at him. Was it so challenging to think of spending time with her? Would she always be a necessary nuisance to others?

Not if she learned to be a secretary and no longer depended on anyone else.

"I can do it myself if you have other things you need to do." She would not be treated as a nuisance. And she saw no reason the children should be, either.

"We can get along without you," Eddie told him.

Missy hadn't realized the two men waited at the door. What must they think of her? First, asking for Wade to stay, then practically telling him to leave? She must sound silly.

She drew her chin in. She was not silly, though perhaps a little confused by her unusual reaction to the events in which she found herself. Caring so deeply about the children and their future, torn between her feelings of being unwanted and her desire to see Wade give the children a home.

Wade returned his coat to the hook by the door. "Let's do it."

The other men left without him.

Linette had told Missy where to find paper and pencils, and invited her to use what she needed. She got four sheets of paper and four pencils and laid them out at the table. Grady had gone upstairs with his mama, but Joey and Annie watched with interest.

"What are we going to do?" Annie asked.

"You showed me a tradition from your family. Now I'm going to show you a tradition from mine." She explained what they'd done when Mama and Papa were alive.

Annie took up her pencil. "But I can't write."

"I'll… We'll help you." The look she gave Wade informed him he was part of this.

His gaze captured hers. "We'll work together." His quiet response brought a rush of heat to her heart. She needed to stop judging him as if he was Gordie. She had to stop letting her feelings of rejection color her attitude toward him.

"Joey writes his name very well." At Wade's softly spoken words, she sucked in a deep breath.

"Fine, put your name on the top of your page." She wrote her name on hers and helped Annie, who sat at her side.

Wade and Joey, sitting side by side, wrote their names.

"Now what?" Joey asked, sounding a bit uncertain.

"Now we start listing all the good things about the past year."

The three of them stared at the blank page, no doubt thinking the death of two people they loved and missed could not be considered good. But her goal was to help them find good despite the tragedy of their lives.

Holding the pencil, her hand hovered over the paper as she realized she needed this exercise as much as they did. "There are things in life that make us unhappy and sad." Her voice was low. She hoped they wouldn't hear the strain that made her throat tight. "Those things are like clouds hiding the sun." To illustrate, she drew a little sketch. "Some clouds are white and fluffy. Some are dark and heavy." She added a dark one to her drawing. "But if we push them aside, the sun is still shining and it makes things bright." She erased the clouds and drew a field of flowers and trees and birds.

Annie nodded. "That's nice."

Joey and Wade wore matching expressions of doubt.

Missy smiled at how alike they were. "Let's see how many good things we can remember. I'll go first." She bent over the paper and wrote "Baby Chloe." "I love my little niece and I am so happy she's here."

Joey's expression relaxed a bit, but Wade's was still tight.

Missy looked at the three who shared the table. "Who wants to go next?"

"Me." Annie edged her paper toward Missy. "Write your name."

"My name?" Missy wasn't sure she understood the child's intent.

"Yes. I'm glad we found you."

Missy's heart stalled. Her gaze slid toward Wade. He watched her unblinkingly, his blue eyes giving away nothing. She swallowed hard. Did he object to the child's request? Perhaps he was concerned Missy would have a bad influence on the children, that she'd suggest they should bombard him with demands for

him to keep them. *No,* she silently informed him. She'd be the one doing the bombarding.

Joey bent over his paper. "I want to write her name, too."

Wade jerked his attention to the boy and Missy turned back to Annie. She wrote her name on Annie's paper.

Wade spelled out her name for Joey to print on his paper and then, to Missy's consternation, he wrote it on his own. She stared at the letters forming her name. Black. Thick. Solid. She tried to make sense of seeing them on his page, in what was supposed to be a list of good things. If she'd given it a bit of thought she might have predicted the children would count her as a good thing. But Wade? She fought to keep from looking at him.

"Is that bad?" Joey asked, misconstruing her silence.

She turned her attention back to the children. "Not at all. I'm so touched I can't think of what to say."

Annie patted Missy's hand. "You'll think of something."

Missy chuckled. "I suppose I will."

Satisfied that things were back to normal, Annie studied Missy's page. "What else are you going to put on yours?"

"You two for sure." She wrote their names.

"But what about Uncle Wade?" At the uncertainty in Joey's voice, Missy held the pencil poised above the paper, wanting to satisfy the boy, but not wanting to give Wade cause to think her too forward.

Then she thought of a solution. "I'm grateful Uncle

Wade brought you here." She wrote that down and sat back, satisfied with her answer.

Only then did she allow her gaze to go to Wade. Her breath stalled at the flat blue of his eyes, like lake water on a cloudy day. Had she offended him by writing his name on her list? Perhaps he saw it as an attempt on her part to link them together.

How could she make it clear that was not her intention? Ah, by reminding him her only desire was to make the season enjoyable for the children.

"I can't think of anyone I'd sooner spend Christmas with than you two," she told them. "Now what else do you want to put on your list of good things?"

"My dollies."

Missy dutifully added it to Annie's sheet and drew two tiny dolls for good measure.

"My ball," Joey said, and he wrote the words, drew a ball and grinned at her.

She grinned right back. This was part of the enjoyment she'd hoped and prayed for. Helping all of them remember the good things.

"Your turn, Uncle Wade," Joey prompted.

"That's easy. You two." He wrote their names and drew two stick figure children.

"What else?" Annie perched her knees on her chair and leaned across the table to watch her uncle. "Something different."

"Hmm." He tapped the pencil against his chin and looked past Missy.

She waited, her heart beating solidly against her ribs. Somehow she knew whatever he decided to put on his list would please the children.

He nodded, bent over the paper and drew a tall triangle.

Two dark-haired little children watched.

"What is it?" Joey asked.

"You can't tell?" Wade pretended to look shocked. Both children shook their heads.

"Humph. I thought you'd know immediately. Maybe this will help." He drew a square shape at the bottom of the triangle and a star at the top.

"A Christmas tree?" Joey sounded as if he thought his guess was foolish.

"Of course it's a Christmas tree. It's a real good thing that I can spend Christmas with you." His look included Missy and she couldn't help but feel pleased. Whether or not he meant to include her in his gratitude, it felt good to think so. To think she might be a welcome addition rather than a necessary nuisance. The words had become a constant echo in her head.

She dismissed the idea as quickly as it came. This wasn't a time for regrets but for rejoicing.

For the better part of an hour, they added to their lists. The children included food, warm mittens that their mama made, the candy Wade had given them. Missy was about to turn the activity toward a prayer for the New Year, or even a play, when Joey grew so serious she feared he would cry.

He sat back. "I forgot the best stuff."

Missy darted a look at Wade. He shook his head to indicate he had no idea what the boy meant, then turned to his nephew. "What's the best stuff?"

For answer, Joey leaned over the paper, pencil in hand. With the tip of his tongue peeking from his mouth, he studiously and carefully drew two stick fig-

ures, a man and a woman. He drew a hat on the head of the man and put a boy and girl between the figures. When he was done he looked up. "The best thing in the world was having Mama and Papa. They loved us."

Tears clogged the back of Missy's throat and she couldn't utter a word.

"They surely did," Wade managed to say, his voice hoarse.

Annie touched the stick figures. "Mama and Papa," she whispered, then sat back and attempted to draw a man and a woman on her own paper. Her efforts were crude but it was clear to them all what she intended to portray.

"The second best thing." Joey turned his attention back to his paper, but he didn't draw anything. "I don't know how to draw God." His voice quavered.

Wade pulled the paper closer, but his pencil never touched the page, either. "How do you draw God?" He shoved the sheet toward Missy.

She shook her head. "You can't draw God."

"Yes, you can." Annie pulled the page toward her and drew a big circle that enclosed all the stick figures and toys and everything. "God is all around us. He's everywhere."

"Indeed He is." She hugged the child tight.

Wade reached across the table and cupped his hand over Annie's head. When he met Missy's gaze, his eyes were full of warmth and life and—dare she think?—regret. If that was what she saw she silently prayed he would turn his regret into action and do something to keep these children.

He reached for Joey and pulled him close. "You two are pretty special," he murmured.

"They certainly are." She knew a warning note had crept into her voice, but she couldn't help it. How could anyone think of letting these two precious children go? To strangers, at that.

She held his unblinking gaze, silently, persistently letting him know her opinion.

He shifted and bent over his paper again to draw a box with four legs, a neck and a head.

The children watched, trying to guess what it was. He added a tail and mane.

"A horse!" Joey crowed. "A funny-looking horse."

"Of course it's a horse." On the ground beside the horse, he drew a cowboy hat, and then laid the pencil down and faced Missy, giving a slight tilt of his head toward the paper.

She understood his message. He was a cowboy. There was no room in his life for children.

"There's nothing in this life that can't be changed," she said in a quiet, firm tone. She didn't know how long she had with them, but whether it was a day or two, thirty or longer, she would continue to urge him to reconsider and find a way to keep the kids.

Chapter Four

Wade shifted his gaze away from Missy. Why must she ruin every occasion with her insistence that he should, could and must keep the children? Did she think it was easy to contemplate giving them away? His arm tightened about Joey until the boy squirmed. Wade relaxed his hold, though everything in him wanted to pull the pair to his chest and keep them there.

He would think only of what was best for them. In the meantime, he had a few days to build a store of memories to take with him into the future...a future that, for him, looked as barren as the rock face of a cliff.

"What's next?" he asked, in an attempt to divert his thoughts.

She startled and looked from him to the papers, paused as if to collect her thoughts. "Now we write a prayer for the New Year." The words seemed to come from a distant spot.

"You *say* prayers," Annie protested.

"You can write them, too."

"Why?" Joey, always the practical one, demanded.

Missy drew in a breath and slowly smiled. "I think my mama and papa thought it would help us remember what we prayed. They encouraged us to put our papers in a drawer or in our Bible so we could see how God was answering our prayers."

The children looked as intrigued as Wade.

Joey leaned closer to Missy. "What sort of prayer did you write?"

Although Missy smiled at the boy, her eyes filled with a faraway look, as if she'd gone back to a time when her parents were alive. "Well, let's see. Mama and Papa encouraged us to be honest about what we prayed, but to try and not be selfish." She chuckled.

Wade realized he was leaning forward, as eager as Joey to hear what amused her, and forced himself to ease back.

"I remember one year I wrote 'Dear God, I know you can do anything, so maybe you could make Eliza be nice to me.' Eliza was my friend."

Annie's eyes were wide. "Did your mama and papa scold you?"

"No." Missy stroked the child's head. Wade realized Annie's hair was braided just as Susan used to braid it, and his throat tightened with longing, loss and a hundred other emotions.

"But later Mama said God might want me to answer my own prayer by being nicer to her. She showed me a verse in the Bible. 'A man—or person—that hath friends must shew himself friendly.'"

"Did you be nice to her?" Annie asked.

"I tried." Regret laced the words.

Wade grinned. He guessed that, just like now, she expected the other person to bend to her wishes.

"Other years, I prayed for different things for the New Year. Like Papa's business to do well. And Mama to get over her illness." Missy's voice cracked.

It was all Wade could do to stop himself from reaching over the table and squeezing her hand in sympathy. Her mother had been ill, but had died in a tragic accident. Indeed, life was filled with tragedy, some of which was unavoidable. Reason enough, he thought, to give these children a good home where such things could be avoided better than he could hope to do.

"What did you pray last year?" Joey asked.

Missy's mouth opened in surprise. "Why, I'd forgotten until just now. I asked God to give me a chance to start a new life and He has."

Joey nodded. "I think I understand. Uncle Wade, will you help me write my prayer?" He shifted his paper toward him.

Wade picked up his pencil and prepared to write.

"Dear God," Joey began. "I know You can't give me back my mama and papa, but could You give me someone to love me."

Wade's heart cracked, and his hand refused to write the final words. He clamped his teeth together and finished the sentence. How could Joey doubt his love?

With a muffled groan Wade caught his nephew's chin and turned his head to face him. "Joey, I love you. You know I do." He didn't care that Missy could hear the agony in his voice, and see it in his face if she cared to look.

"Then why do you want to leave us? Where are we going? Can we stay with Missy? That might be

okay." Hope and despair wove through Joey's voice as he spoke.

Wade's eyes stung. He would not look at Missy for fear of openly shedding tears and having her see him as less of a man. He cleared his throat. "Joey, all I can tell you right now is I'll make sure you are in a good place. That's what I promised your mama." He pulled the boy into his arms. His heart squeezed out a meager beat as Joey remained stiff.

Wade knew his answer had not satisfied Joey, but it was the best he could give.

Annie, clinging to Missy, suddenly sat up straight. "Help me write my prayer."

Missy picked up a pencil. Wade wondered if she felt the same degree of dread over what Annie might want as he did. But then, why should she? She did not have the same heart-and-soul connection to these children who were all that remained of his family.

His lungs tightened and his chest muscles froze, even as he forced himself to come to his senses. He reminded himself of the facts. He had spent a lot of years on his own, his solitude broken briefly by visits to his sister and her family. It wouldn't be that hard to return to the lonely life of a cowboy.

But nothing inside him believed it.

Annie leaned over the table, watching Missy write as she dictated, "Dear God, I want to stay with Uncle Wade."

Someone might have poured scalding water over him, so great was the burning pain he felt. Wade jolted to his feet, managed to scrape out the words "Excuse me," and strode from the room toward the front door.

"Where's he going?" Annie's voice thinned with fear.

"I don't know, but I'll find out," Missy said.

"Maybe he's leaving." Joey's voice dripped with resignation.

Wade grabbed his coat, but before he could get his arms into the sleeves, Missy snatched it from him and returned it to the hook. "Wade Snyder, are you planning to walk out of these children's lives?"

He had no idea if she meant now or when the adoptive couple came, but in either case, the answer was the same. "I will do what I must."

"Why do you think you must?"

He dragged his gaze to hers, expecting a challenge. Instead, he saw sympathy that threatened his resolve. He jerked his eyes away. "I promised my sister."

"Am I wrong in thinking you promised to give them a good home?"

He nodded.

"You can do that."

"No, I can't." He reached past her, grabbed his coat again and left the house without a backward look.

He heard the door open and close behind him and knew Missy followed him. He ground his teeth together. Why couldn't she simply accept that the decision had been made? Why couldn't she believe he was acting out of concern for the children?

Despite his long strides, she trotted to his side. "Wade, I don't understand why you aren't willing to make a few sacrifices in order to give these children a home."

He kept moving, resisting the temptation to break into an all-out run.

She dogged his every step. "All you need is a housekeeper or a wife."

He jerked to a stop and turned to her. "Do you really presume to know what I need and offer a solution?"

Uncertainty flickered across her face for an instant, then her lips tightened and her eyes challenged him.

He didn't give her an opportunity to answer. "You have no idea how hard it is to think of letting them go to another family. How could you? You've never had to face this decision. But I have my reasons and I don't care to share them."

Her eyes narrowed, as if assessing him. He could almost hear the gears turning in her mind as she no doubt tried to interpret his words.

He pressed his hand to his forehead. He'd just given her one more thing to gnaw on by hinting that he had other reasons he couldn't keep the children—other than being a wandering cowboy and having no home or wife.

"Let it go," he told her, preempting her questions.

She shook her head. "I can't. I know what it's like to be a nuisance and it bothers me to know these adorable children are being made to feel that way."

"A nuisance?" Who would consider her such when she was so eager to be helpful? So loving and kind and a pleasure to watch? Grateful for the opening to divert the conversation away from himself, he asked, "Why would you feel you were a nuisance to anybody?"

She looked away, perhaps thinking of denying her words, then shrugged her shoulders and brought her gaze back to him. "When my parents died my brother became my reluctant guardian. He never let me forget that he didn't much care for the role that had been thrust upon him." She swallowed loudly. "I was a necessary nuisance." Fire came to her eyes. "Of course,

Vic saw me as a tempting morsel. He wanted me, but not because he cared." She crossed her arms over her chest and looked away.

"Who is Vic?"

"Vic Hector was my brother's partner. A snake of a person. He thought I was part of the bargain when he and Gordie threw in together. A few weeks ago, he moved into our house. He thought he owned Louise, too. You know what he told her?" Fury colored Missy's words and brought a blush of pink to her cheeks. "He said he would sell her baby as soon as it was born. Can you imagine?" Her body nearly shook with anger.

"Vic is the reason we fled to the Eden Valley Ranch," she continued. "God helped us escape and led us through the journey. He provided a place for baby Chloe to be born." Missy pinned Wade with a hard look that blasted through his defenses and pierced his thoughts. He tried in vain to rebuild the barriers, but was distracted by the way her fists balled and her breath came in bursts.

"Don't you see? God can provide a way for you to keep Annie and Joey if you but ask."

"I expect He could. However, I am not going to ask."

"Because you have your reasons?"

"That's correct."

She gasped and her eyes narrowed. "You said you were married. I assumed your wife was dead. Was I mistaken?" She pressed her hand to his arm.

He shook it off. "You understand nothing. My wife is dead. Has been for six years." His head told him to leave, to walk away from this conversation, but his feet remained rooted to the ground.

"Dead? Then I don't understand why you don't re-marry or—"

Would she not drop the subject? She was like a dog with a tasty bone. "Are you applying for the job?"

"Me?" Missy stepped back two feet. "No. I won't ever again be a necessary burden to someone. No." She shook her head hard. "I would never settle for a marriage of convenience, which is what you are suggesting."

He lifted one shoulder. He hadn't suggested it at all. He simply wanted her to stop insisting that he should find a way to keep the children. "It's what you're suggesting on my behalf."

"That's different."

"How?"

She didn't get the opportunity to answer as, in the distance, the house door banged shut.

She jerked her gaze away. "The children… Are you coming back in?"

When he didn't answer, she met his eyes again, her own full of hopes and wishes and, as he looked deeper, a hint of a challenge. He averted his gaze before she could see his doubt, the depth of his failure, his sorrow, the emptiness of his heart.

If only he could allow himself to think of marrying again. It would enable him to keep the children.

But both were out of the question.

Missy walked back toward the house. She hoped Wade would follow, but whether or not he did, there were two children there wondering why the adults who were in charge of them had disappeared. No doubt they would fear being left.

She well understood the feeling. For months after her parents had died, her insides had knotted whenever Gordie was late returning home. She'd worried about being alone. At least Gordie had to give her a home. What would have become of her if he hadn't been there?

She shook the thought away. That time was no more and would never be again, because she meant to have a way of being on her own. If only she could give the same security to the children. But they were so young they would need a home for years to come.

Wade didn't have to enter a marriage of convenience, but surely he could court a young woman of his liking who cared about the children.

He'd neatly avoided her question as to why he wouldn't remarry. Curiosity made Missy's steps slow and she half turned, intending to ask him the question again. But he was on her heels and hurried past her to hold the door open.

"The children await," he said.

She took her time entering the house as she studied him. "Something awful must have happened."

He met her look with wide-eyed innocence, as if he didn't understand what she meant. She might have been convinced except for the twitch at the corner of his right eye. Maybe if she discovered what had happened, she could help him see it didn't matter when it came to the children.

She didn't get the chance.

"They're back!" Annie crowed, rushing to her uncle, who swung her into his arms. Joey, however, hung back, a wary look on his face.

Missy removed her coat, then bent over to hug the boy. "I'm sorry we took so long. We were talking."

He remained stiff.

She understood his uncertainty about his uncle Wade and even her. "Joey, I promise you I won't leave without telling you. Nor will your uncle." She glanced over her shoulder, hoping Wade would follow her lead.

He knelt beside her. "I promise you that, too." He held out an inviting hand to Joey, who shrugged away from him.

"But you will leave." A shudder rattled through the boy, and Missy almost considered settling for a marriage of convenience for the sake of giving these children the home and security they so desperately needed. Only the searing memories of her past stopped her.

Her eyes lingering on the sullen child, she straightened. "Who wants to hear about the rest of what my family did?"

"I do." Annie jumped up and down.

Missy kept a hand on Joey's shoulder as she led them toward the kitchen. "We made up plays. Would you like to do that?"

Annie bounced ahead. Wade stayed at Missy's side, his attention mostly on Joey. But when he briefly glanced at her, she knew she wasn't mistaken in seeing sorrow and regret in his eyes, as deep as the ocean.

He loved these children. He didn't want to part with them. But something had happened to convince him he must. Again she vowed she would find out what.

Having made up her mind, she entered the kitchen. Then her steps faltered. It was the same room she'd been in many times since arriving at the ranch. The same sage and dill scent. The same polished black

stove and array of coats on hooks next to the back door, where the men normally came in from doing chores. Even the same basket of potatoes on the cupboard.

But it was not the same room from which she'd followed Wade. Three chairs were overturned. The papers they'd written memories and prayers on had been torn to shreds and scattered across the floor. One pencil lay broken in two beside a table leg.

Thankfully the others weren't there to witness the scene. Linette might have been offended at the way her home had been treated, and Grady frightened at the anger displayed.

Wade strode into the room and took in the destruction, then slowly turned to confront the children.

Annie sidled close to Missy.

Joey stood alone and defiant.

"What happened here?" Wade started off sounding surprised, but ended on a harsh note. "Who is responsible for this mess?"

"Joey said—" Annie began.

Wade silenced her. "No tattling. Joey, is this your work?"

"What if it is?" Anger, frustration and emotions Missy couldn't name flew across Joey's expression, and her insides clenched in sorrow.

"I don't care if you leave. I don't need you. I don't need anybody." Joey threw the words out boldly, but failed to convince Missy he meant them.

She guessed from the strained look on Wade's face he was no more convinced than she. *Oh, Wade, listen to your heart. Find a way. They're worth it.*

At Joey's words, Annie pressed hard to Missy's side. Overwhelmed by a thousand memories of shar-

ing the same uncertainties, anger and sorrow of these children, she grabbed the nearest chair and sat down. Annie climbed to her lap and they clung to each other. How sweet the comfort from those trusting arms.

Missy wanted to pull Joey to her knee as well, knowing he was frustrated and had turned it to anger. But Wade must deal with him first.

Please, God, let Wade see this for what it is. A cry for assurance.

Wade sat on a chair facing his nephew. "I understand you're upset and worried, but you can't do this. It's wrong. A person must control anger, not let it control them."

"Who says?" Joey gave him a defiant look.

"Me."

"Why should I listen to you? You don't care about us. We're just a nuisance."

At the word Missy had recently used, Wade's gaze came to hers—so full of sadness and despair, she slid her chair close. He was hurting every bit as much as Joey and Annie. Missy's arms ached to be able to comfort all of them. They were each hurting, trapped by something out of their control. At least that was the way she thought they all viewed the situation. She pressed her hand to Wade's arm and gave him a look that she hoped conveyed her sympathy.

"You are what these children need," she whispered to him. "You can be what they need. For your sake as much as theirs."

His eyes searched hers, seeking assurance that her words were true, perhaps even seeking courage to follow the path that would keep them together.

He smiled, though there was more regret than joy

in the expression. He turned back to Joey. "You aren't a nuisance to me, and you should listen to me because I'm your uncle and I care about you." He reached for the boy, but Joey again shrugged away.

"No, you don't. You're just saying that." He kicked the nearest object, which happened to be the back of an overturned chair.

Wade gave Missy a helpless look, as if to ask what he should do.

She didn't know how to help them. He knew the children far better than she. All she could go on was her own experiences. In this position she'd want…

She'd want what she couldn't have—her parents. Someone who loved her more than their own pursuits. Maybe Wade didn't deserve these children, for he'd made it as clear as the air atop the mountains that his interests were more important than their needs.

Except she was convinced there was something more than personal interests holding Wade back, just as it had with Gordie.

Wade gave a slight nod, as if accepting that Missy had nothing to offer. He turned back to the boy. "Joey, I love you. You know that."

The boy grunted in disbelief.

"However," Wade continued, "I cannot allow destructive behavior such as this. You will clean it up, then when Mrs. Gardiner comes down, you will apologize for breaking her pencil."

Joey glowered at Wade and made no move toward obeying.

Missy held her breath, waiting to see what Wade would do if the boy outright defied him.

Wade continued to look at him, his expression firm but unyielding.

Joey shuffled his feet, then with a drawn-out sigh put the chairs aright, gathered up the scraps of paper and took them to the stove.

Annie leaned back to look at their uncle. "Joey said you weren't coming back. I said you were. He said maybe this time but not next time." Annie's voice caught and she turned back to Missy arms, sobbing. Through her tears she managed to get out a few muffled words. "He said you didn't care and then he got mad."

Joey scowled at his sister. "Tattletale." He was about to say more, but at a warning look from Wade, settled for wrinkling his nose. "Who cares? Christmas is over and it wasn't any fun."

Wade closed his eyes, but not before Missy saw the pain in them. Her heart went out to him. Whatever his reasons for not keeping the children, she didn't doubt his love for them.

Help him.

She knew it was what God would want her to do. Comfort him as Louise and others had comforted her when her parents had died and Gordie got burdened with caring for her.

She rubbed her hand along Wade's arm, feeling the tension in the knotted muscles. Beneath her palm they began to relax. Slowly his eyes opened and locked with hers.

Her heart tipped a little and leaked out an emotion that tightened her throat until she couldn't swallow. It frightened her to think of caring about this man. If he didn't have room in his life for helpless children,

he certainly wouldn't have room for a young woman who longed for so much—acceptance, value, heart-and-soul-deep caring. And yet, despite his arguments to the contrary, she glimpsed exactly what she needed in this man.

If only he would give it.

She sucked in a deep breath. She would not allow herself to need what she couldn't have. No. She would keep her eyes firmly on her goal of becoming a self-sufficient young woman. But in the meantime, perhaps God had given her a task.

"Does Christmas have to be over?" she asked. Perhaps in helping Wade and the children, she could undo some of the hurt she'd endured.

Chapter Five

Missy's question was so unexpected Wade couldn't think of an answer, especially as his attention remained trapped by her hand gently rubbing his arm. He couldn't tell what she meant by the gesture, but surely she didn't know how it touched the very depths of his heart, reaching past the defenses he'd erected right to the core of his hurts and failures. Why hadn't he seen what Tomasina needed? Why hadn't he been enough for her?

His face grew wooden. His chest muscles tightened. He'd never before admitted how it hurt to not be enough. Was he not worth as much to her as a child would have been?

At the thought he felt the hurt and anger build in him.

Just as it had in Joey.

Wade scrubbed his lips together and tried to think how he could make Joey see it wasn't the boy's fault that his uncle couldn't give him what he needed. It was Wade's inadequacies that were to blame.

But Joey had shifted his attention to Missy and her question.

For the first time since they'd returned to the house, Joey showed something besides anger. Only because of Missy, Wade pointed out to himself, reminding him yet again of his insufficiencies to understand and meet the needs of others. But even he had to admit a degree of curiosity about her question.

"What do you mean, it doesn't have to be over?" he asked.

She favored the children with a gentle smile full of so many good things, then turned her smile upon him and offered him the same.

He smiled back with hope and expectation, feeling as if she really cared how he felt.

Again he was struck by her ability to do that.

Her eyes remained gentle as she spoke. "I heard a song back in Montana, 'The Twelve Days of Christmas.' I guess it's a way to make Christmas festivities last longer. I believe it originated as a game, where you have to remember what was given each day until the end." She softly sang the words to the song, causing the children to giggle at the various gifts given.

Wade chuckled, too, enjoying the entertainment every bit as much as the children did. Missy had a fine singing voice, the prettiest blue-green eyes that danced with joy, and a way of looking at him that could almost erase six years of regrets.

When she finished, Annie cocked her head as if deep in thought.

Missy flashed a grin at Wade as if to say she could hardly wait to hear what his niece would think of the song.

"Maids a-milking doesn't sound like fun, but I'd like to see lords a-leaping. But I don't know any lords."

Missy's merry laugh rang out. "I don't, either." She flashed a teasing look at Wade. "But maybe we could see one cowboy leaping."

He laughed and sputtered at the same time. "Or maybe not."

When Joey chuckled, Wade wished for a way to convey his gratitude to Missy. The best he could do at the moment was nod. But he'd thank her properly just as soon as he could.

"Do we go hunting French hens and pear trees?" he asked, in an attempt to keep his thoughts on the suggestion.

She chuckled. "I haven't seen any pear trees around here, or French hens, for that matter, though Linette has some ordinary hens out in the chicken house."

"Then what do we do?" He asked the question that had the children straining to hear the answer.

She tipped her head and grew thoughtful. "I don't know. Perhaps you have suggestions." She let her gaze go to both children and then back to him.

Him? He could think of nothing he'd sooner do for twelve days then spend time with Missy and the children. But the children would want more than sitting around talking.

"Could we have a party?" Annie asked, half eager and half cautious.

"A party with just us?" Missy asked. The way her eyes flashed, as if hit by bright sunlight, Wade suspected she liked the idea as much as he did.

Annie thought for a second. "Maybe we could invite all the children."

As they spoke, Joey edged closer to Missy.

Fearing the boy would withdraw if Wade acknowledged it in any way, he settled for quirking an eyebrow at Missy. She gave the slightest nod, as if to indicate how fragile the moment was, and assure him she would proceed with caution.

She turned her attention to the boy, a look of tenderness on her face that made Wade yearn for something that he couldn't—wouldn't—identify. "Would you like that, Joey?"

"It'd be okay." He barely managed to sound disgruntled.

"Then let's ask Mrs. Gardiner for permission."

"But that's only one day," Annie stated. "There are twelve days of Christmas."

Wade grinned at his niece. How he enjoyed these children. He was so thankful that Missy had just offered him a Christmas of twelve days to enjoy them, he almost hugged her.

"We've already had two days. Doesn't that count?" she asked Annie.

The girl sighed dramatically. "I guess so."

Missy flashed Wade a look so full of amusement that he almost choked. This woman had the power to unsettle him. He'd best be on guard or she'd have him agreeing to things he didn't intend to agree to.

Linette and baby Jonathan returned to the kitchen then, with Grady, Louise and Chloe right behind them.

"Can I ask?" Annie said.

Wade nodded.

Annie jumped from Missy's lap and went to Linette.

Missy smoothed her skirt and slowly brought her attention to Wade. But this time he did not feel ac-

cused by her look. Instead, he felt as if they were allies. Enjoying the children together, regretting it was temporary and determined to fill the days they had with memories to carry into the future.

Would she miss them as much as he would?

Would she miss him? He certainly would her.

Shocked as he was by the thought, he suddenly realized something. If he would miss her after such a short time together, what would these children experience? Had he made life more difficult for them by asking Missy to help care for them? Should he persuade her to take over their care once he left? He could come back and visit the three of them.

He pushed the thought aside before it could take root and grow. She had plans that did not include any of them. Besides, there was a couple in Fort Macleod eager to adopt the children. It was what Susan would have wanted. A real family with a father and mother, not something temporary.

The only regret Wade allowed was that he couldn't keep them himself. Couldn't give them what they needed.

He didn't examine the thought any further to decide if he meant for the children, for Missy or for all three.

Linette's pleasant voice interrupted his musings.

"A party would be a lovely idea," she said, thankfully providing an escape from his thoughts. "Would you like to invite the other children?"

Missy nodded. "If you don't mind."

"Not at all. I'll ask Eddie to arrange the delivery of messages to the girls in town and to the twins and Belle." She meant Blue and Clara's two little girls, Mercy and Abel's twins and Grace and Ward's little

girl. "We can ask the Jones children directly." Cassie
and Roper Jones and their four children lived nearby.

Missy's genuine smile gave Wade pause. How eager
she was to entertain a group of children who weren't
in any way related to her. She certainly was a generous, giving woman. One who could deal with disappointment, yet still find a way to make others happy.
Vastly different from Tomasina.

Not that he blamed his wife for what had happened.
He slammed the door on such thoughts.

"After dinner let's make invitations to send to the
others," Missy said, and the children nodded. "But first
let's help Linette make the meal."

Wade's world felt right and good as Joey and Annie,
under Missy's patient tutelage, helped prepare the food
and set the table.

During the meal Wade and Missy sat facing each
other, with Joey and Grady beside him, Annie and
Louise and Chloe beside Missy, the others surround-
ing them.

There was a time Wade had dreamed of a warm and
welcoming home similar to this. Not as large, with perhaps not as many people living under the roof, but a
woman with a big heart, and children to fill it.

He ducked his head as Eddie asked the blessing.
And Wade offered his own prayer.

*Lord, I thank you for my many blessings, but please
keep me from longing for things I can't have. Give the
children a loving home and keep my heart from breaking when they leave. And Missy—*

He couldn't bring himself to pray her out of his life,
though the time would come when they'd part. His life
would suddenly be empty and he'd be alone.

No need to get all sentimental and sorrowful. He'd find the forgetfulness he'd need by riding after some cows. He always had in the past.

Somehow, he was less certain that he'd find it so easily again when he left this place.

Subdued by thoughts of the future, he passed the food and helped Joey cut his meat. Thankfully, the boy did not object.

The meal passed in a pleasant murmur of conversation. Several times Wade found himself checking to see if Missy enjoyed a tale told by one of the others as much as he had. He was not disappointed. Her eyes danced with merriment and her lips twitched as Eddie told about the antics of the barn cats.

"How is Thor?" Linette asked, and Wade jerked his attention in her direction.

"Thor?" Louise and Missy questioned at the same time.

"Our pet fawn. Jayne and Seth rescued it." Linette referred to one of the newlywed couples living in a log cabin on the ranch. Wade had met them Christmas Day. "Of course, he isn't a fawn any longer and roams the woods freely. He used to hang about playing with the children. I just wonder if he's okay."

"Seth said Thor paid him a visit the other day and Daisy said he played chase with her before he left."

Joey perched on the edge of his chair. "A pet deer. Will I get to see him? Can I play with him?"

"I can't promise," Eddie said. "But he often shows up when he hears children outside playing."

Joey wriggled. "Will he come if he hears me?"

"He might, especially if Grady is with you."

Wade knew Joey would be wanting to go outside

and play at first opportunity. In fact, he glanced toward the door as if wondering if he could skip the rest of the meal.

Missy smiled gently at the boy. "We need to make invitations first, remember?"

He nodded, his expression half argumentative, half resigned.

Grady settled the matter. "Thor usually comes later in the afternoon, anyway."

They finished the meal and Missy insisted she and the children would clean up. She soon had the three young ones laughing as they raced each other to do their chore first.

Again Wade admired Missy's patient guiding hand with children. She'd make a great mother. And no doubt a great wife. The idea of her marrying sliced through his thoughts as he quickly skimmed through the marriageable young men in the area that he was familiar with. And there were lots of them. Such as Lane and Ward's younger brother and a dozen others—cowboys, settlers, freighters. But somehow Wade knew none of them would appreciate Missy's attributes the way they should.

"How many invitations do we need to make?" Joey asked.

"Let's see." Missy counted all the families. "Four." She turned to Linette. "Have I forgotten anyone?"

Linette shook her head.

"Okay, that's one for each of us to make."

Annie counted out loud, pointing to herself, Joey and Grady. "There's only three of us."

Missy lifted her hands in mock surprise. "You didn't count me. I'll make one."

"Then what about Uncle Wade?" Annie asked. "He needs to make one, too."

"Yes, that's true. What about it, Uncle Wade?" Missy gave him a look so full of teasing challenge that he almost choked on the coffee he'd been lingering over.

Eddie and Nate, both rocking their babies, chuckled.

"She's got you dead to rights," Eddie said.

"No point in fighting it. I tried and I lost. You will, too." Nate seemed certain of whatever he meant, but Wade had no idea what it might be. He had no intention of losing anything. Especially his good sense.

"But you only need four," he pointed out, hoping that was reason enough to be excused from the activity.

"You can make the fourth and I'll help the children."

He opened his mouth to protest Missy's offer, but she held her palms toward him before he could get one word out. "Oh, no need to thank me. I don't mind in the least." And with an airy laugh, she vacated her chair and swept her arm in a wide arc, welcoming him to take her place.

He didn't mind helping them. In fact, it quite appealed. But for some reason, as he sat in the offered chair he felt as if he committed himself to more than making a party invitation. As soon as he acknowledged the thought he realized how silly it seemed. He turned his face toward Missy just as the children did, waiting for her instructions.

She smiled at each of them, but her gaze clung to his longer than the others. Warmth and sweetness. Home and comfort. Peace and belonging. How could one glance convey all that?

He dragged his gaze from hers and stared at the

paper in front of him. Now was not the time nor the place to take leave of his senses, he cautioned himself. Not that there ever was such a time.

A man must do what a man must do and that meant keeping his barriers up. Allowing himself no dreams of what he'd once wanted.

Missy gloried in the way Wade looked at her. Realizing she treaded on dangerous ground, she'd jerked away, hopefully without him realizing, and then her gaze returned. Everything she wanted heated her eyes until she could barely blink.

He'd smiled as if he understood. Then shifted his attention to the papers she'd placed on the table.

Of course. They were here for a purpose other than to get lost in each other's gaze.

She hustled her thoughts into order. "Let's fold the paper in half. On the front, we can draw a picture, and inside we'll put the details of the party."

She let the children fold their sheet. Annie's was almost square. Both boys' papers were cockeyed, but Wade bent over his, concentration evident in his pose, and folded it precisely.

"Done." He sat back and gave her a look of triumph.

She laughed. "Good job." She could feel the twinkle in her eyes as their gazes caught and held.

She pulled herself together, handed out colored pencils. "Decorate the front."

"How?" Joey made it sound like an impossible idea.

"However you like. Stars. Christmas trees. Party things."

Grady and Annie bent over their paper and were soon hard at work. Wade stared into the distance for

a moment, then picked up a pencil and began to draw. Missy resisted an urge to lean over his shoulder and look at his sketch. Instead, she turned her attention to Joey, who was stuck for a plan.

"I can't draw," he complained.

"But I expect you can color. So color the page."

"Just color it?" She might have suggested he leap off the roof for the surprise he showed.

"Why not? Isn't some pretty gift wrapping paper just colored?"

He looked at her as if she might be teasing, but when he saw that she meant it, he grabbed a red pencil and began to scribble over the paper.

She shrugged. It was getting done. That's all that mattered. She moved to Annie's side. The girl was drawing a row of figures—odd-looking people with big heads and no body, only legs and arms. An assortment of boys and girls, Missy guessed. The curly loops on some heads indicated girls, while bald heads indicated boys.

"These are all the people coming to the party," Annie said.

"That's a good idea." Missy moved to Grady's side. With a green pencil, he was drawing a Christmas tree. It was lopsided and crowded to the side of the page to make room for a manger.

"'Cause it's Jesus's birthday," he explained.

Only after she'd admired the work of the others did she let herself look at Wade's sheet. She'd expected something as crude as the drawing he'd done of his horse, but she immediately realized he was quite an artist, for he drew a reasonable likeness of her holding

hands with Joey and Annie in a circle of other children. "How did you do that in such a short time?"

"They're just caricatures. They don't take long at all."

"But they're so good. It looks like you spent hours on them."

"Nope." He spoke with obvious pleasure at her admiration. "It doesn't take any skill. Just the shape of the face and a few details. I used to do it in school when I got bored." He grinned crookedly. "It got me into trouble often enough. Teachers didn't like me not paying attention and they liked it even less if I did an unflattering sketch of them."

Missy tried to imagine him in school, but he was so forceful and strong she couldn't picture him as a child.

"Why didn't you draw like this when we did our thank-you list?"

He quirked an eyebrow. "I did something the children could relate to."

It continually amazed her that he understood the children and their needs so well. "Do you do this often?"

He shrugged. "It helps pass the time when I'm alone watching cows."

"Do you save them?" She wondered if he used scraps of paper and threw them in the fire when done. What a shame it would be to waste his drawings.

Another shrug. "I keep a few. Leave most of them at Stuart's place."

The friend who owned the ranch where he planned to go. Hearing his name reminded her of just how soon Wade meant to leave. All that prevented him from going immediately was the children, and he expected

to have them sent to another family soon. He'd said he thought to get word any day.

She felt the disappointment in her chest. He'd never given her reason to think he might stay and yet she'd clung to that hope.

Would she never learn to guard her heart?

Yes, she would. She'd learn to be a secretary and take care of herself. She'd need no one and expect nothing from anybody.

"Now what?" Joey asked, pulling her attention to the children and their finished artwork.

"Now we write the details on the inside. Party at Eden Valley Ranch, Thursday, December 28 at one o'clock in the afternoon. We'll put individual names on each one. I'll help you write it," she said to Annie, before the child could protest.

"I can write it myself," Grady said.

"Me, too," Joey echoed.

With much prompting, they wrote their invitations. Several times Missy and Wade glanced at each other, sharing their amusement and admiration of the children.

This was how family should be. The thought filled her with such longing that she ducked her head and pretended a great interest in arranging the pencils. Family should cherish each member. Caring for one another should not be a burden. Oh, if she had a family like this she would gladly serve them, wholly love them and enjoy every daily task.

However, this family was not hers. Nor would it be. She could try and protect her heart from the sorrow she'd know when they were sent away.

Or she could enjoy them for a time knowing it was

temporary, knowing she'd miss them all like a giant toothache when they left.

All? Even Wade?

Yes, she admitted in the secret corners of her mind. She'd miss Wade. Hopefully she would forget him quickly.

She feared she wouldn't.

"Can we take one to the Joneses?" Grady asked.

Missy brought her attention back to the children, had each write the name of the recipient on their invitation. Wade's was chosen to go to Cassie and Roper's children.

How Missy would like to keep that picture. Would Cassie think she had fallen for Wade if she asked for it back?

She had not fallen for the man. How foolish could she be?

After donning their winter wear they left the house in the direction of the Jones family, who lived past the other buildings.

Joey and Grady raced ahead, chasing each other. Annie hung back, holding Missy's hand on one side and Wade's on the other.

Again the notion struck her that this was how family should be. But before she could dwell on it, Annie dropped their hands and ran after the boys.

They passed the cookhouse, from which wafted the scent of cinnamon. "You haven't had a chance to taste Cookie's famous cinnamon rolls," Missy told Wade. "You'll get a chance on Sunday, after the service."

"If I'm here Sunday."

The reminder quenched every thought of sharing the upcoming day with him.

"Do you expect to hear from the Bauers by then?" She thought to point out all the reasons the couple wouldn't come. It was winter. Fort Macleod was a two days' ride away. It was Christmas season. The stage-coach wasn't running. He knew all that and still hoped the Bauers would come. As if he couldn't wait to send the children away.

Missy recognized that the resentment she felt stemmed from her own experience. In this case, she didn't doubt Wade's love for the children. It would be difficult for him to turn them over to the adoptive family and yet he meant to do exactly that.

"They seemed very eager to get the children," Wade said. "I guess if they want them badly enough, they'll find a way to make arrangements."

With that, the subject was dropped.

As they passed the barn on one side, some horses were outdoors and ran to the fences to watch them. On the other side were two log cabins—one where Jayne and Seth lived and behind that, Sybil and Brand's. Brand's dog, Dawg, woofed at the children and ambled out to join their play.

Wade and Missy continued in mutual silence past the bridge toward the Jones house. Cassie opened the door at their knock.

"Come in. It's so nice to have company."

"We brought an invitation," Annie said.

"It's for the children," Grady added.

Daisy and her sister and brothers joined their mother, crowding round. Annie handed the invitation to seven-year-old Billy, who was so impressed with being chosen to receive it that he puffed out his chest and read it aloud.

"A party! Can we go?" Daisy asked.

"Of course. It sounds like fun," Cassie answered.

Missy wondered if it also sounded to her like a chance for some quiet.

"Would you care to come in?" Cassie asked.

Missy glanced at Wade. She'd rather hoped he would suggest a walk—just the two of them—but he nodded. No need to be disappointed, she told herself as her insides grew empty and needy. Maybe that was the root cause of her problems in the first place—always wanting and needing what she couldn't have.

"Can we go out and play?" Neil asked. At twelve, he often worked alongside the men, but still enjoyed free time to be a child.

"Away you go, all of you."

After scrambling into coats and boots, they stampeded outside. Soon they were all playing tag, throwing snowballs and chasing each other.

Cassie stood beside Missy and Wade in the doorway and watched them. She sighed. "I thank God every day for the gift of these young ones."

Wade nudged Missy. She refused to look at him, knowing he meant her to realize that being adopted could be a very good thing for the children. Yes, she silently admitted, if they didn't have family who were able to provide a home if they so chose.

Cassie closed the door and ushered them into the kitchen. Signs of a happy family life surrounded them. A doll sat on one chair as if waiting to be remembered. Four empty glasses were on the table. A collection of papers and pencils, plus an assortment of well-worn books filled a bookcase next to the table.

Missy looked about the room. It reminded her

of how her home had been before her parents had died. Would she ever get over missing them? No, she wouldn't. Nor could she hope to again find the peace and joy and love she'd known when they were alive.

She sat across from Wade, at Cassie's invitation. Feeling as if her emotions would fill her eyes, Missy avoided looking at him. But of their own will, they sought him out. She feared her hunger and hopeless longing filled them.

His blue eyes managed to say more than she could bear—understanding, a shared regret over what they had lost and were about to lose in giving the children to be adopted, and an echo of her own empty heart.

She'd lost her family. He'd lost his. Different circumstances but the same pain.

As Cassie made tea and chattered, a thousand things were spoken into the silence.

"Do you take milk or sugar?" Cassie's words jerked Missy back to the here and now.

"No, thank you, this is fine." She hoped Cassie wouldn't notice the tremor in her voice. Or the way Wade looked at her, for that matter.

They drank their tea, ate a cookie and talked, though for the life of her Missy couldn't have said what they talked about, so lost was she in the twirling confusion of her own thoughts. Why did she feel this particular attraction to Wade? Of course he was a handsome man, and probably drew women's glances wherever he went. But it was more than that. More than the sense of power and purpose emanating from him. It was the way their gazes so often collided, the sense of seeing into his heart and having him see into hers and understand it. It was the way he treated the

children. How even his drawing spoke to Missy in the secret places of her heart.

She glanced about, saw the invitation propped on the nearby cupboard, but could not bring herself to ask Cassie to save it for her.

Wade pushed aside his empty cup. "Thank you for the tea and cookies. Now if you don't mind, I'd like for Missy to show me around the ranch. I've only seen the inside of the house and barn."

"There's a lovely view from up the hill. You cross the bridge and go past the wintering pens." Cassie seemed pleased with the idea. "Don't worry about the children. Daisy will keep an eye on them and so will I."

They thanked her again and stepped out into the bright winter sunshine. Earlier Missy had hoped he'd ask to take a walk around the ranch. Now, though, she found it difficult to breathe, the air getting stuck at the knot in her throat.

A walk, just the two of them? What had she been thinking to agree to that?

Joey ran past. "Look. Thor is coming."

She followed the direction he indicated. Sure enough, a deer trotted from the woods. She could make out a few spots.

Thor ran up to the children. Dawg woofed a greeting and then he and Thor butted heads playfully.

Thor bounced toward Grady. The deer and the boy soon engaged in a game of chase that had Missy laughing. She turned to share her amusement with Wade, only to find him watching her with serious eyes.

She couldn't look away, trapped by the emotions she read. Her pulse bumped as if she'd stepped in a hole. Something inside her stirred to life, a feeling un-

like any she'd ever before experienced. A longing that went far beyond wanting a home and acceptance. This feeling danced across her heart with a joy she could hardly believe existed.

"Look, Uncle Wade." At Joey's call, Wade slowly pulled his attention from her, his gaze clinging till the last second, leaving her breathless and a tiny bit afraid. He would soon ride out of her life and she'd be left with a heart emptier than what she'd grown used to.

She tried to shift back to who she was and what she'd wanted when she'd arrived in Eden Valley. She pressed her hand to the pocket of her dress beneath her coat, but felt no familiar rustle of paper. When had she last reached for that bit of advertising? Christmas Day? It seemed an eternity ago.

Wade chuckled at the way Thor chased Joey and then stopped, inviting the boy to chase him.

Thor would no doubt mature and leave the security of the ranch. The children would miss him, but he was, after all, a wild creature, not intended to be confined to a corral or even a yard.

Something about that thought seemed to warn Missy. She, too, must move on and follow her plan. Yes, she would miss the children and their uncle, but reminded herself that this was only an interlude.

She would do well to remember what was real and what was not.

Chapter Six

Wade watched the play of emotions on Missy's face. He had experienced something between them that made his insides ache as though chilled by a cold north wind. It rang with familiarity, like a dream he'd once cherished. He'd even thought he'd achieved the dream.

He shook his head, hoping to clear his thoughts. But the action had little effect. He reminded himself of all the reasons he could not wish for such things, although he wanted them clear to the core of his being.

Nor would he give the wish a name.

Had Missy felt it, too? Was that what her serious look indicated?

He could not follow that line of thought. Instead, he watched the fawn and children playing together and remembered his intention to go on a walk with Missy. "Shall we cross the river?"

She nodded and fell in beside him. They retraced their steps as far as the bridge, then tramped across it, pausing momentarily to watch the water swirling past the icy, snowy edges. Soon it would turn cold enough to freeze it over.

There should be a lesson for him in that, Wade decided. Today the water flowed. Tomorrow it would freeze. Today he entertained hope and acknowledged soul-deep desires. Tomorrow he'd remember the reasons he must deny them, and his heart would again grow a shell of ice.

They ventured onward, past the wintering pens where many of Eddie's prize cattle fed, while the main part of the herd ranged in snowy pastures. A bunch of pigs squealed and jockeyed for the best position at the feed trough.

Missy paused to watch them and laughed aloud as one pig was pushed aside and ran around frantically, seeking an opening.

Wade was so relieved to hear her laugh that without thinking of how she'd interpret his actions, he draped an arm about her shoulders and pulled her to his side. She hesitated, then relaxed there.

"I've seen cowboys at the table act like that," he said, which made her chuckle.

She looked up at him, her eyes dancing. "Are you the cowboy who elbows the poor fellow aside?"

He fell into her gaze, like a man falling into a warm body of water. "I might be," he acknowledged regretfully. "Sometimes the pickings are a might thin and if you let a greedy man at the food before the others, there's not enough to go around." Captured by the interest and encouragement in her eyes, he continued, though only about half his attention was on his words. The rest was on the power of her gaze. "I knew a man who would take about half of what was served. I've never figured out how he could pile so much on his plate and not spill it. Practice, I suppose."

"They say practice makes perfect."

He did not want to argue, but he knew sometimes all the practice in the world didn't make things perfect... or even satisfactory. He ignored the thought, wanting to think only of this moment and the sense of camaraderie he shared with Missy.

She pulled her gaze away from his. "Did you want to go farther?"

"Sure."

They continued on. The path before them was less trampled and the snow crunched beneath their feet. They climbed toward the crest of the hill. Missy watched the ground before them, picking places to step where the snow wasn't too deep.

Wade kept his attention on their surroundings. "Stop." He caught her arm and pulled her to a halt.

"What?" She looked about as if expecting some danger.

He pressed a gloved finger to his lips and then pointed to their right. Sitting on a branch not thirty feet away was a snowy owl, its beady yellow eyes watching them unblinkingly.

"Oh." Missy pressed a hand to her mouth and gave Wade a look that signaled her pleasure. "What kind of owl is it?" she whispered.

He told her. "They're the heaviest ones in North America."

Her eyes sparkled as she stared at the owl, which stared right back. Then it silently flew past them with a sweep of its mighty wings.

Startled by the size of the bird flying so close, Missy stepped back, bumping into Wade's chest.

He caught her and steadied her.

"Oh, I'm sorry." Color stained her cheeks as she tried to right herself and pull away, but he turned her to face him and held her in the circle of his arms, looking down into her eyes.

Their gazes melded. The moment froze. His heartbeat ticked with urgency and hope. If he could stay here, alone in a snow-encased world with Missy, perhaps he could forget his past failings and simply live. He let her gaze burn into him, search all the hidden peaks and valleys of his heart, except for one corner— the knowledge of how he'd failed as a husband.

His resistance must have shown in his eyes for she blinked and pulled away. She turned and smoothed the fingers of her gloves. "Seeing that owl was special. I'm glad we came this way."

He, too, was glad they'd come, though he wasn't thinking of the route they'd followed. No, his thoughts went more toward the few seconds when he'd felt as if life lay before him, an open road that beckoned.

Missy took a step forward, giving him a questioning look as if to ask if he meant to continue.

He could think of nothing he'd sooner do at the moment than prolong this interlude, and fell in at her side. "Have you heard of John James Audubon?" When she shook her head, he told her about the man who'd studied birds and drawn them with such detail. "He hoped to draw every bird in North America."

"Did he succeed?"

"I don't know, but he drew a lot. He drew the snowy owl after observing it for a long period. He said he watched one at the edge of an ice hole waiting for fish to appear, and when they did, the bird caught them using its feet." Wade spouted off information like a

talking encyclopedia, but he couldn't help it. Having Missy at his side, watching him as he spoke, unleashed his tongue in a way totally unfamiliar to him.

They continued upward until they reached the crest of the hill. Before them lay a snow-covered vista that rose to the mountain peaks and contrasted with the blue of the sky. They both breathed deeply, taking in the beauty and serenity before them.

She shifted her attention to him. "How do you know so much about snowy owls?" she asked.

He grinned crookedly. "The winter days get long. Stuart has a very fine library, so I pass the time reading."

"And drawing." She studied Wade, her eyes awash in blue-green. "It sounds very peaceful."

"It is."

Her eyes narrowed slightly, and he feared she might suggest there were other, happier ways to pass the time. Knowing he teetered on the edge of acknowledging he'd like nothing better than a home filled with joy and love and laughter, he turned the conversation to other things. "How did you learn about this secretarial course you want to take?" Speaking the words emptied his heart in a whoosh, leaving it echoing with wishes and regrets. If only he could be what she needed, what the children needed. But he could not be selfish and put his desires ahead of their needs.

"I saw the advertisement in a ladies magazine back in Montana, and knew that's what I wanted to do. The only thing that kept me from going immediately was Vic. I couldn't leave Louise to deal with him alone." Missy's voice grew harsh at the mention of the man.

"How did Vic become part of your life?" It seemed such a man would be driven from her presence.

"When my parents died, my brother wasn't ready to accept the task of working hard for a living. He met Vic one night and Vic persuaded him there were easier ways to make money than through honest labor." She shrugged, though it was more a gesture of defeat than dismissal.

Wade wanted to pull her into his arms and shield her from the dark side of life.

She stopped and confronted him. "Do you know that man followed us all the way to Fort Macleod?"

The idea made Wade shudder. "Sounds like a determined man."

"A mean, selfish, hard-hearted man with absolutely no human decency." She swallowed audibly, her eyes flared with dislike. "Do you know what he did?"

Wade shook his head. He had no way of knowing.

"He kidnapped Louise right in the fort. Talk about gall. He had to know the Mounties would hunt him down. He would have taken the baby, too, but Louise managed to convince him Chloe would cry and make it impossible to hide from the authorities."

Despite knowing Louise and her baby had escaped, Wade felt his insides ice over. "What happened?"

"Louise flung herself from his horse when she saw two Mounties approaching. Thank God she wasn't hurt."

Wade caught Missy's arms. He couldn't help himself. "He might have taken you."

"If he'd seen me first he probably would have. The man is a snake. Nothing is beneath him."

"At least he's behind bars now." Kidnapping was

a capital offense. Vic would never be a threat to her again.

"I certainly hope so."

Her words made no sense. "What do you mean? Didn't they apprehend him on the spot?"

"I wish they had. But he rode away and the Mounties' first concern was Louise's safety. By the time they set out after him, he had a good head start. When we left, they had not brought word of his capture."

"He's free?" Wade looked at the vast open spaces before him, this time seeing the trees that could even now be sheltering a man with evil on his mind. Wade pulled Missy to his chest, wrapping his arms across her back, bending his head over hers in an attempt to hide her.

"Maybe Petey—the stagecoach driver—will bring news of his capture when he returns." Her voice was muffled against his chest.

Wade struggled to keep from tightening his arms about her even more for fear of hurting her. He glanced over his shoulder. A man could sneak up on them at any moment. "We need to get back to the ranch."

The tone of his voice caused her to jerk away and stare up at him. "Surely we aren't in any danger. Vic will be running and hiding if he isn't already captured."

Wade searched her gaze, wanting to keep her here in his arms, knowing he must get her back to the shelter of the ranch house. "He doesn't sound like the sort of man to give up." Vic might be ready to forsake his interest in Louise, seeing as she was married, though Wade wondered if that mattered at all to such a rogue. But Missy was another story.

"You are so beautiful that I can understand if he doesn't give up trying to get you for himself." Wade hadn't meant to speak the words aloud and wished he could pull them back when he saw the shock and surprise in Missy's eyes.

Would he never learn to understand what others needed?

She laid splayed fingers on his chest. The color of her eyes deepened and a smile curved her mouth. "Thank you for those kind words."

Their gazes fused and their hearts spoke far more than any words could.

The white owl flew past them toward the trees, seeking shelter. Wade would be wise to do the same. He turned his feet toward the path, tucking Missy against his side. "Stay close. That way you'll be safe."

His words mocked him. Would he fail to protect her just as he'd failed Tomasina?

Missy pressed to Wade's side. His worry had fractured her peace. She'd simply assumed Vic would have been captured by now, never to bother her again. But perhaps she was wrong. Her concern was laced with the knowledge that it seemed to matter to Wade. And for no reason that she could fathom. He wasn't obligated to take care of her. He didn't have a duty to protect her. Yet he showed more concern than anyone had since her parents had died. Except for Louise, of course. But even Louise had had her reasons—to keep peace in the home, to protect herself and then her baby.

They hurried back to the yard where the children, the dog and the fawn still played. She pulled away from

Wade, not wanting others to see and assign their own meaning to their closeness.

"Joey, Annie, Grady, it's time to go back," he called, making Missy note how fast the afternoon had passed.

Daisy called to her siblings. "We need to go, too."

Already the sun was dipping toward the mountains, throwing dark, sinister shadows across the landscape.

Missy shuddered.

Wade glanced about, then took a step toward her, misunderstanding her shiver for worry.

"I'm okay," she said. "Just getting cold." It didn't take long for the afternoon to lose its warmth. But it was more than the cold filling her insides with a wintry chill. It was the step back to normal. Normalcy might look good for the children, playing with friends as they were. It was less attractive for her. The few moments up the hill weren't her usual life, knowing she must forge her own path for the future, depending on no one, was. But for a brief spell, mattering to someone had been enjoyable. It was what she truly wanted in the deep, secret places of her heart. But she could not have it and would rather not face disappointment again in seeking it.

The children raced ahead to the house. Wade and Missy followed at a more sedate pace, though she got the impression he would have preferred she run the whole way. "You're worrying for nothing," she told him.

"You can't know that. I certainly don't."

"Rest assured, if he showed up I would not let him harm the children."

Wade ground to a halt. "But what harm might befall you? That's a concern."

She buried his words deep inside. She'd mentioned the children in the hopes he would say something exactly as he had. He had not disappointed.

He didn't wait for her to respond, but caught her elbow and hurried her along, not speaking again until they reached the door. He held it open and paused to look back as though he thought Vic may have followed them.

"I need to find Eddie." Wade closed the door behind her. His footsteps thudded away.

She shivered. Surely Vic was not a danger.

Louise was in the sitting room by the window, rocking little Chloe. "I'm glad to see you enjoying yourself."

"Well, I was until I told Wade about Vic, and he got nervous that the man might still be following us."

Louise stopped rocking. She pulled Chloe closer. "Surely that's not possible."

"I wouldn't think so and said as much to Wade. But he wasn't convinced and now I wonder. Do you think Vic is still a danger?"

Linette came into the room in time to hear Missy's question. "It's wise not to take any chances until we're certain that man has been captured. I'll let Eddie know and he'll alert the cowboys to keep a watch. That will make it almost impossible for anyone to get close."

Missy explained that Nate had already told Eddie, but relieved at her concern, she went to supervise the children. But as she played a game with them and assigned them chores to help with supper preparation, her thoughts kept harking back to the time on the hilltop when Wade had been so tender, so caring. It might

be temporary but it was a moment she would cherish for the rest of her life.

Wade returned for supper, then hurried out as soon as he had eaten.

"He's going to watch the place for a few hours," Eddie said. "The men have been taking turns on guard."

Missy hadn't known that and wanted to protest, to say it wasn't necessary and she didn't want to inconvenience others, but Louise spoke first.

"Thank you. It's nice to know we're safe."

"I'm taking the next shift," Nate announced. "You and Chloe will have to manage without me for a few hours."

Louise said, "We'll manage," but her eyes said she wouldn't like it.

Missy stared at her plate. This wasn't only for her sake, but she felt she had become a burden to everyone on the ranch.

Nonetheless, she had two children to take care of. It was her full responsibility now that Wade was out. She smiled as they turned to her after the dishes were done.

"Can we play a game?" Joey asked.

"Or you can read to us." Annie looked expectant.

The two glanced at each other and grinned, sharing some secret only they understood.

"Tell us a made-up story," Annie said, bouncing up and down as she spoke. "Like Uncle Wade did this morning."

What she wouldn't have given to be a little mouse in the corner so she could have heard that. "Fine. Get ready for bed first. Mind you wash really well." As she helped them prepare for the night, she tried to think what kind of story she would tell.

What kind had Wade told?

Would it be prying to ask?

She led the children upstairs and tucked them into their cots, then sat on a chair between them.

"Uncle Wade told about a cowboy who loved a lady," Annie said.

"Is that a fact?" Missy hadn't even had to pry to get the information.

"She was very beautiful." Annie stumbled over the word. "And she could sing and play the piano." She propped herself up on her elbow to consider Missy. "Can you play the piano?"

"Passably." She followed the direction Annie went with her questions, willing to play along because it was make-believe. Nothing would come of it.

"She could cook," Joey added. "Cookies and cakes and candy."

Missy chuckled. "Surely she could make a meal, too."

"Yup, fried chicken and pie. Lots of kinds of pie."

"What was her favorite pie?"

He mused a moment. "I guess apple." He nodded. "Yes, it would have to be apple."

Annie continued the story. "She and the cowboy got married 'cause they were in love, and they had a dozen kids. How many is that, Joey?"

"Twelve. Six boys and six girls. And he played lots of games with them."

Missy's amusement and pleasure ran clear through her, erasing debris and trash left behind by Gordie's often cruel comments. "Wow. That sounds like a wonderful story. I don't think I could tell a better one."

"Tell us about a little girl they had," Annie begged,

her brown eyes wide. "Tell us how much they loved her."

"That's easy. The day little…" She paused, waiting to see if they would give a name.

"Annabelle," Annie said.

Missy hid her smile knowing it was Annie's full name.

"The day Annabelle was born, the mama and papa looked at her and smiled. The papa said, 'She's just as beautiful as her mother.' The mama said, 'My heart is flooded with love for this perfect gift.'"

The children hung on her every word, so Missy continued.

"The papa knelt by the bed. He took the mama's hand in his and pressed his other palm to the baby's head. 'Let's thank God for this precious gift and ask Him to bless her every day of her life.'" Missy's parents had often told her that they did that exact thing the day she was born. Unfortunately, their untimely death had left the prayer unanswered.

She continued. "They introduced little Annabelle to her brothers and sisters. You see, she was baby number twelve. Many people thought they wouldn't be so happy to have another child, but they were and her brothers and sisters adored her." Missy continued on with a story that fulfilled the desires of her heart and perhaps those of the children, as well. She ended, "And when she was grown, she fell in love with a cowboy as strong and handsome and special as her papa. The cowboy loved her very much and they lived happily ever after."

The children lay back on their pillows, staring at the ceiling, quiet as they contemplated her story.

"Does everyone live happy ever after?" Annie asked.

Joey didn't give Missy time to answer. "'Course not. That's just in fairy tales. Isn't that right, Missy?" He confronted her with a hard look that reminded her of the incident earlier in the day.

She understood his anger. *Please, God. Show me a way to help him deal with his feelings.*

"Not everyone lives happily ever after, but remember I told you how God is always with you. He promises to lead us and take care of us." Linette kept a Bible in each room and Missy pulled a copy from the nearby drawer. "Why don't I read some of His promises to you?" She turned to Psalm 139 and read, "'Where shall I go from thy Spirit? Or whither shall I flee from thy presence?'" She skipped a verse. "'If I take the wings of the morning, and dwell in the uttermost parts of the sea: even there thy hand shall lead me, and thy right hand shall hold me.'" She lowered the Bible and looked at the two intent children. They had obviously been taught to listen to the word of God. "God is with us wherever we go and He will guide our steps if we let Him." She might have been speaking to herself. She would trust God and follow His lead. No matter where it took her or how difficult it was.

"Now you two need to go to sleep." She kissed each of them. Annie hugged her around the neck. Joey lay stiff and unresponsive. She hugged him nevertheless and was rewarded when he relaxed in her arms. She tiptoed out of the room even though there was no need for quiet. But it was how her mother had always said good-night.

The memory was bittersweet. Knowing she wouldn't

be able to sleep, Missy descended to the sitting room, where a lamp burned to welcome Wade when he returned. The others had left. The new babies required that their mamas get sleep whenever they could. Nate would be leaving during the night hours.

Missy prowled about the room, studying the paintings on the wall that Linette had done. Summer scenes of flowers in an English garden—a marked contrast to the view out the window here during daylight hours.

She touched the yarn in the basket Linette kept at her feet. She'd had little time to knit in the past few days, but a pair of socks was partially done.

Missy paused before the window, but saw only her own reflection. If she leaned closer, she could make out lit windows in three of the buildings down the hill. The ranch was settling in for the night, quiet and peaceful. But inside her, thoughts rolled and clashed, and memories awoke. Memories of her parents brought to life by the story she'd told the children. She longed for the love she'd known when they were alive. Only now she wanted something more than loving parents. She rubbed her arms where Wade had held her close.

She wanted a love of her own.

She shook her head and wandered down the hall. A love such as she wanted existed only in fairy tales.

Reality was standing on her own, finding her happiness without depending on others.

She stepped into the library, grabbed the first book her hand touched and, unable to read the title in the darkness, hurried back to the sitting room. She settled into one of the green wingback chairs where the light would allow reading and looked at the title.

"Wives and Daughters." She laughed aloud. Just the

sort of book she did not want to read. She half rose, intending to seek something more suitable, but sank back down, curious about the contents. She opened the volume to the frontispiece—the picture of a woman reaching for a new bonnet—and saw that the book had been released in serial form in *The Cornhill Magazine*. She eyed some of the chapter titles. At "The New Mama," she decided to start reading. Soon she was interested in the life of a little girl who was much loved by her father, though Missy grew impatient with her simpering ways.

The outer door rattled, startling her from her reading. She glanced up to find Wade standing in the hallway, looking at her.

The world tipped a little, then righted itself. She stared at him as if he'd walked from the pages of her book.

He took his hat off and studied her with unblinking intensity. "I thought you'd be asleep."

"I started reading." She lifted the book without breaking eye contact.

"A good story?" He sounded a little distracted.

"So-so." Silence descended upon them, which neither seemed inclined to break, and yet Missy wasn't uncomfortable because of it. In fact, her cheeks grew warm and she squeezed the book, determined to ignore an urge to go to his arms and thank him for caring enough to stand guard in the dark, cold night.

Nate strode into the room. "Anything suspicious out there?"

Wade jerked his attention to the other man. "It's all quiet."

Nate pulled on his outer wear. "I'll have a look

around. Get some sleep. Both of you." And he stepped out into the night.

Missy got to her feet. What was she thinking to be sitting in the dim room, alone with Wade?

"Good night." His softly spoken words stopped her.

She slowly turned. There were so many things she wanted to say. A thousand things. She settled for one. "Thank you for watching for Vic." With that she hurried to her room.

She had but two tasks while here—take care of the children and get Wade to see he should provide them with a home. How had her thoughts and actions gotten so far off course?

Chapter Seven

Wade hurried up the stairs and into his assigned bedroom. He lit the lamp and went to the doorway to the children's room. They slept peacefully. Annie had her two dolls tucked in her arms. Joey lay with his arms tossed to his sides as if on the defensive.

Wade understood why the boy would feel that way. Life had pulled the rug out from under his feet, though, if Wade were to be true to his beliefs, he'd have to say God had done it. But that made God sound unkind and petty. Better to blame life.

Satisfied the children were settled, he turned back to his own bed and in a few minutes crawled under the covers. During the long dark hours of patrolling the perimeter of the ranch yard, he'd had plenty of time to talk sense into himself.

He understandably felt protective of Missy. To know there was danger lurking out there and do nothing to prevent it from descending upon her would be irresponsible. If he could help another person avoid disaster, even in some small way, it would make up for failing Tomasina. There was no more to it than that.

He'd about reasoned himself back to common sense when he'd stepped into the house and saw Missy sitting in the big armchair waiting for him. At least that had been his first thought.

Someone to welcome him home. Would he ever put that dream to rest and accept that it would never be?

She'd smiled up at him in a way that made his heart lose its moorings and his head forget all the things he'd just told himself.

Thankfully Nate had appeared before Wade could say or do anything that would take him beyond the boundaries he'd laid out for his life.

The next morning he was as anxious as the bouncing children to go downstairs. They could hardly wait for tomorrow so they could have their party.

"What will we do today?" Annie asked.

"Do we have to do something?" He thought of the pleasure of sitting quietly with Missy at his side, talking and sharing. Learning about each other. Whoa! His thoughts were running away from what his life allowed.

"But Missy said we could have twelve days of Christmas," Annie insisted, while Joey sat back, a doubtful look on his face.

Seeing their different expectations—Annie hopeful, Joey awaiting the worst—Wade shifted his own wishes for the day. "I'm sure we can think of something." Hadn't Missy said something about a play? He'd like to see her create such a thing. He'd even like to help her do so.

No. It was an activity for the children's pleasure. Not for his.

He heard the clatter of the stove lids and knew the household was astir. "Go get dressed. We'll have breakfast, then discuss what we want to do today."

Annie scampered away, while Joey dragged his feet across the floor.

Wade stared after him, troubled by his nephew's attitude. If only the adoption hadn't been delayed. The sooner the boy was settled, the better. For Joey, at least. For Wade, every extra day with the children was a gift. He drew to his heart the thoughts of forgetfulness that he had practiced and perfected over the years.

Though he knew all his practice would be in vain when he said goodbye to the children and Missy.

He tried to tell himself there was no reason he should include Missy. No reason but the truth. He had grown exceptionally fond of the young lady in a matter of days. It would be difficult—if not impossible—to push her memory from his thoughts.

He dressed and accompanied the children downstairs to the kitchen. He ground to a halt in the doorway at the sight of Missy at the stove, three pots before her. She was singing "The Twelve Days of Christmas" as she worked.

His heart beat faster in eager response despite his efforts to keep his thoughts focused on the reality of his life and decisions.

She turned, a smile lighting her eyes like the sun filling the sky. "Good morning. I trust you all slept well."

"You haven't forgotten," Annie said.

Her gaze slowly went to the child. "What haven't I forgotten?"

"The twelve days of Christmas you promised us."

Missy chuckled. "I haven't forgotten." Her gaze returned to Wade's, full of welcome and invitation.

He swallowed hard. Surely he mistook her look.

"How did you sleep?" she asked, likely intending to include them all, though her eyes never left Wade.

"With my eyes closed," he replied, almost choking from a tight throat.

She laughed. "Good to know." She shifted her attention to Joey. "You ready to help me make breakfast?"

At first the boy hung back, determined to remain sullen, but Missy held out her hand to him. "Come along. I need someone with a strong arm to stir the porridge."

Joey could no more resist her than he could fly. There was something about her eagerness for life that attracted them all.

Soon she had the children busy with chores. Wade sat at the table, content to watch. She filled a cup with steaming coffee and set it before him.

"Thanks," he said. "You're good with the children." He could picture her with a dozen of her own.

"You think so?" She waited for his affirmative answer, then rushed on. "I enjoy them." Annie pressed to her side and Missy planted a kiss on the top of her head. "They are both very special." She reached out and brushed her hand over Joey's hair.

The boy ducked his head to hide his pleasure.

Wade envied Joey.

Now where had such a strange thought come from? But it was true. He wished Missy would run her hand over his head. He shifted his gaze and stared off into nothing. Nothing but the memory of long, lonesome nights following even longer days of regrets and dis-

gust at how he'd failed to take care of Tomasina. What would Missy think if she knew the truth? Would she brush her hand along his arm in sympathy, or jerk back in shock and silent accusation?

He didn't care to find out the truth.

The others joined them then and Missy served breakfast.

"You don't know how much I appreciate your help," Linette said. "But I feel a little guilty at leaving you to do so much of the work."

"I don't mind in the least," Missy assured her.

Louise added her thanks and Missy reassured her, as well. "I haven't forgotten how much Chloe cries in the night."

"She's getting better." Louise quickly defended her daughter.

Missy laughed. "I wasn't criticizing her." She caught Wade's gaze and raised her eyebrows. "Remind me to never do so."

At her teasing, warm look, he felt his face freeze, his mouth half-open and his eyes wide. He couldn't blink. Couldn't move his lips. Could not think.

"Uncle Wade, you look funny," Annie observed, and he jerked his mouth shut and managed to shift his gaze from Missy. Of course she didn't mean for the glance to be so personal, so...

He couldn't think of a word to describe how it felt, but throughout the rest of the meal his thoughts hopped about like a man standing barefoot on ice. He had lost his mind. That was the only explanation for it. And he needed to find it again real quick. He could not do it here when his eyes kept seeking Missy, following her every move. When his thoughts were stuck on her

words and expressions as if they were sustenance to a starving man.

The table was cleared, coffee finished. Missy supervised the children doing dishes, though he suspected she could have done the task in half the time without their help.

Wade had to get out of this room. "My horse needs some tending. I need to grease the wagon axle. And I might as well chop some wood to add to your store." Yes, he had things to do outside, none of which he'd thought urgent until this very moment.

"That's not necessary." Eddie protested. "I've got cowboys to chop wood."

"I'll do my share."

Joey and Missy stared at him. Missy was surprised, shocked, perhaps a little disappointed. Or was he only wishing she was? But he was certain Joey scowled at him.

"I'll be back," Wade assured the boy.

Joey shrugged and gave him a good view of his back. His message was clear—he didn't want Wade to leave and didn't want to admit it. But the boy couldn't cling to him forever.

The thought did little to ease the tension pulling Wade's own shoulders forward.

He shifted his gaze back to Missy, who dropped a hand to Joey's shoulder. "We'll be busy getting ready for the party. Don't worry about us."

"He won't," Joey mumbled.

How wrong the boy was. Wade would miss the children every day. He'd miss this time spent with Missy. He'd be the loneliest man on the face of the earth.

He hurried from the house before he blurted out

his regret. Before he allowed any of them—himself included—to believe things could be different.

Missy told herself she wasn't disappointed. She had no cause to think Wade might want to spend the morning with them helping prepare for the party, but she was and she did.

Annie, thankfully, played in the soapy dishwater and paid little attention to her uncle's departure. Not so Joey. He saw every goodbye as a reminder that there would soon be a final one.

Missy must focus on the children's needs. That was not only her job, but her desire. She wanted to make their stay as enjoyable as possible.

She rubbed her temples at the realization of how she had fallen down in pursuing her goal of persuading Wade that the children belonged with him.

She'd had opportunities to discuss the matter with him but had gotten sidetracked by her own weakness. Such as a few minutes ago, when she'd felt as if the two of them had shared something special that isolated them from the others. And the day before, when they'd been entirely alone, but her thoughts had selfishly clung to the moment, enjoying the sweetness it held.

But from now on she would focus on keeping the children busy and happy. And she'd confront Wade at each and every opportunity in an attempt to get him to see that they needed him.

She knew just the thing to occupy the children. She went to Linette and whispered her request.

The woman nodded. "Excellent idea."

Annie and Grady watched with curious, eager eyes. If Joey felt either he hid it rather well.

"Who would like to make candy to give out at the party?"

Grady grinned and nodded.

Annie bounced up and down. "I would. I would."

"Joey, how about you?" More than anything Missy wanted to stir a little enthusiasm in the boy. But Joey only shrugged. Her heart went out to him. He couldn't see past the rejection he felt from his uncle.

No matter how much it hurt Joey to feel rejected, she wished for a way to help him understand those negative feelings needn't ruin his life. He had so much to live for.

Ignoring his lack of response, she clapped her hands. "Great. Let's get the kitchen clean and then we'll make candy. Annie, you sweep the floor. Grady, you put the pots away. Joey, you dump out the water."

The kids hurried to do their assigned chores, with Missy assisting and guiding their efforts.

"What kind of candy are we going to make?" Annie asked as her broom pushed crumbs into a pile.

"Hard rock candy. Have you made that before?" She brought out a large pot for the syrup.

Annie paused to watch her. "I helped Mama make fudge. Papa said fudge was his favorite."

"Fudge is good. I think it might be my favorite, too."

"I think I helped my first mama make candy," Grady said, sounding confused. "Maybe. I'm not sure. Sometimes I can't quite remember her."

"Come here." Linette hugged the boy to her side. "You will never forget her. And if you need to refresh your memory you have the picture I drew for you."

Cheered by her words, Grady hopped away to look into the big empty pot. "Can I help?"

"You are all going to help. After all, this is your party."

Both children grinned, pleased to be considered so important in the scheme of things.

Now to draw Joey into the proceedings. "Joey, what do you know about rock candy?" Missy looked about. "Joey?" He wasn't in the room. "Did he not come back from dumping out the dishwater?" she asked Linette.

"I haven't seen him."

"He should have been in before now. I better see what's keeping him." She went to the door and called him, but she got no response. And she couldn't see him anywhere. "That's odd."

"Maybe he went to find his uncle," Linette suggested.

"I'll check." Missy grabbed a warm shawl and stepped out into the cold. She called him again, but heard nothing but the squawk of a raven and the crackle of bare branches in the wind. She shivered, and not just from the cold.

What if something bad happened to Joey? She was supposed to be taking care of him and yet he'd disappeared without her even noticing. What if Vic had made it to the ranch and thought taking the boy would serve his evil purposes? Missy shook away the idea. Perhaps Joey had gone after his uncle. She hoped so, though it meant she'd have to confess her failure to Wade.

She skirted the house, intending to make her way downhill. At the corner she heard the sound of someone chopping wood, and stopped. The woodshed was

to her right, and Wade was swinging an ax over and over. After splitting a log, he neatly stacked the pieces, then positioned another chunk of wood.

He moved with a rhythm that was almost musical. Missy couldn't look away. Something about him held her mesmerized. Power. Strength. Determination. A great wave of longing rose within her, making it difficult to breathe. He straightened, wiped his brow, then picked up another piece of wood and put it on the chopping block.

She jerked her attention back to finding Joey. He was obviously not with his uncle. Rather than bother Wade, who certainly bothered her, she turned aside. She'd find Joey on her own. After all, it was her responsibility.

She circled the house. Joey did not answer her calls. Perhaps something like a snowy owl in the woods behind the house had caught his interest. She followed a narrow trail of animal tracks for a distance, but seeing no boot tracks, she turned back.

A sound to one side brought her to a halt and she strained her ears to hear it again. A crashing, as if someone was pushing his way through the bushes.

"Joey?" She followed the sound.

"Papa, Papa."

Wade looked up as Grady trotted down the hill in search of Eddie. Wade watched the boy, letting everything he knew about Grady underscore what he'd been telling himself. His adoptive parents loved him and he loved them. He had a good home with Eddie and Linette. Wade was doing the right thing in getting an adoptive home for Annie and Joey. "Papa." Grady's

call turned shrill and brought Eddie from the barn. Now it sent a shiver up Wade's spine. Something had obviously alarmed the boy.

Wade turned his attention back to the house, but could see nothing to explain the way his heart picked up speed. Nevertheless he waited to hear what had brought Grady in search of Eddie. Wade couldn't hear the words, but something about the boy's wild gesturing made him rest one foot on the chopping block and watch. Seemed something was amiss.

When Eddie glanced in his direction, Wade's nerves tingled. He was on his way over before the rancher waved to him.

"What's up?" he asked, doing his best to sound casual. He glanced around and saw no danger, yet he knew something was wrong. He felt it in the marrow of his bones.

"Grady says Joey and Missy are—" Eddie began.

"They're gone," Grady exclaimed. "Missy and Joey."

"Gone?" Wade must have chopped wood too long for his arms felt spongy. "Where?"

"Don't know. First Joey went out and didn't come back, then Missy went to find him. When she didn't come back, Mama sent me to get Papa." The boy grabbed Eddie's hand. "I'm not going to disappear next, am I?"

"No one's disappeared and you certainly aren't going to." Eddie's expression grew hard. "Let's see what's going on."

Wade was several yards ahead of him.

By the time he reached the house he had a good lead on Eddie and he burst through the door into the kitchen.

Linette sat holding the baby. Louise rocked Chloe. Annie stood beside the table, looking at a book someone had given her. At first glance things appeared as normal as potatoes and gravy, except for the guarded expression in the eyes of both women.

And the burning urgency in the pit of his stomach.

"How long—" Wade halted when he saw Annie, who seemed unaware of the tension in the room.

"Annie, why don't you take the book back to the library and look at some of the other books there," Linette suggested.

Annie slowly closed the book and sighed. "You want to say adult stuff, don't you?" With another weary sigh, she dragged herself from the room.

Eddie and Grady clattered in and Grady was sent to keep Annie company.

Linette spoke before Wade could voice his question again.

"I might be concerned over nothing, but they've been gone half an hour or more, when I expected them to be right back."

"No, you're right to be worried. It's cold out there and who knows what they've encountered," Eddie assured his wife.

"Or who," Wade added, his heart beating as hard as the blood pushing through his veins.

"I have someone watching but there's a hundred different ways a man could sneak onto the ranch." Eddie shook his head. They were both thinking of Vic.

"That's hardly reassuring, dear." Linette gently scolded her husband.

But she could have saved her breath. Nothing Eddie

or Linette or any of them said could be worse than the dreadful pictures racing through Wade's head.

He remembered all the awful things Missy had told him about Vic. His cruel intentions toward Missy, Louise and the baby.

Wade met Louise's gaze. Her mouth twisted as if she'd tasted something bitter. No doubt her reaction to the possibility of the pair falling into the hands of Vic. "Find her. Find them both."

"I won't be back until I do." He strode from the house into the cold.

Eddie followed. "They're out there somewhere and we'll find them."

Wade didn't answer, just stood outside the house, trying to find a clue as to where they'd gone. He studied the packed snow in the yard. There were too many footprints to detect just one or two sets. He circled the house with his head down, looking for something, anything. He made his circles wider and wider until he reached the edge of the yard next to the thicket of trees that he guessed went on for some time. A person could get lost in there.

He looked down and saw them—small fresh boot prints.

"Here," he called. "Missy went this way." She must have had her reasons. Whatever they were, he meant to follow her tracks. He trod a narrow trail made by animals. He and Eddie reached a little clearing with lots of deer and coyotes tracks, but he could not discern any more tiny boot prints. He had not seen Missy's tracks for the last hundred feet, but neither had he seen any evidence of her leaving the trail, so she must have come this way.

He carefully circled the clearing, again looking for a clue. He reached the edge without discovering any.

Eddie waited, knowing he could destroy any signs if he wasn't careful, and he seemed to understand this was something Wade needed to do.

"I can't see anything." Wade straightened and looked around, as if Missy and Joey might appear in the trees. "They can't simply disappear."

"No, they can't, and at least there is no sign of this Vic you're worried about."

Wade did not find Eddie's words comforting. What if he'd missed a clue? Something as obvious as horse hooves that blended into the deer tracks. It would be a mistake a youngster would make. He was fairly confident he would have noticed something like that. To be certain, he scoured the area again, all the while praying, *God, give me eyes to see.*

And God did. In an area where the snow had not yet buried the leaves, he detected a faint depression. "I found it." He wasn't certain, but hoped he saw two different sized tracks. Eddie jogged over and they bent under the branches and climbed over the fallen trees. "Why would either of them come this way?" He didn't expect an answer from Eddie and got none.

"Missy, Joey," he called. Did he hear an answer above the sound of his harsh breathing and the rattle of them scrambling through trees? He couldn't be certain and pushed on, aware they made enough noise to frighten off anybody lurking around the area. There was only one reason the idea didn't bring relief. If Vic had threatened Missy and Joey, Wade would like to get his hands on the man and make sure he would never do it again.

Wade paused once more and signaled Eddie to be still. "Missy! Joey!"

A faint sound came from his right.

"Over here," he called to Eddie. He battered his way through the bushes and drew to a halt when he saw them.

They sat on the cold ground, Joey wrapped in Missy's arms. They turned tear-streaked faces toward him.

With a groan of agony at the sign of their sorrow, and a sigh of relief that they were safe from Vic and all in one piece, Wade dropped to the ground beside them and wrapped his arms about them.

"You were gone so long," he murmured. "I was afraid..." He wouldn't name his fears, but Vic had been only a part of them.

"We needed a little time." Her words whispered against his cheek. "I'm glad you came."

At the strain in her voice his relief ended. "Are you okay?"

"I'm cold."

"How long have you been sitting on the ground?" In the few seconds he'd been there the chill had seeped clear to his innards.

"A little while."

Eddie took in the scene. "Come on, Joey, I'll take you home and your uncle will help Missy get up."

Joey hesitated, darted a glance at Wade. "Don't be mad at Missy. She came looking for me." He hung his head. "I tried to run away but I just got lost."

Wade rested his hand on Joey's head. "I'm not mad at either of you. Only glad you're safe and sound. But it's cold sitting on the ground so let's go back."

Joey scrambled from Missy's lap and began to follow Eddie.

Wade got up and reached out to help Missy to her feet. She took his hands and pulled herself up, but as she tried to stand she crumpled against him.

"I'm sorry but my legs seem to have fallen asleep. I'm sure I'll be okay in a minute or two." But she clung to him, unmoving. She wasn't going anywhere under her own steam for a bit.

He scooped her up in his arms. "Let's go home." He meant back to the ranch. He had no home. Nor, for that matter, did she. His arms tightened around her. If only he could offer her a home, but he knew his limitations.

"I'm sure I can walk," she protested, as she settled one arm about his neck.

"Sure could have fooled me."

"I feel like such a baby."

"Not to me." Then, fearing she would take his words in a way he hadn't meant them, he added, "I've held babies and they're a lot lighter."

She chuckled and pressed her forehead to his cheek. "Wade, I do believe you just called me heavy. I don't know if I should be offended."

"No need to be." His voice seemed to come from an unfamiliar spot behind his heart.

"Okay." She rested her head against his shoulder. Her voice drifted sleepily.

"You're awfully cold." He could feel it clear through their layers of clothing. Was she chilled enough that she was in danger?

"I was there a long time."

"Tell me what happened." He needed her to stay awake; and besides, he truly wanted to know. He

turned his back to the branches and pushed his way through, huddling forward to protect Missy.

"It was pretty much as Joey said. He was upset and decided to run away." She tried to sit up, nearly unbalancing both of them. "Wade, you need to stop seeing the children as a nuisance."

"I don't."

She went on as if he hadn't spoken. "They need you. You can't give them away." Her words seemed a little slurred and, worried, he tried to pick up the pace. But it was difficult to beat his way through the bushes with his arms full.

"I'm not letting the Bauers adopt them because it's easy, but because it's for their best."

Missy caught his chin and turned his face toward her, almost upsetting him. He had to stop walking to keep his balance.

"How can it be for their best?"

"What can I give them?"

"Your love and your care." She squinted at him. "Though if they're only going to be a nuisance and a hindrance to you, perhaps it's best if you do give them away to a loving family. A mother and father who…" Her voice drifted off. She'd forgotten what she meant to say.

"Especially a father who—" No, he would not say it. Would not confess his failings. He could not bear to look weak and inadequate in her eyes.

"A father who what?" she prompted, suddenly alert.

"I only meant they need a mother and a father."

"No, you meant something about the father."

Would they never reach the trail, where he could pick up the pace and put an end to her prodding?

She patted his shoulder. "What were you going to say?"

"I've said it all." Where was the clearing? He didn't recall it being so far away. "You know I was worried Vic might have found you."

"Good try, but I'm not changing the subject. I know you love these kids, so there has to be some reason you're giving them up besides your agreement with the Bauers. You said they need a father. You could be their father."

"They need a father who understands their needs."

She didn't say a thing. Not a blessed thing, after he'd almost confessed his deepest, darkest, most shameful secret.

"Now you have nothing to say?" He stopped walking to look into her face. Despite the way the cold made her foggy from time to time, her eyes were sharp and focused at the moment and drilling into him as if she saw things. Things he didn't care for her to see.

She shook her head and gave him a pitying look. "Wade, I have plenty to say."

"Humph. I suspected you might."

"I've been in a situation very like what Joey and Annie are in, and I can tell you what they need." She impaled him with her fierce look. "They need someone to love them enough to stick with them even if it's hard."

Missy and Wade did silent battle with their eyes.

"They need more than that. Everyone does." He pushed onward, desperate to reach the ranch house, and ignored the way she studied him. He would not look at her, would not reveal any more, would not let her words get under his skin. But oh, she could be as

persistent as a burr under his saddle. Knowing that, he shouldn't have been surprised when she continued.

Her words were slow and measured. "I think we are no longer talking about a five-year-old and a seven-year-old, are we?"

Where was the clearing? Had God moved it?

"Would you by any chance be talking about your wife?" Missy prompted.

He almost dropped her. "If you aren't the most persistent, nosiest woman I've ever met my name isn't Wade Snyder."

"So what shall I call you?" Her voice dripped with teasing sweetness.

He almost choked. And then he finally saw the clearing. It was about time. "I don't know why I was concerned about you. You'd likely tell the cold to forget about bothering you."

She grinned. "I tried." She batted her eyes. "I failed."

His anger fled and he laughed. "I'll get you to the house and you'll get warmed up by the stove."

She settled into his arms as he trotted down the path toward the ranch house.

Eddie was watching for them and held the door so they could enter, "How is she?"

Wade caught a chair with his foot, dragged it to the stove and lowered her into it.

The ladies gathered around her. Linette draped a blanket around her shoulders as Louise eased her boots off and gently massaged her feet.

"She's fine," Wade muttered, though he wondered if anyone heard him.

A little hand took his. Annie. He smiled at her. Joey

sat at the table, wary and watchful. Keeping Annie's hand in his, Wade crossed to the table, sat beside his nephew and draped an arm over his shoulders.

He pulled him close and the boy came to him. No words were needed.

From across the room Wade sensed Missy's gaze on him and felt her insistence.

If he thought he could give these kids what they needed, he would keep them. But they deserved so much more than a man who feared the day he would fail them.

Chapter Eight

Although she was no longer as cold as she'd been sitting on the ground with Joey on her lap, Missy let the ladies fuss over her, and clutched the cup of warm tea they placed in her hands. Being carried back to the house in Wade's arms had warmed her from the inside out. As she'd sat comforting and counseling Joey, she'd been struck by how much the boy cared about his uncle.

"Why can't we stay with him?" Joey had asked through his tears.

"He doesn't have a home."

"I don't care. We could go with him. I can ride a horse."

"But what about Annie? She's pretty little."

Joey had sighed. "I guess so."

Missy had tried to help him believe it wasn't because Wade didn't care about them. But she knew Joey would always feel it was. Just as she felt she'd been nothing but a burden to Gordie. In hindsight she could see that perhaps her brother was simply unable

to deal with the difficulties thrust upon him by their
parents' death.

But it wasn't her fault and she didn't like being
treated as if it were. She could hardly blame Joey for
sharing a similar feeling toward Wade.

She should have gotten up and returned to the
house, but she hadn't wanted to put an end to the way
Joey was coming around to accepting what life had in
store for him. Not even when her legs had grown numb.

How embarrassing it was to discover she couldn't
stand when Wade had helped her to her feet.

Her cheeks warmed. Thankfully the others would
put it down to sitting so close to the stove and not realize it was due to remembering the moment she had
collapsed against him.

Her breath had caught halfway up her throat when
he'd swept her into his arms. Funny how comfortable
she'd felt there. Her half-frozen brain had not found one
word of protest. In fact, she could have almost settled
there and gone to sleep. With a great deal of effort,
she'd managed to resist the temptation.

But at least it had provided an opportunity for her
to discuss the matter of him keeping the children. In
the closeness, he'd almost confessed his reasons for
believing he could not do so.

She knew there was more to it than he'd said. How
he didn't think he could give them what they needed.
If he would tell her, then she could assure him his reasons didn't matter. No reason should prevent him from
keeping the children.

"I'm warm now," she said, letting the blanket slip
from her shoulders as she looked around the kitchen.

"Where's Joey?" He'd been beside Wade a few minutes ago.

"The children are all in the library," Linette said.

"Joey's okay?" Missy's gaze went to Wade for an answer.

He nodded. "He's fine. How are you?" His look seemed to say he meant more than just her possible frostbite.

She wasn't sure how to answer. Did he mean how had she liked being carried home? Her cheeks grew even warmer. She glanced about the room again in order to avoid looking directly at him. She spied the big pot she'd brought out before she'd gone in search of Joey. "Oh, I told the children I'd make candy with them and I haven't."

"There's all afternoon," Linette assured her. "First we'll have dinner."

Missy jumped up. "I'll take care of the meal."

Linette waved her away. "Louise and I made soup while the men went in search of you."

"I'm sorry. I should have been here to help." She watched Wade out of the corner of her eyes, saw a flicker of something vaguely regretful.

Was he thinking of all the time that had been wasted finding her?

Their gazes collided and the warmth in his made the blood rush up her neck. *Oh my.* That was not a look of regret at all.

If she wasn't dreaming, it was a secret look of sweet reminders of a time he'd held her in his arms. Could it be? Was it possible he'd actually enjoyed it? She tried to swallow but her mouth had dried up like cotton. She tried to pull her gaze away but could not.

Annie trotted into the room. "Can I come in now? I want to see Missy."

Missy dragged her attention to the child and held out her arms. "Come and see me then."

Annie raced across the room into her embrace. "Joey said you were cold. You don't feel cold to me. You're nice and warm." She snuggled against her.

Missy chuckled, her head bent over the child. Yet even without looking, she felt Wade's gaze on her. She would not look up at him. Could not risk being again captured by his eyes.

Her heart ticked a demanding rhythm against her ribs, and slowly she gave in to the compulsion. She lifted her head enough to look at him through the curtain of her eyelashes.

He indeed watched her, a faint smile on his lips.

What was he thinking? She'd sure like to know.

"Are we still going to make candy?" Annie asked.

"We certainly are. But first, dinner. Maybe you'd like to help." She included the two little boys hovering in the doorway.

Annie scrambled from Missy's arms. "We can set the table."

The children hurried about, carrying dishes, pouring a jug of water and then helping Linette and Louise take the food to the table.

In the meantime, Missy folded the blanket and put it on the rocking chair in the corner of the room. She put away her empty teacup and spent unnecessary time straightening a shelf. Anything to keep her mind away from the man across the room who followed her every move with eyes full of...

She would not admit he had a longing look in his eyes. Because that simply made no sense.

Soon the entire household gathered for the meal. Nate came in from outdoors. "What's this I hear?" he asked. "I'm busy in the harness room and miss all the excitement."

Eddie chuckled. "Turns out it wasn't as exciting as it might have been, for which we are all grateful."

A murmur of agreement came from the other adults at the table. Seeing the growing resentment in Joey's eyes, Missy looked at Wade and tipped her head to the boy.

He nodded in understanding. "Do you think it will snow?" he asked Eddie.

The rancher gave his answer a great deal of consideration, but his look indicated he understood the need to change the subject. "It's been a while since we've had any substantial amount. I suppose we are due for more."

"We ran into a storm on our trip here," Missy added. "Did you happen to get the same storm?"

The conversation shifted to record snowstorms, previous winters and then the experience of Eddie's first winter in Alberta.

Joey's eyes lost their hardness and he listened to the stories with interest.

Missy allowed herself a long, inquiring glance at Wade, intending only to signal her relief over Joey's change in attitude. But within two seconds she felt a pinch in the back of her heart at Wade's probing, possessive look.

She quickly diverted her attention. Possessive? The last thing either of them wanted was to belong to any-

one. No, both of them were clear on their desires—
he wanted to live the life of a lonesome cowboy; she
wanted to gain her independence.

She told herself she'd only imagined the look. But
when she slid her gaze back to his her breath caught
in the back of her throat at the longing she glimpsed.
Then he blinked and it was gone.

It was only a trick of lighting coming through the
window and catching his eyes.

She knew a rush of gratitude when the meal ended.

Annie jumped up. "Can I help do dishes?"

Linette laughed. "When was the last time I heard
anyone so anxious to do the dishes?"

Annie sighed. "Missy said we'd make candy after
dinner, but I know she won't let us until the kitchen
is clean."

Missy joined the others in laughter.

Grady and Joey jumped up and began to gather the
used dishes.

Missy pushed herself back from the table. "I better
get to work or they'll have it all done without me." She
glanced around at the half-empty cups of coffee. "Take
your time. There's no rush," she said to the adults, then
laughed at the protest on three little faces. "Come on,
you three, let's get this done."

Soon the last dish had been dried and put away.
The table didn't have a single crumb on it. Linette and
Louise had gone to the sitting room with their babies.
Nate had left with a comment about more harnesses
to clean and repair. Eddie had departed after kissing
his wife and baby. He had things to do.

Only Wade remained, his presence making Missy's
nerves tingle. He had a newspaper open before him

but she couldn't help notice he had not once turned a page, and every time her eyes darted toward him, he was watching her.

What was he thinking?

If they'd been alone she might have had the courage to ask him. Did he question her ability to take care of the children if Joey could so easily run away? Or was he thinking it had been pleasant to hold her in his arms? Was she the only one who had found it so?

It didn't matter what he thought at the moment. She had children to entertain. "Who knows how to make hard rock candy?"

The three shook their heads.

"My mama used to make it every year for Christmas." This was the first time since her parents' death she'd attempted to make it, but she could hear her mama's sweet voice instructing her. *Thank you, Mama.* "First, we measure the sugar. Annie, you're the youngest, so you go first." She supervised as the child measured and poured sugar into the big pot.

"Next is the syrup. Joey, you can measure that." The sticky liquid was a little more challenging to handle, but he managed with her assistance. She found her attention distracted by Wade's watchfulness and almost measured out too much. Why must he sit there, making her nervous, watching every movement she made?

But if he left she'd wish him back.

So he could share the time with the children, she told herself.

"Good job," she said, as the last drop of syrup dripped into the pot.

"Now it's your turn, Grady." He measured in the water.

She carried the pot to the stove and pulled a chair close. "Who wants to stir it?"

Three hands shot in the air. Annie bounced up and down on her feet. Grady managed to looked patient and Joey hovered between a scowl and a plea.

Missy smiled at how each of the children's personalities was so clearly revealed.

Wade grinned. "The face reveals the heart," he said.

If that was so, did the fact that his expression showed interest and his eyes longing mean he wanted to be part of their lives?

The children's lives, she quickly amended. But her thoughts had flown immediately to imagined scenes of sharing other occasions around a kitchen table where they all belonged. Together.

She slammed the door of her mind against those thoughts with such vigor she shuddered. She knew it was impossible. Not what either of them wanted.

"You can take turns again." Annie climbed to the chair and Missy stood at her side, making sure she didn't burn herself.

"The nice thing about this candy is you don't have to stir it all the time." She recalled her mama saying the same thing. "The bad thing is it takes a long time to boil to hard ball stage."

"How long?" Joey asked, as she indicated he could have a turn.

"I can't say. It takes its own time. We just have to be patient."

She helped Joey down and Grady had his turn. The sugar had all dissolved. "Now we let it boil."

The trio lined up before the stove, waiting anxiously.

Wade rattled his paper, drawing her attention to him. He said, "Waiting is hard."

Losing parents was hard. Not knowing where they'd live or with whom was hard. Making candy was not.

The look between Wade and Missy went on and on, his gaze dark like deep, still waters, as if he read her thoughts. As if he agreed. It was strange how they concurred on many things, yet not on something as major as whether he should keep the children or give them up for adoption.

Not that it was any of her business. Except she'd made it so simply because she identified with what the children felt, and because she knew he could give the children the love they needed.

He was a man with a deep capacity to love and yet he shied away from it.

Why? What was he afraid of?

The candy mixture boiled. The children waited, rocking on the balls of their feet.

Missy tried to reassure them. "It will take time, but it will be worth it in the end." It was the same message she wanted to give to Wade. Keeping the children might require some changes in his life, but it would be worth it.

She had the children grease two cake pans, and after a few minutes she scooped a bit of syrup from the pot and dropped it into a cup of cold water to test it. "Not hard enough yet. Who wants to taste it?"

Receiving three eager replies, she repeated the process twice and made three tiny samples.

They savored the sweet treat.

"Ahem." Wade cleared his throat.

"Do you want some, too?" Her words croaked from a throat that had grown tight.

"I like sweets as much as anyone."

"Very well." She made another sample, then carried it to him on the tip of the spoon.

She expected him to take the spoon, but he opened his mouth as the children had done.

She gulped. There was something about feeding him the treat that threatened her barriers. But he waited, his eyes watchful, perhaps a little challenging.

Pasting on a smile, she leaned in close and put the spoon in his mouth. He sucked the candy off.

She pulled the spoon back and stood there immobile, trapped by a thousand warring emotions. Awareness of his powerful presence, wariness of his secrets, longing for something she felt here in this room.

Something that was impossible for her to have. She thought of the advertisement for secretarial school and reminded herself of her goals.

Missy turned back to the stove, ignoring the reluctance in her heart to end the moment.

"What color shall we make it?" she asked the children.

They agreed on red and she added the coloring. A few minutes later it was done. She added peppermint flavoring.

"We need to pour it into the pans." She grabbed pot holders and prepared to pick up the pot.

Wade scrambled to his feet. "I'll do that." He took the mitts from her hands and gripped the pan, but didn't lift it.

She met his look, saw something fleeting. Like concern. Like home... She jerked away, her feelings con-

fused by the memories triggered by candy making, memories of her mother, of her childhood. Missy did not expect to ever again have that sense of security and love. But for the moment she could not understand why, any more than she could force herself to recall why she meant to go to secretarial training.

Wade hoisted the pot and poured red candy syrup into the pans.

"Now we wait for it to cool," she said. "It will take a while. Why don't you go play? I'll call you when it's ready."

Not until the children left the room did she realize she'd arranged to be alone with Wade. She twisted her hands together.

"Is there any coffee left?" he asked.

She shook the coffeepot at the back of the stove. "Some, but it's been sitting here since dinner. I'll make a fresh pot," she said, grateful for something with which to occupy her hands and mind. Even after she set it to heat she remained at the stove, staring at the pot.

"Didn't anyone ever tell you a watched pot never boils?" His words jangled through her head.

If she didn't watch, then would he expect her to sit and visit with him? And why should she find the idea so frightening, and at the same time alluring.

"My experience has been that the minute I turn my back on a pot it boils over."

"So you'd sooner be safe than sorry?"

Something about his tone of voice—as if he meant far more than making coffee—made her turn to confront him. He still sat at the table, the paper folded neatly at his elbow, his chair turned at an angle so he

could stretch one leg out before him. There was no mistaking the challenge in his eyes.

"Always!" she said, meaning so much more than a watched pot.

"In everything?"

"I'd say so."

"So you make a plan and stick to it, taking no risks?"

The seconds ticked by as he searched her face. What did he see? Could he read her reasons for following her plans and avoiding risk? Could he even begin to guess how painful it was to be the victim of life's tragedies?

"I don't care for the result of things not planned."

He nodded, "I think the coffee has started to boil."

She jerked around, grabbed a towel and pulled the pot to the side just in time to keep it from boiling over.

She poured him a cup, then touched the side of one pan of candy. "Still too warm."

"Might as well sit down and rest your feet."

She could think of no reasonable excuse to say no and sat across the corner from him.

He shifted so she was directly across from him.

She should have poured herself a cup of coffee even though she didn't want one. At least it would have given her something to do with her hands.

"No aftereffects from this morning?" he asked.

Too many to count, she silently replied. An awareness of him that had grown to overwhelming proportions. A remembrance of his arms about her that would likely last for days. Confusion of her thoughts.

"Your legs are working okay now?"

Of course he only asked about the physical effects of sitting on the cold ground. "They're fine, thanks. Good thing you came along to rescue us."

"Yes, good thing."

At the husky tone of his voice, her gaze found his.

Neither of them spoke and yet she read volumes. A portion of her brain—the little that remained rational—warned her it was only her imagination causing her to think she saw an invitation in his eyes.

Missy turned to check the temperature of the candy.

"It's ready." She called the children. "Now we go outdoors."

They all marched outside. Wade followed on her heels. "I gotta see this."

Missy grinned at him. "Have you never made hard rock candy?"

"Not that I recall. Like Joey said, our family liked fudge."

"It's not near as much fun to make as this. Wait until you see the children break it. It was my favorite thing about the candy."

"Even better than eating it?"

She nodded, her eyes warm with challenge. "Some things are better than candy." Would he realize what she was implying?

"Is that a fact?"

For a moment she thought he was going to ask her to tell him what.

Love, home, belonging. They would answer the question, but she didn't want to say the words aloud. He would think her an impossible dreamer. And perhaps wonder if she was a bit confused, when her plans included none of those things.

She put the pans on the ground and handed the cloth-wrapped hammer to Joey. "You can break the first pan." He swung the hammer down and crowed

with delight when it fractured the candy like broken glass.

Grady and Annie took their turns, then slowly, hesitantly, Missy handed Wade the hammer. "Give it a try."

He grinned as widely as any of the children and broke the corner pieces of the second pan.

She glowed with satisfaction at giving them all this simple pleasure.

He tapped the candy again and again as the children cheered him on. He grinned at her. "You're right. This is fun."

She tried and failed to ignore his wide smile. Swallowed hard and reminded herself of her goals. Somehow she managed to gain balance. "It might surprise you to know I'm right about a lot of things."

His smile faded. "I guess it would depend on the situation."

She didn't want to be the first to end the look between them. Seemed he didn't want to be, either. Her heart rattled inside her chest as the seconds passed.

"Missy, now what do we do?" Annie asked.

Missy couldn't say who broke away first, but no doubt he was as relieved as she to be free of the moment.

"Now we taste it." She handed a piece to each of them. Wade, too, though her fingers burned from touching his palm.

She tasted a piece as well, and added her sound of approval to those of the children.

Wade quietly watched her as he savored his share. "Nothing sweeter than good candy," he said, as if he'd understood all the things she hadn't said, and wished to inform her he didn't agree.

He had not changed one bit in his plan to give away the children.

Her heart sank like a stone.

As she turned away from him she remembered a saying her father had often repeated. *A man convinced against his will is of the same opinion still.* She'd do well to remember that. If she wanted Wade to realize he could provide a home for the children, it would take more than words. She needed to prove it.

"Let's put the rest in a bowl to serve to your guests tomorrow."

The children turned to follow her back inside.

She glanced over her shoulder. Wade still stood in the yard. He looked at the hammer in his hand as if surprised to see it there. "I'll put it away." He tossed her the cloth and trotted past her to stow the hammer in the nearby toolshed.

Then, to her surprise and disappointment, he strode down the hill.

Telling herself she hadn't expected him to follow her or to spend the afternoon together with the children, she returned inside.

After all, she was being paid to take care of them.

Wade did his best to not hurry away. Not that he was anxious to leave Missy and the children behind. Quite the opposite. He was enjoying their company far too much and beginning to picture them in his life for more than a few days.

He reached the barn and grabbed a fork. The floor was clean but he spent an hour cleaning it even better.

Brand entered the barn and leaned against a wall. "You trying to get away from your thoughts?"

"Just trying to help out."

He grunted. "Looks like more than that to me. Let me tell you something."

Wade thought to tell him not to bother, but despite his casual manner he guessed Brand kind of said what he wanted whether or not the listener cared to hear it.

Brand continued, "There's three things you can't run from. Your family. Your thoughts." He let a beat or two of silence fill the air, so that Wade paused and looked at him.

"And your past," Brand concluded. "Sooner or later you have to stop running from it and face it." A slow, dreamy smile curved his mouth. "And ain't no better reason to do it than for a good woman."

Brand's look was benign, so Wade couldn't judge if there was a hidden meaning or if he spoke only of his own experience.

Wade put the fork back in the corner. "Guess I'll go see if there's anything else needs doing."

The other man grunted and straightened. "There's a broken plank on the far pen. Always find driving in spikes helps ease my mind." And he sauntered away without a backward look.

Well, that was strange, Wade thought. But he didn't mind fixing a fence, so he grabbed tools and spikes from the tack room and left the barn. In the yard he paused to look toward the big house, but all he saw was the reflection of the clouds in the windows.

He wasn't running from his family or his thoughts

or his past. Well, maybe a little from his past. But what choice did he have? It held nothing but regrets and failures, and he sure hoped to avoid them in the future.

He hustled across the bridge toward the wintering pens. His glance went unbidden to the path he and Missy had followed up the hill. Where she'd fallen into his arms. A smile came from his heart to his mouth. She was a good woman, all right. Far too good for the likes of him. She deserved a man who would never fail her. Not that marriage was in her plans. She'd made that plain from the first night.

Brand was wrong. Pounding in nails did not clear Wade's thoughts. With every blow of his hammer he drove home another memory of Missy. How she felt neither too light nor too heavy in his arms as he carried her home. How she'd leaned her head against his shoulder. The feel of her fingers on his palm as she gave him a bit of candy. By the time he'd repaired the fence he was grinning like a crazy kid full of hard rock candy. Good thing he worked in solitude or people might wonder if he was addled.

He sauntered back to the house after putting his tools away, wondering what the evening had in store and what Missy had done the rest of the afternoon.

The children raced over to greet him as he stepped inside. He swung them both into his arms. How sweet it was that Joey didn't protest.

He gave them each a little whisker rub, ignoring their pretend protests, then shifted his attention to Missy.

She smiled, her eyes soft with approval. If playing

with the children brought that look to her face, he'd play with them every waking minute.

He set the pair on the floor. Of course he couldn't and wouldn't. That was only foolish dreams.

And yet over the meal and as the evening wore on he found himself looking to her more and more often, yearning for signs of approval, and he was rewarded time and time again until he thought he might actually stand up and cheer.

The children yawned.

"Grady, it's time for bed," Linette said. "Come along."

"You two, as well." Missy held out her hands to the pair.

Wade rose, but she smiled and said, "You rest. I'll take care of them."

He settled back into his chair, though his gaze followed them to the stairs. He listened until their footsteps faded away.

The minutes dragged by. How long did it take to put two children to bed?

Finally his ear picked up a footstep in the hall above. It could be Linette. Or Louise, who had taken Chloe upstairs a bit ago. Air eased from his lungs as Missy descended. He stood as she stepped into the room.

She stopped and looked at him, waiting, it seemed, for him to say something.

His mind went blank, then he said he first thing that popped into his befuddled brain.

"Would you like to go for a walk?" In the deepest part of his brain, he knew he shouldn't have asked her to walk with him. But he couldn't pull the words back and, for the most part, didn't regret the invitation.

She stood motionless, not answering.

Would she find some excuse? For both their sakes, she should, but he held his breath, waiting for her response.

Chapter Nine

"I'd like that." She turned aside to get her coat, but not before Wade saw a flash of light in her eyes. As if she thought walking with him was a good idea

His breath whistled past his teeth as he hurried to join her.

They stepped outside. The air was crisp with winter's breath. There was just a slice of moon, but it was enough to turn the snow silvery and cast enough light for them to walk easily. At the same time it provided enough of an excuse for him to tuck her arm around his and hold her close. That and concern about Vic, of course. The man had still not been spotted.

"It's beautiful out," she said. "So clear and still."

Unlike his thoughts, he mused wryly. He couldn't remember when he'd felt so muddled, yearning after things he knew he must deny himself. An ache the size of the great outdoors grew within him, the desire to open the vaults of his past and lay before her all his secrets.

They passed the cookhouse, where Cookie and her husband could be seen sitting at the table, a lit lamp

between them. Cookie's hands were busy with some sewing and Bertie held a book.

"Likely the Bible," Missy commented. "He speaks at church on Sunday."

"Guess I'll get a chance to hear him." Wade welcomed the idea, even though he knew every day he delayed his departure made his resolve more tenuous.

To their right, light glowed from the cabin where Jayne and Seth lived. Missy told him how Jayne had accidently shot Seth while attempting to learn how to shoot a gun. "That's how they met."

Wade laughed. "That will be a story to tell their grandchildren."

Her laughter joined his and if he wasn't mistaken, she pressed closer to him.

If so, he informed his befuddled brain, it was only to share body heat.

Yellow light filled the three windows of the bunkhouse. Wood smoke drifted from the chimney. Someone played a lonesome tune on a mouth organ. They paused to listen, then without speaking continued across the bridge toward the hill they'd climbed last evening, though neither of them suggested that direction. They could have just as easily gone past the Jones house and walked that trail.

"We gave the children the third day of Christmas," Missy said at last.

He welcomed the safe topic, coming, as it did, before he started blurting out his past. Would she condemn him as Tomasina's parents had, as his own heart continued to do? Would she agree that he had failed as a husband and as a man?

"I surely do appreciate the way you entertain the

children," he said instead. "I'm sure Linette appreciates your help with Grady, as well."

"I'm enjoying it. You know you're welcome to take part in any activity we do."

At her invitation he longed to say he'd be there each and every moment, but he had to maintain a few boundaries. "I'll be there when I can, but I feel I need to help out around the ranch to repay the Gardiners for their kindness."

"Of course. I understand."

The pigs snorted as they passed. The cows mooed softly. In the distance a wolf howled and Missy's arm tightened. He gladly pressed her closer to his side. "It's a distance off," he assured her. His senses were alert for something more sinister than a wild animal. There was nothing more deadly than a rogue man.

"Have you seen wolves up close?" she asked, her voice full of concern, which weakened his already faltering boundaries.

He had difficulty forcing the words from his tight throat. "Once or twice."

She shuddered and clutched his arm.

He closed his eyes and allowed himself to momentarily think of protecting her and shielding her for more than this one fragile moment.

"How close? Were they attacking you?"

"Too close for comfort. They were after a calf that had somehow wandered too far from its mama. Would have gotten it, too, if I hadn't been walking by."

"You chased them away? How many were there?"

"There were four and they turned on me. They like to corner their prey, but I scared them away with my gun." He did his best to make it sound harmless, when

in reality one had lunged for his throat and he'd escaped only because he'd happened to be carrying a pistol and shot it. Wade would spare her that bit of information.

A rustle came from the nearby trees and she drew back with a jerk. "What's that?"

"I'm sure it's nothing." But he wasn't convinced. He'd come out with no means of protection and the talk of wolves had made him tense, but he'd protect her barehanded if he must.

A dark shadow leaped from the trees.

Missy screamed.

Wade shoved her behind him and widened his stance. Nothing was going to get to her without going through him, and he was prepared to tear any attacking animal limb from limb before that happened.

The animal stopped two feet away, woofed and panted. "It's only Dawg."

She released pent-up air and leaned against Wade's back.

He pulled her around into his arms. "There was never any real danger."

"Not for me, but you were prepared to stop a wild animal." She tipped her face toward his. "Thank you."

"There's nothing to thank me for."

"Is that you, Wade?" He recognized Brand's voice.

Wade and Missy broke apart, but she continued to clutch his arm.

Then Brand and Sybil came into view. Dawg plopped down beside his master. "Did the dog scare you?" Brand asked.

"A little," Wade confessed.

"A lot," Missy corrected. "We were just talking

about wolves. My nerves were already on edge when the dog appeared."

"Sorry about that," Sybil said. "He's completely harmless, unless someone threatens Brand. Then you better watch out."

Wade tucked the bit of information under his hat. Not that he thought he and Brand would ever come to any sort of disagreement. "No harm done."

"You're headed up to the courting hill, I see." Sybil and Brand smiled at each other as if they shared a secret.

"Courting hill?" Wade tried to think what she meant.

"Oh, yes," Sybil went on. "There's been more than one couple climb that hill, stop at the top and slowly or instantly fall in love.

Her words sent his heart into a gallop, which he instantly ordered to stop. He had no intention of falling in love with Missy. Nor her with him, for that matter. "We were just getting some fresh air and talking about tomorrow."

"I see." Brand sounded doubtful. "Well, Sybil and I have had our share of fresh air. You're welcome to the courting hill." The pair continued toward their cabin.

With one accord, Wade and Missy shifted direction. She seemed no more eager to make use of the courting hill than he. Though he was tempted to see what would happen if they went up there, he'd forbidden such things in his life.

They crossed the bridge again and turned onto the trail passing the Jones home. Through the front window they glimpsed Cassie and Roper sitting together

in rocking chairs. Missy's steps slowed as she continued to look toward the house.

She'd said she wanted to become a secretary and be on her own. Perhaps she was having second thoughts after seeing all the happy couples here.

Not that it mattered to Wade.

"Are you ready for the party tomorrow?" she asked, after they'd passed the house.

"Is there something I needed to do?" Had he missed a task he was responsible for?

"Just show up and enjoy yourself with the children."

He could tell she had more to say by the way she caught her breath.

"Something that you do very well, I might add."

"What? Show up?" Did he sound as surprised as he felt? Surely he was good for more than that.

Her peals of laughter so startled him that he turned to stare at her.

She tried to speak, but instead, laughed again.

He crossed his arms and regarded her with a great deal of patience. He sure would like to know what was so funny.

She managed to control her amusement, but still grinned widely. He wished he could see her eyes better in the evening light. Then he might be able to guess what this was all about.

"I didn't mean that you just show up, like a bad penny or something. Not at all. Sorry I laughed, but your reaction struck me as funny." She sucked in a deep breath. "I meant that you are so good with the children. It seems you understand their needs. And you're so patient with them. Yet at the same time, you obviously enjoy them."

Her words brushed over him, touching bruises and wounds with a healing balm. For a moment he was speechless, then, aware that she watched him closely, he said, "I do enjoy them. Always have. Even when they were babies. Do you know how special it is to watch them go from one stage to another?" He shrugged. "I was blessed that Susan allowed me to be so involved in their lives."

"So were they, I would say." Missy continued to study him until he had to look away. This time he was grateful the dim light didn't allow her to see the emotions he knew were in his eyes—regret and sorrow at the loss of his sister and the impending loss of his niece and nephew. Nor could she see the warning in his eyes to not pursue the direction she headed with this conversation.

She patted his arm. "You're a good man, Wade Snyder. You should remember that."

She could have blown him over with less effort than it took to blow out a candle. When had she gone from pressing him to keep the children to admiring him? Not that he was complaining. It felt downright good to have someone say such kind words. Good thing he hadn't confessed his past, or she would not be quite so free with her praise.

They ventured on, her arm tucked about his, and now it felt entirely different. He could almost let himself think she liked him. The thought warmed the recesses of his heart. "What are the plans for the party?"

"I thought we'd play a few games, have some treats. Can you think of anything else?"

He was pleased to be able to say he could. "I have popping corn."

"Oh, that would be delightful."

He glowed with pleasure.

The night had grown darker, the path harder to see. "We better turn around."

"I suppose so." But she stared off into the darkness.

"What's wrong?" he asked.

She shuddered slightly. "Nothing, I guess. But I always miss my parents this time of year, and now my brother is gone and I've had to leave the house I've always lived in. I had to leave behind everything but what I could pack into a small trunk. I had two special Christmas ornaments I didn't bring. I never even thought of it at the time. My only concern was to get away from Vic before he harmed any of us."

Vic! Wade grabbed Missy's elbow and hustled her back along the trail. "We should have never come this far. I don't know what I was thinking."

"Humph. I hope you were thinking how nice it would be to walk with me."

At the injured tone in her voice, he relented. "Of course I was, but I plumb forgot about Vic. How is that possible?"

"Maybe because he isn't much of a risk. You know the Mounties always get their man. Vic is no doubt rotting in a jail right now, awaiting his trial." She was definitely aggrieved.

Wade slowed his steps and pulled her to his side again, but his ears strained to catch any sound. Not until they reached the house did he relax. Even then, he opened the door and ushered her in with urgency.

Missy knew she shouldn't be annoyed, but she was. Clear through. She and Louise had left Montana to es-

cape Vic. The horrible man had followed them to Fort Macleod and caused fear and havoc, and now he was ruining her stay at Eden Valley Ranch. He wasn't even here and yet he was exerting control over her.

No doubt they would soon receive word he had been captured, and then she could start to live her own life without fear. A secretary was what she'd be.

She slammed an inner door to the thoughts that had sprung up unbidden and unwelcome as they walked by Cassie and Roper's house. A home. Children safely tucked in bed. A man sitting nearby, sharing the little joys and trials of the day. More than a man, a husband.

Home and family were not part of her plans.

Freedom and independence were.

She entered the Gardiner house and called a goodnight to those still in the other room, then turned her steps down the hall. Before she reached the doorway to her bedroom, she heard Wade call good-night and then his footsteps sounded on the stairs.

He was, as she said, a good man, but for some reason he seemed to think otherwise. If only Missy could make him see what she saw in him, then perhaps he'd make the effort to keep the children.

She wakened next morning to the sound of a floorboard next to her bed squeaking, and jerked instantly awake, her heart pounding. Her first thought was that Vic had found her!

Instead of his hoarse rasp she heard a child's high-pitched voice. "I'm awake but Joey isn't," Annie whispered.

Missy fell back against her pillow and pressed her palm to her chest in an effort to calm her heart. She

would not be so frightened by the possibility of Vic showing up if not for Wade's reaction last night.

She held the covers open, inviting Annie to join her. The little girl crawled in and arranged her two dolls on the pillow. She shuffled down, pulled the quilt to her chin and stuck her icy feet against Missy.

Missy shivered. "Does your uncle know you're here?"

"He's still asleep."

He'd taken a watch again, which cut drastically into the amount of sleep he got. Missy's throat stung. Here she was again, being a burden to everyone. Vic was a threat partially because of her presence here. Louise had Nate to protect her.

Vic had pursued her ever since Gordie had taken up with him following Mama and Papa's deaths. Louise had often come to her rescue.

Again Missy wondered if she was the reason Louise had married Gordie.

She muffled a groan. Never again would she be a burden to anyone. Never. Secretarial school was her pathway to establishing that independence.

But in the meantime, the men took turns watching the place, missing their sleep, carrying long guns when they normally didn't. Surely all this caution was for nothing. She'd tell Wade and Eddie there was no reason for concern.

She shivered again as she pictured Vic jumping out from behind a tree and grabbing her.

"My feet cold?" Annie asked, without taking them away.

"Like ice." Though it was not Annie's cold feet that made her shiver.

"Mary likes Martha. They're best friends forever," Annie said, and proceeded to tell her all the things her dolls liked to do. Then Annie rose on her elbow and studied Missy.

"Today is the party."

"Uh-huh. You're letting the cold air under the blanket."

Annie lay down again. "The others aren't coming until after dinner, right?"

"That's right."

Annie let out a long-suffering sigh. "What will we do this morning?"

Missy would have liked to say they'd sleep a few more hours, but she understood how long the morning would seem to the children. "I suppose we could make cookies for the party."

"Goody." Annie bounced, again letting in a rush of cold air.

Missy threw back the covers. "Run upstairs and get dressed. Then you can help me make breakfast." She'd heard the faint cries of an infant during the night and knew the newborns had kept their mamas up for hours. As soon as Annie departed, Missy scrambled into her clothes and hurried to the kitchen to begin breakfast.

"I'm back," Annie said.

"Good. I need someone to measure out raisins for the porridge." She handed a cup to Annie and let her tackle the job on her own.

"I'll help, too."

Missy glanced up as Joey entered the kitchen, and saw Wade beside him. His hair had been slicked back, turning it a chocolate brown. He was freshly shaved and considered her with unblinking blue eyes.

"Good morning." His deep voice thrummed inside her chest.

"Good morning," she managed to reply, as a dozen conflicting thoughts flooded her mind. How good it was to see him standing there. How his presence made her muscles go all twitchy. "I regret that you feel you must keep watch every night. I'm sure it's unnecessary."

He shrugged. "It's not an unpleasant task. Gives a man plenty of time to think." The way he studied her face brought a rush of heat up her neck.

What was wrong with her? The man said a simple, straightforward thing and she immediately thought he meant her. Likely he had lots more important things to think about.

"What do you want me to do?" Joey asked, drawing her attention away from Wade.

She turned back to her task. "You could put jam in these dishes." She tried not to be aware of Wade crossing toward the stove. He stood very close behind her and reached past her right shoulder with a tea towel in his hand to lift the coffeepot. Then he sidestepped and poured himself a cupful. When he took a sip a moment later, he sighed. "Good." He patted her shoulder. "Sure do appreciate having hot coffee waiting for me."

She'd been stirring the porridge, but her hands grew still. Her muscles tightened. His words confounded her almost as much as his touch. "It's nice to be appreciated," she managed to squeak out.

The air between them grew still, expectant, even though the children clattered about and chattered.

Missy turned, silently questioning the sudden change,

and her lungs refused to work at the look in his eyes. She could almost describe it as surprised, even curious.

"I expect you often hear how much you're appreciated."

She lifted one shoulder—half dismissive, half regretful.

He smiled slowly, with the power of the dawning sun, and she blinked as if she'd stared into its blinding brightness. "Well, if they don't say it I know they have overlooked it, for you are the most helpful creature I've ever seen."

Her mouth grew slack. Her tongue refused to function. Helpful? Not burdensome? She let herself drown in the depths of his sky-blue eyes.

Still holding her gaze, he sipped again from his cup. "Good." He went to the table and she returned to preparing breakfast, but something inside her had shifted and she was at a loss to say what it was.

Apart from slipping in for dinner, which he ate hurriedly, then left again with a murmur about some chore, Wade forced himself to stay away from the house until the party began. After that, he would not deny his desire to be where he could watch Missy, catch her eye from time to time and maybe even speak to her once in a while.

Three wagons drew up to the house at the same time as the Jones children trooped across the yard. The guests had arrived, so now he could reasonably head indoors.

The party gave him a good reason to be present. He intended to help Missy make this an event the children would remember years after they became part of an-

other family. His hurried steps ground to a halt as pain sucked at his insides. He drew in a slow, strengthening breath. A man must do what was best, not what felt good. To do otherwise was simply selfish.

He resumed his journey, entering the house several minutes after the last of the guests.

The adults congregated in the kitchen, visiting, while the children gathered in the sitting room, where all the furniture had been pushed back so they had room to play.

Missy glanced up as he entered, then resumed giving instructions for a game of Button, Button to the children, who sat in a circle on the floor.

He paused, wondering what he could do to help. Joey saw him and shifted to one side, making room for him. "Come and play with us, Uncle Wade."

"Sure." He sat cross-legged beside his nephew, awkwardly aware that even folded, his legs took up a lot of area.

The children all held their palms together in front of them. Wade imitated the pose.

Missy circled the room pretending to drop a button into the hands of the children. He'd played this game as a child and knew what to expect. She'd drop the button into one pair of hands and Neil, who was "it," had to guess where it was.

She paused in front of Wade's legs and leaned over. He held out his hands and she brushed hers across them, as she had with the children. She didn't give him the button, but did give him a whole lot of disconcerting thoughts. Never in all the times he'd played this game had he ever experienced such a reaction. His heart raced. His mouth grew dry. His head pounded.

Maybe he was getting sick. Or maybe he was a foolish man who overreacted to a simple touch.

That was it. Nothing he need get concerned about.

She was done and stood to one side as Neil went around the circle. He had three guesses. On the second, he pointed at Joey. "You have it." He'd guessed right.

The game continued for a time. Wade laughed and cheered with the rest of them, but his attention constantly sought Missy.

They switched to a more active game. Always on the go, Missy grew flushed as she directed the children, making sure everyone was included, even little Pansy, Cassie and Roper's two-year-old.

The game switched again, this time to Blind Man's Bluff. The children called for Missy to be blindfolded.

Wade stood back against the wall, letting her try to catch one of the children.

Daisy called Missy, teasing her toward her. But at the last second Daisy darted out of the way and Missy caught Wade.

Her hands rested on his forearms and she grew very still as if she'd forgotten to breathe.

"Guess who it is," Joey called.

"I think it's your uncle Wade." She sounded as if the blindfold had slipped to her mouth, muffling her words.

"That's right. Now Uncle Wade is 'it.'"

She pulled the scarf off her eyes and handed it to him. "Play with them while I prepare the treats." And without a backward look, she hurried to the kitchen.

Wade would have followed, demanding to know if she was upset about something, but the children

clamored around him and he turned his attention back to them.

A few minutes later they were called into the kitchen and the children wolfed down cookies and milk. Then Missy handed out the hard rock candy, which earned her many thanks.

The adults seemed in no hurry to leave and the children were content playing together. Missy served cookies and tea to the adults and answered a hundred questions from the children. Then, one by one, the guests left, with an invitation to return Sunday evening to jointly welcome in the New Year.

Missy sank to a chair and puffed out her lips in a sigh.

It was the first time she'd sat down since the party began. She must be exhausted. She poured so much into their lives, and not just for Annie and Joey. She'd given Wade something, too, though he wasn't prepared to give it a name. It was enough to acknowledge that much.

Perhaps he could also give her something as repayment besides the few dollars he meant to pay her.

But what did he have to give?

Chapter Ten

The thought came to him over supper. When Missy started to get up to get more potatoes, he rushed to his feet.

"I'll do it." He refilled the bowl and took it to the table.

She blushed.

He hesitated before he returned to his place. Did she think because he'd helped he thought she couldn't manage? Then it hit him. She kept trying to do everything because she was afraid she'd be considered a nuisance if she sat and let someone else do it.

Well, he'd soon disabuse her of that notion.

"I think Missy deserves a break tonight after all she's done."

"Absolutely," Linette agreed, and the others echoed the same.

"Oh, no. I'll do my share," Missy protested.

Wade sat back, prepared to point out if the others didn't how she'd done more than her share, but a chorus of protests echoed around the table.

Linette summed it up perfectly. "You've done more

than your share and we've noticed. It's been truly appreciated, but it's your turn this evening to sit back
while we clean up."

Wade grinned as she finally accepted the offer.

He helped gather the dirty dishes. He took the scraps
out for the cats waiting at the back door. After years
of living on his own, he knew how to clean the place
up, knew how to wash dishes, even knew how to bake
a passable batch of biscuits.

That gave him an idea. He'd make breakfast tomorrow. It meant he'd have to get up early and likely have
to argue with Missy about whether or not she should
help, but this was one thing he could do to show his
gratitude to her.

The next morning, he tiptoed from his room before
he heard anyone else stir. He'd added wood to the embers in the stove and had flour measured out when
Missy flew into the room, strands of her blond hair
hanging about her face as if she'd hurriedly put it up.

He grinned, kind of enjoying this version of her.

"What are you doing?" she demanded, tucking back
one wayward lock.

"Making biscuits for breakfast." He spoke so matter-
of-factly that he had the pleasure of seeing her speechless.

For all of five seconds, which was likely a record.

"I can make breakfast," she sputtered.

"Seems so. But I can, too. I've done it most every
day for about six years now."

"But you don't need to."

He kept his attention on chopping lard into the flour,

thoroughly enjoying her reaction. "Nope, I don't need to. I want to."

She stood in the middle of the floor, her hands twisting, her mouth opening and closing without uttering a word.

His enjoyment of the moment grew. He stirred in milk until he had the right consistency, then rolled and cut the biscuits and placed them on a cookie sheet. He checked the temperature of the oven. Perfect. He put the biscuits to bake, then began preparing the potatoes to fry.

Still she stood there. "Why?" she finally managed to ask.

"Why what? Why am I making potatoes? Don't you like fried potatoes?"

"I like them fine." Exasperation dripped from her voice. "Why are you making breakfast?"

Then and only then did he turn and face her full on, and immediately wondered if it was a wise move. The bewildered look in her eyes made him want to pull her into his arms and pat her head. Thankfully, he resisted the urge.

"I guess you could say I want to show my thanks, and this was all I could think of to do."

"Thanks?"

He grinned. She seemed to have lost her ability to say much. "For all you've done."

"What have I done?" Suspicion crept into her voice.

"I could mention a lot of things, but I need to get the potatoes frying." He turned back to the stove.

"Maybe you could mention a few just to clear up my confusion."

He chuckled at her dry tone. "Okay, but don't dis-

tract me. I've got a meal to make here." He prepared a fry pan for the potatoes. "Go sit down and I'll bring you coffee."

She hesitated. Then, with a half-annoyed sigh, she sat.

He poured coffee, added a generous amount of cream and took it to her.

She stared at the contents. "How did you know I take cream?"

He shrugged. "Just know, I guess." Just as he knew a hundred tiny details about her. Like how one eyebrow lifted slightly when she was talking about her past. How she always put her fork down precisely beside her plate between bites. How she hummed as she worked, though he wondered if she was even aware of her habit.

She lifted the cup, sipped a mouthful and sighed in pleasure. "Good coffee." Her eyes narrowed. "Now what is this all about?"

"Missy, you have been so good to all of us, taking care of the meals, taking care of the children, even giving them a party they will remember for a long time. I just thought it was time someone did something for you and showed you our gratitude. That's all."

He returned to the stove. Annie and Joey skidded into the room, took in the sight of him at the stove and Missy sitting at the table, but said nothing. Grady entered more slowly.

"Could the three of you set the table, please?" Wade asked.

They did. As the other adults joined them, he fried eggs, then served up a breakfast of golden biscuits, crispy fried potatoes and perfectly presented eggs. A

fine breakfast if he did say so himself. He grinned at
the approval of the others.

"I'm glad you gave Missy a break from all the cook-
ing," Linette said as she scraped up the last of her meal.
"She's done a fine job and we truly appreciate it, but
I feel up to taking over again."

Louise spoke. "I'm feeling fine, too. Why don't we
take turns cooking or at least work together?"

Missy started to protest. "I can do it. After all, you
have new babies to care for."

When the meal was over, little Chloe started to
fuss. Louise lifted her from the basket and handed
her to Missy. "You sit and enjoy your little niece while
Linette and I do the dishes."

If Wade wasn't mistaken, tears glistened in Missy's
eyes as she sat in the rocking chair, the baby cradled
to her shoulder.

If they were alone, he would have asked the reason
for those tears.

Smelling sweet and clean, the baby nuzzled into
Missy's shoulder and made little sucking noises. Annie
leaned against Missy's other shoulder. Not saying anything. Not doing anything. Simply enjoying the contact.

Tears stung Missy's eyes as she caught a momen-
tary glimpse of what life could be like—with a home,
a baby, children and a man who appreciated her.

She blinked twice and tried to ignore the fragile and
very temporary hope that rushed through her. Like a
flash in the pan.

Joey stood before her, his expression half wary, half

hopeful. He didn't say anything, though she could see how much he wanted to.

"What is it?" she asked gently, sensing how he expected to have his dream dashed, so he hesitated to voice it.

"It's just…" He swallowed loudly, but spoke no more words.

"Yes? Go ahead. You can tell me."

"About Christmas. You know. The twelve days thing." He swayed slightly, reluctant to continue. She considered him a seven-year old worrywart.

"I haven't forgotten," she said. "This is day five. Where do you suppose we'll find five golden rings?" Unbidden, unwelcome, her gaze went to Wade and locked there. Was he thinking of the symbolism of a golden ring? Giving the promise of home and family and forever love?

She jerked her attention back to Joey so fast her head spun.

His shoulders slumped. "Gold rings don't sound like any fun."

"I agree. So why don't we forget about the rings and do something you'd like?"

He nodded, his eyes full of eager expectation.

"What would you like to do?" she asked him.

He giggled a little. "Have five picnics."

She laughed. "That's funny."

He grinned back, then sobered. "But you can't have picnics in the winter."

"I don't believe that. Do you?"

He shook his head.

"Do any of you?"

Linette and Louise murmured no, but it was Wade

she looked to. He had moved to the door as if he meant to leave, but he had not donned his coat and now he grinned at her. "If you're going on a winter picnic I'm coming."

Joey ran to his uncle and grabbed his hand. "When are we going?"

Wade looked to Missy for direction. The way his eyes danced with anticipation made her wonder— maybe even wish—that he meant to enjoy her company as much as he would the children's.

"If I may make a suggestion?" Linette said.

"By all means." Missy was only too grateful for someone to bring her thoughts back to normalcy.

"You could take a wagon and go to a special place." She described a sheltered spot a few miles from the house. "We've picnicked there in the summer and I've often thought it would be pleasant in the winter, too."

Out of the corner of her eyes, Missy watched Wade as Linette described the place. He looked every bit as eager for the outing as she.

"Go about noon," Linette advised. "That way you enjoy the warmest part of the day. Help yourself to whatever you need for food."

"That settles it," Wade said. "We're going."

Grady was included. The children offered to help.

"I'll get the wagon ready, then be back to assist," Wade told them. But before he reached the door, he turned. "On second thought, maybe this isn't a good idea."

The excitement in the room came to a sudden halt.

He gave Missy a considering look. "I know you think Vic has been caught, but you can't be sure."

Heavy disappointment—both hers and the chil-

dren's—weighed down her heart. Would she always be to blame for things going wrong?

No. She could not bear to disappoint them all. She rose, handed Chloe to Louise and confronted Wade. "We're having a winter picnic with or without you."

Linette gasped. "You won't be safe."

"I'll take a gun." Realizing the children were listening, wide-eyed, Missy sent them a comforting smile, though she felt anything but soothing. "There's no need to worry. We'll be perfectly safe. We could even take Dawg along to protect us. Would that make everyone happy?" She turned and glared at Wade, silently daring him to refuse to accompany them.

He stood, twisting his hat in his hands. She could almost see him twisting her words about in his mind at the same worried pace.

Finally he released a heavy sigh. "I wouldn't think of letting you go alone."

"Good." She turned back to the children, ignoring the regret in his eyes. "Let's get ready."

With a deep protesting murmur, Wade left the house.

Torn between her victory and her regret at the loss of her joy, Missy organized the children. She sliced bread and meat and they buttered the bread, added a piece of meat, some salt and pepper, making sandwiches for all of them.

Linette filled a syrup bucket with cookies.

"What will we drink?" Joey asked.

"We could heat milk over a fire for hot cocoa."

The children cheered at the idea so she gathered together the ingredients and a suitable pot. She hadn't asked Wade, but they'd surely be able to have a fire.

By the time they were done, she had filled a sizable crate with picnic makings. Linette had given them several blankets, as well.

The children went to the front window and pressed their noses to the glass to watch for Wade.

"He's coming now," Joey called.

Missy's heart skittered up her throat. Maybe this *was* a mistake. Not because she had any concern about Vic, but apart from the children, she'd be alone with Wade, and a bit of the morning feeling lingered—a faint wish for what she'd glimpsed.

He wasn't planning to stay...unless she could persuade him to reconsider his plans. But even that wouldn't change things. They each had separate paths laid out for themselves.

She'd best remember that.

Wade pulled up to the back door and strode in. When he spied the box he hoisted it to his shoulder. "Is this it?"

"Isn't it enough?" she asked, somewhat briskly.

"Sure hope so. A man can get might hungry being outdoors."

She couldn't tell from his voice if he meant the words to be regretful or teasing, and he'd turned his back to take the food to the wagon so she couldn't tell by his face. Might as well believe he was teasing. "I promise you won't starve," she called after him.

He put the box in the wagon and turned to grin at her. "Can you also promise me I'll have fun?"

Her heart forgot to beat as their gazes locked, hers full of impossible longings, his full of impossible promises.

She jerked away to shepherd the children into warm

coats and boots. "Don't forget your mittens and hats."
Once dressed, the children rushed out, and Wade lifted
them into the back of the wagon.

Taking her time, still wondering if this was wise,
Missy made her way to the rig. Of necessity she accepted his help to climb in. But it was totally unnecessary for her heart to speed up and her mouth to grow
dry.

This was only about seeing that the children got the
best Christmas she could help them have. How hard
could it be to remember that?

As they drove down the hill toward the barn, Dawg
ran up to them in front of Brand.

"Can Dawg come with us?" Joey asked.

Before Brand could answer, the dog jumped up beside the children with a silly look on his face.

Brand shook his head. "No one would ever believe
he was once unsociable." He patted the animal. "Have
fun."

Missy wasn't sure if he meant the dog or the hu-
mans occupying the wagon, but from the lonely note
in Brand's voice she thought it likely the first.

They continued on toward the harness shop, where
Eddie stepped out to wave goodbye.

Grady, seeing the length of leather in his hands,
called out, "What are you making, Papa?"

"I promised you a halter so you could work with a
colt. Thought you might want to help make it, but I see
you have other plans."

Both Wade and Missy turned to study the boy. He
glanced at them. "Is it okay if I stay with Papa?"

"Whoa." Wade pulled the wagon to a halt. "Of
course. Jump down."

He waited for Grady to join Eddie, then drove onward, a grin on his face. "It's nice to see how close Eddie and Grady are. You know, with Grady being adopted."

She nodded. "I understand adoption has worked out well for the Gardiners. It's not that I'm opposed to the idea of adoption. It's just…" She shrugged. "It's not the only answer." His grin faded, replaced by a grim look. "It seems we are always going to disagree on this matter. But I don't want to ruin the day with arguments and disagreements."

"Nor do I."

"Then let's not talk about this anymore."

She nodded. She'd stop, but only for the afternoon.

Turning her attention to the scenery around them, she sighed. "It's a beautiful country. The snow, the mountains, the trees."

"It is. You should see it farther up the hills." He pointed toward the mountains. "Even up higher where it's too rugged to build a house. The views are something to behold."

"Tell me about it."

He told of riding into the mountains for days, of quickly flowing streams, waterfalls and ice that never melted. "The wildflowers are like nothing you've ever seen and there are so many beautiful wild creatures— bighorn sheep, grizzly bears eight feet tall when they rise up on their hind legs, elk with horns out to here." He held his hand at a distance from his head to indicate the size.

Missy listened, mesmerized as he told story after story of the animals he'd seen and encountered, the

tales coming to life before her eyes. Before she knew it the wagon halted.

"This must be the place," Wade said, bringing her thoughts from mountain adventures back to the here and now.

He jumped to the ground. "Wait while I tamp the snow down for us."

She watched, amused as he danced about on the white blanket. "Here we go loop-de-loo, here were go loop-de-lay," she sang.

He gave a sheepish laugh. "I should make you get down here and help me."

Her heart beat faster as she envisioned herself holding his hands and dancing in abandonment to the music in her mind. She gulped away the feeling and shook her head. "I'll wait."

The children didn't want to stay in the wagon and joined their uncle in a crazy jig. Even Dawg chased around in circles. The children's giggles grew wilder as they enjoyed the freedom of the moment.

Missy sat back and watched them. It wouldn't matter a bit to her if the day ended right here, so great was her pleasure in seeing the three of them together. This was one of those times when anything she could have said about Wade keeping the children would have been redundant.

"There." He stood still, his hands on his hips. "What do you think?" He turned to the children and they imitated his stance, bringing another smile to Missy's lips.

"It looks good," Joey said, all serious.

"Yup. Looks good," Annie echoed.

"Then let's picnic." Wade crossed to Missy's side in three strides and reached up to lift her from the wagon.

He swung her high, making her squeal. "Put me down."

"I am." But he took his time about it, his eyes locked with hers.

She didn't know if she was flying or drowning. And then her feet hit the ground. Her thoughts, though, did not hit solid footing. She couldn't think what she should do next.

Wade had no such problem. He trotted to the back of the wagon and tossed out firewood. "Kids, help me make a fire."

The "help" was getting under foot, dropping pieces of wood and falling over them amid a lot of giggling.

Missy might have offered to assist, but watching the children tumble about and Wade trying to sort them out was far too much fun. She leaned against the wagon wheel, a huge smile on her face.

Wade handed Joey another piece of wood. "Put it on that side. If we make a nice open tent of sticks, the air will draw through it and it will burn nicely."

Joey tried to position the wood, got off balance and fell, scattering the whole lot.

Wade sat back on his heels, pushed his hat off his forehead and rolled his eyes.

Missy chuckled softly, not wanting any of them to think she mocked them.

"I'll fix it." Joey gathered up the scattered wood and did his best to re-create the tidy pile Wade had made.

As the boy worked, Wade shifted his attention to Missy, and seeing her amusement, his eyes darkened. His gaze went deep, so deep she could almost feel it delving into the secret places of her heart. For a tender,

expectant moment, she almost threw open the doors and let him see.

What was there to see? She had told him everything of importance.

Except, a tiny strident voice insisted, *that you'd give anything to be part of this forever and ever.*

No. She swiftly denied the idea. She knew better than to beg for disappointment and rejection. She'd learned that lesson several times over.

She broke free of his gaze and pushed away from the wagon to assist Joey. "It looks pretty good," she said, after helping him make a few adjustments. "Is it ready to light?" Only then did she allow herself to look again at Wade.

He hadn't moved. His eyes were watchful. Knowing.

What had he seen? Or thought he saw? Surely she'd closed herself to him in time.

He lit the fire, positioned a log for her to perch on and sat beside her. The kids sat on a smaller log and stared into the fire…for about three minutes. Then Joey said, "I'm hungry."

"So let's eat." Wade brought over the box of food. "Do you want to save the cocoa for later?"

Annie and Joey decided they would.

Missy suspected they hoped it would prolong the outing, and she had no objection. There was something quietly soothing about sitting around the fire eating sandwiches and cookies.

Annie turned to Joey. "Did Mama and Papa take us on a winter picnic? I don't remember."

Joey grew thoughtful. "I don't recall. Uncle Wade, did they?"

Wade's hand, halfway to his mouth with a cookie, fell to his knee. "Not when I was there, though I remember they liked to bundle you two up and take you for a ride in the sleigh with bells jingling. You recall that?"

Both children grinned and nodded.

"Tell us other things you remember, Uncle Wade." Annie said the words, but Joey nodded eager agreement.

Wade slowly finished his cookie. Then he leaned back on his hands, his elbow brushing Missy's and disrupting all her noble intentions.

"Joey, you walked early. Your papa was so proud of that. 'Not even a year old and look at him go,' he would say. Your mama had a different opinion. 'Now I won't be able to keep him out of anything.'" Wade laughed. "And she was right. One day when I was there and she was preparing for Christmas, you managed to pull over a whole bowl of flour." He tipped his head back and chuckled. "What a mess. You should have seen yourself. Sputtering out flour. Your skin and hair all white. About the only thing not white was your eyes." Wade shook his head. "You sure did keep your mama going to get ahead of you."

The children ate up his stories, the food completely forgotten.

Missy shifted so she could watch Wade, too. She wanted to say to him, "You should see yourself and what you have to offer these children."

"What about me?" Annie asked.

"Well, you were a little more content to sit and watch Joey. More than once your mama said how glad she was for that. But as soon as you could walk you

wanted to help. Why, I don't suppose you were more than two when you'd push a chair up to the cupboard and insist on helping your mama with whatever she was doing. And she was such a good teacher." He grew somber. "You know she taught me lots of things, too."

"Like what?" Joey asked, hunger to know more about his parents drawing him to Wade's knees.

Wade ruffled the boy's hair. "She taught me that very same song Annie sang on Boxing Day at the manger. She taught me Bible verses. In fact, because of her help, I won a prize one year in Sunday school for memorizing the most verses. She even taught me how to braid a girl's hair."

Joey sat back, a look of shock on his face. "She did not."

Wade nodded. "Yup. She did."

"You didn't do it, did ya?"

Wade leaned over to whisper close to Joey's ear. "Not when my friends were looking."

"Whew."

Missy pressed back a laugh.

Wade unwound from his position next to her. "Come on, you two. Time to work off that meal. Who wants to play tag?"

"Go ahead. I'll tidy up." Besides, Missy would prefer to watch them. And she needed time to deal with the vast emptiness that tore at her insides when Wade moved from her side, leaving her feeling so very alone.

She slowly drew in a calming breath and reasoned with herself. She *planned* to be alone. Had developed her plan over the course of the past few months. Being alone meant she wasn't a burden to anyone, nor could they disappoint her or leave her suddenly and without

explanation. Being alone was the only way to protect her heart.

Wade paused in front of Missy, the children hanging from him, Dawg at his heels.

She looked at him, even knowing it would undo the progress she'd made toward persuading herself she wanted to be alone. Needed to be alone.

He gazed at her with such knowing eyes he must surely see her confusion. Her deepest longings. Longings that must be denied if she meant to guard her heart.

The moment stretched endlessly between them until he spoke.

"You want to play tag, too?" His voice was so full of invitation.

"Yes, do, Missy, please do," the children begged.

"Okay." She knew in the bottom of her heart that this was going to be a mistake. Every moment spent enjoying Wade and the children made her more and more uncertain about following her plan. A fact that frightened her more than she cared to admit.

Chapter Eleven

Wade grinned clear through when Missy agreed to play tag with them. He had plans. As soon as he was "it"—and he'd make sure that was soon—he would catch her, thinking he could hold her in his arms and she would look deep into his eyes as she had done several times over the course of the day. Each time he felt he learned a bit more about her.

He caught her but she spun away, chasing after Joey. He could reason it was about the game, but he suspected it was more. From the glistening tears earlier in the day, to the moments their gazes had locked and he'd felt as if he was spinning on an out-of-control merry-go-round, he'd seen something in her eyes that intrigued him. At first he'd thought it was longing for the joy these children had. She understood too well how fleeting such times were.

As the afternoon passed, he grew to believe it wasn't longing he saw but regret.

His heart settled in the depths of his chest, as heavy as unrisen bread dough. Was he part of her regrets?

Did she feel the same draw to him as he did to her? Did she fear it would upset her plans?

He could have told her not to worry. His plans did not include following the desires of his heart. Yes, he freely admitted, he was attracted to her in an unusual, first-time-ever way. It felt as if a portion of his innermost being had a Missy-shaped vacancy. But Missy deserved more than he could give her. Just as the children did. So it was a good thing their plans did not include each other.

The children had begun to slow down. Even Dawg flopped down, too tired to run any more.

"Time to make cocoa," Wade said.

The four of them hunkered down around the fire. He hung the kettle of water over the flames to heat while Missy added the cocoa and sugar. They poured the steaming liquid into cups and cooled it with milk.

Missy started a game of What Do I See as they enjoyed their drinks.

It was Wade's turn. He wanted to say, "I see a young lady who won't look at me. What is she hiding? What doesn't she want me to see?" Instead he made them guess he saw the black grease on the wagon axle.

The fire had burned to coals. "It's time to head back." He let Joey and Annie throw snow on the embers, enjoying the sizzle. Then he beat them out and buried them properly.

He hated to leave. He'd hoped to draw Missy out and failed. Ah well, there was always tomorrow.

The next day was Saturday. Breakfast was prepared by the three women working together. Over the meal,

Eddie asked, "We might not get many more days as pleasant as this. Does anyone want to go to town?"

There as a general chorus of assent.

Missy did not answer. Wade raised his eyebrows questioningly.

She ducked her head and would not look at him.

"A trip to town sounds like the perfect way to celebrate day six of the twelve days of Christmas," he said loudly enough for all to hear, as if he didn't mean the words for Missy alone.

She looked up, her eyes full of surprise and a hint of regret. What he wouldn't do to get rid of that look. Somehow a trip to town sounded like an opportunity to do so.

"Can we really go?" Joey asked, already half expecting to be disappointed.

"Missy, what do you think?" Wade meant to push her to show her usual enthusiasm.

Her gaze went to Joey and she smiled. "It sounds like fun."

Wade let out his pent-up breath. "Then it's settled."

A short time later, the wagon on runners pulled up to the door. Eddie helped Linette and the baby to the seat. Nate assisted Louise and little Chloe into the back and the three of them settled along one side. Grady climbed up and crowded forward.

Wade lifted Joey and Annie in and they scurried to the other side. He tucked away a secret smile as he helped Missy in and followed. He sat with his back to the rear corner of the wagon, one shoulder protectively pressed to Missy, and pulled warm fur robes over them. This was his idea of a nice way to spend some time. Of course, he wouldn't get a chance to ask

her why she seemed to put up invisible barriers every time he met her eyes, but maybe knowing he couldn't would make her relax.

Louise and Nate talked to Missy with the ease of old friends and Wade sat back, content to simply listen.

After a few minutes, Louise shook her head sadly. "About this time every year, I remember how your parents would have a New Year's Eve party for their children's friends."

Wade felt a jolt go through Missy. "I'd forgotten that. What a fun time we'd have."

Linette glanced over her shoulder, shifting as little as possible to avoid letting cold air under the covers. "I hope you enjoy our party just as much."

"I didn't mean to beg for an invite," Missy protested.

"Nonsense. I expect all our friends to be there. And that includes everyone in this wagon, just in case you might think otherwise."

"Thank you," Louise answered. "We'll be there." She nudged Missy with her foot.

"Yes, thank you," Missy said.

Wade added his thanks, while trying to decide if Missy looked forward to the event or worried she might be included only out of necessity. What had she called herself? A necessary nuisance. Perhaps by now she was beginning to believe she was never that, but so much more. He wished he could find words to help her see it.

They reached town and Eddie stopped at Macpherson's store. They left the wagon and headed their separate ways. Linette wanted to visit the church and see how much work was left to do before it could be used. Louise wanted to find a bit of ribbon to put on one of

Chloe's sweaters, and Nate stuck close to her side. Eddie needed to go to the livery stables and take care of something. Grady went with him.

Missy and Wade stood in front of the store, the children confronting them.

"What do we do?" Annie asked. Her meaning was clear: What fun activity was there to be had?

"Missy, have you had a good look at the town?" Wade asked.

"Just a passing glance."

"Then let me show you around." Not that there was a lot to see. Although the town had gone from a store and a livery barn and a handful of houses a year or two ago to two streets full of houses and a number of businesses. It took them little less than an hour to complete the tour and return to the store.

A man was just heading around the back with a wagon. Seeing Wade, he called out, "Say, you think you could help me load a few things?"

"Sure thing." He swung up beside the man and turned to tell Missy he'd be back shortly, but she and the children stepped through the door of Macpherson's store without a backward look.

All the while he helped load feed and lumber into the stranger's wagon, Wade's thoughts followed Missy. He'd hoped for a chance to talk to her, though he did not know what he could say to make her see that she was valued.

She had to believe it inside before any words he or anyone else spoke would ring true.

The wagon loaded, the man thanked him and drove away. Wade jogged around the store and in the front door.

The kids were admiring something in the display

case and Missy was talking to Macpherson. She leaned over the counter, her voice low, as if she didn't care for anyone else to overhear the conversation.

The door banged shut. When she turned around and saw Wade she straightened, then spoke again to the shopkeeper. "Thanks. I'll let you know when it works out."

She joined the children at the display case, but if Wade didn't miss his guess, she looked rather pleased with herself. Something about the situation set his nerves on edge. What sort of dealings would she have with the store owner?

Wade stepped to her side. When she tipped her face toward him and smiled, every troubling thought melted away. He'd only been imagining she harbored a secret that kept her from taking and enjoying all that life offered.

"The children are admiring all the pretty things." She joined them hovering over the display.

He elbowed close to her to see what caught their attention. Several fancy pins and hair doodads for women. A shaving brush and razor; a pretty ornament with a lady sitting in a rocking chair; a silver-and-ivory brush and comb and mirror. He failed to see what had them pressing their noses to the glass and was about to suggest they move away when he saw it.

A frame for a picture. Fancy gold-colored metal curlicues around a place for a special image. He knew the children were seeing that frame holding the photograph of their parents, and he signaled to Macpherson.

"How much?" he whispered.

The amount was enough to make Wade reconsider, but he knew how they'd appreciate it. "I'll take it." He handed over the necessary coins.

Macpherson opened the case from the back and took out the frame. Two pairs of eyes followed its journey. The children edged to the counter as Macpherson wrapped the frame in brown paper and tied the package with a string. Finished, he handed it to Wade.

Wade shook his head. "It belongs to them." He indicated the children.

Macpherson lowered his hand. Both Annie and Joey took the package.

"You carry it," Annie said.

Her brother clutched it to his chest. "Thank you." He held out his hand to shake Wade's. When Wade took it, he got the feeling the boy had crossed an invisible line toward manhood.

Annie signaled Wade to bend down, and when he did, she hugged him around the neck. "Thank you."

"You're both welcome." He watched them move away to sit side by side on a narrow bench, their eyes glued to the package.

Missy touched Wade's arm. "How did you know? I couldn't figure out what held their attention and they refused to tell me."

He shrugged. How did he know? He couldn't say. He just knew. The fact sent a warm glow through him. He might even believe he'd finally succeeded in understanding what someone needed. He quenched the thought lest it make him careless and cause him to think he could do it again. He might well do it another time, but could he do it when it was absolutely necessary? He wasn't willing to test and see whether or not he could. There was too much at stake.

Missy seemed to read his thoughts. "Don't let doubts mar the moment."

"Huh?" He pretended not to understand.

She grinned and patted his arm. "I think you know what I mean."

If she kept touching him he would lose the ability to understand anything. Worse, he'd forget to keep his heart corralled by his regrets.

Eddie came in and announced they would be heading home soon.

Wade hurried to the back of the store as if he urgently needed something, but then stood before the array of shovels and hammers and saws without a single thought in mind.

How had he gone from being concerned about Missy's regrets to running from the way she saw through his defenses?

He filled his lungs with the smell of linseed oil and leather and hopefully, at the same time, filled his mind with caution. He reminded himself of who he was and the things he could and could not have.

At the moment, he had to fight to recall why he denied himself those things.

He turned to join the others. His roaming gaze caught on a display of brown bottles behind the counter. The skull and crossbones on the labels reminded him of his reasons and he ground his teeth.

Some things could never be forgotten. Nor should they.

Missy waited for Wade to rejoin them. He seemed distracted. Perhaps he'd forgotten what he'd come in to buy. She smiled to herself. She might be partially responsible for his state of mind, but she didn't regret it. Not for a moment. She'd been hoping and praying

for him to see how capable he was of providing for the children. Having him understand what they wanted without any of them saying a word must surely have proved it to him.

And she didn't mind putting in a word or two to help him see it.

The whole day had been rather successful for her.

She'd mentioned to Macpherson that she was looking for a job to pay for her secretary school.

He'd immediately shown interest. "I've been wanting to visit my daughter and her family. Seems a long time since I've seen them. You could run the store for me while I'm gone. It's not busy this time of year and if you need help, Claude Morton will come." He'd nodded in the direction where Claude and his wife ran a sort of stopping house, a place where, according to Wade, travelers could get fed. Claude's wife, Bonnie, also provided baked goods for the store.

"I'm taking care of the children at the moment, but Wade expects to make other arrangements soon." Missy's throat had grown so tight at that point that she couldn't go on for several seconds, and when she'd finally spoken, her voice had a thin tone. "But I would be only too happy to run the store for you when that happens."

"How long before you can do so?"

She'd struggled to think of a reply. Her heart had ached even to think about it. But the man had deserved an answer. "I'll let you know as soon as I can."

"Good enough."

She knew she should be rejoicing. This was an answer to a prayer. But by the time it happened she would have said goodbye to Wade and the children, and—

against her better judgment—she had grown extremely fond of all three. She would suffer the agony of loss yet again.

Surely, when she became a secretary, that was something she would never again face.

Conversation on the journey home was full of news and events of the little town. Linette was particularly excited about the church. "Now if we could only find a preacher to come here," she said.

"God will provide in His time," Eddie assured her. He turned to the others. "Time and again we've seen God work things out that, at first, looked like a mistake. Even our marriage." He chuckled and gave Linette such an adoring glance that she pressed her head to his shoulder.

"Do I sense a story?" Wade asked.

"Yes, you do." Eddie held the reins, but the horses needed little guidance so he shifted to more easily talk to those in the wagon. "You might say Linette is my mistake wife."

Missy gasped. Poor Linette, being called a mistake. And yet she didn't seem to mind. Was it possible a person got used to being necessary but a mistake? The notion burned through Missy. Some might be prepared to settle for such, but not her. She would never accept being a convenience or a necessary nuisance.

Eddie continued. "I was expecting another woman— my former fiancée—to arrive, but instead, Linette stepped from the stagecoach, thinking I was expecting her. You see, she'd sent a letter and thought the message to my fiancée saying to come was my reply to it. As soon as I learned of Linette's mistake and her

belief that she was to become my wife, I said she could return as soon as the weather allowed travel."

The whole time Eddie talked, his wife watched him with such love that Missy blinked away tears. Linette obviously felt cherished. How Missy envied her.

"By that time, I had lost my heart to her." Eddie bent his head to Linette's. "What looked like a series of regrettable mistakes was really God's hands at work, just as it says in Romans 8, verse 28. 'All things work together for good to them that love God.'"

God's hands at work. Missy repeated the words over and over. She knew the verse he quoted. Had memorized it at her mama's knee. But surely it didn't mean things like parents dying too young, or include evil men like Vic.

"Mr. Eddie?" Joey waited for the rancher to acknowledge him. "Our mama and papa died." He struggled to find the words he wanted to say.

Eddie cupped the boy's head. "And you want to know what good can come of it."

Joey nodded.

Annie hung back, watching, hoping.

Under the warm fur robe, Missy reached for Wade's hand and squeezed it. She could have voiced the same question and she waited for a satisfactory answer, feeling more than a little like young Annie—hoping for understanding. But Missy wasn't a child. She was an adult who realized bad things happened and there was no explaining why.

"I can't say how things will work out for you. But I can promise you God is true to His word." Eddie grew thoughtful. "Sometimes good is happening and we can't see it. Maybe we won't notice it until much

later. You see, God doesn't promise things will always be easy. But He loves us and sometimes that has to be enough."

Missy clung to the words. Yes, it was enough. But not always. There were days when she longed to experience the end result immediately.

Wade turned their joined hands over and weaved his fingers through hers. She realized how long she'd clutched his, but she could not let go. She turned to speak softly, hoping no one else could hear. "It's hard to see the good in everything."

He shifted his head close to hers and answered in a low voice, "It's impossible."

At his blunt words, an argument rose inside her. "But we must trust."

"Sometimes we just have to forge ahead and do our best to not repeat our mistakes." The muscle at the side of his jaw twitched.

She wanted to reach up and smooth away the tension, but could not with an audience. "And yet don't we grow stronger every day?" She ached for him to see what he had to offer.

"Is that your experience?" His eyes probed hers.

She blinked but couldn't tear away from his look. She meant for him to find hope in what lay ahead. She didn't mean to apply the words to herself.

A knowing look flickered across his eyes. "Have you grown strong enough to take risks in the future?"

She was grateful they arrived back at the ranch before she could respond, because she had no answer. At least not one she was willing to give.

In her heart of hearts she knew it was fear that drove her plans, not courage or strength. Because if she was

bold and free of her fear she would plot an entirely different course.

Except what she pictured for the future did not depend entirely on her being brave enough to face her fears. It depended far too much on someone else confronting his.

As Wade helped her down, she took the opportunity to speak softly for his ears alone. "I ask you a similar question. Are you brave enough to step into a future that offers no guarantees, yet is full of hope?"

Before he could hide the surprise in his eyes and find a reply, Missy thanked him and followed the ladies into the house.

The discussion circled endlessly inside her head, prowling like a restless animal. Embracing a future with no guarantees required courage and faith. A coil of fear tightened within her. Some risks were too great.

Chapter Twelve

Wade rose Sunday morning with a head full of restless thoughts. Missy's question had haunted him throughout the night. Was he brave enough to step into a future with no guarantees? No doubt she referred to him finding a way to keep the children. However, his wayward brain had thought of other things he longed for, but which, if he should step in that direction, offered no assurances of success.

He ached for a peaceful, loving home.

He saw a woman and children in that home. The woman was not Tomasina. Despite his love for his late wife, she had never given him the peace he wanted. There had always been tension in the air from so many sources. Disappointment in not having children, but other things, too. Dissatisfaction with their surroundings. Resentment at how many hours he worked on the farm. Boredom because she refused to occupy herself.

No, the woman he saw in his impossible dream was blonde and busy. Very pretty, with a joyous laugh that rang out often. She was surrounded by children whom she lovingly touched and patiently guided.

The direction of his thoughts made his stomach burn. Had Missy accused him of being afraid? She'd be surprised to learn he had good reason.

He brought his thoughts back to the children who had already prepared for church. Wade had even braided Annie's hair.

She'd examined herself in his little mirror. "Looks nice. Thanks, Uncle Wade."

Silently, he thanked Susan for teaching him this skill. Neither of them could have guessed how and when he'd use it.

"You two go on down and wait for me. No running around. Be sure you stay clean."

Hand in hand, they sedately walked out of the room. Their footsteps on the stairs were slow and measured. He grinned. They meant to obey him. He washed and shaved, combed his hair back and looked at his reflection in the mirror. Not bad for an old guy.

That thought sobered him. He was twenty-six. Missy was only eighteen. Likely she saw him as a father figure.

He turned from the mirror and descended the stairs, each footstep hard enough to send a jolt clear to the top of his head. As if he could drive away all his foolish thoughts.

The others, including the children, had already left the house. As he stepped outside, he saw them enter the cookhouse. He followed after them, keeping his gaze on the ground ahead. After all, a man must guard his steps if he meant to stay on the trail he'd chosen. He reached his destination, kicked the snow and dirt from his boots and entered.

Cookie grabbed him in a bear hug. "I've wondered when you'd visit me."

His lungs could not work. His heart pounded a protest until she released him, leaving him gasping for breath.

Wade held out his hand to her husband, Bertie, relieved the man settled for a quick handshake.

The children waited for his welcome to end, then Annie raced toward him. He caught her in his arms and pulled Joey to his side. Only then did he allow his gaze to go to Missy.

She smiled and his heart tipped sideways.

"Good morning," he murmured. He could say nothing more because of the others crowding through the door. Which was probably a good thing, as he felt a sudden, inexplicable urge to tell her the darkest secrets of his heart.

"We're going to have church." Annie sounded excited as she took his hand and led him toward a bench.

Joey and Missy followed and then a crowd filled the benches—the cowboys of the ranch, the newly married couples, the Jones family, two families from nearby ranches and the couple and their two little girls from town. Apart from those from the neighboring ranches, he'd already met them.

Somehow, as he and Missy took their places, a child ended up beside each of them, pressing Wade's shoulder to Missy's on the crowded bench. And somehow, he didn't mind. It seemed a perfect way to spend a Sunday morning.

Cookie stood at the front. "So glad to see all of you on this, the last day of 1882. It's been a good year

and next year will be just as good or better because of God's grace. Let's sing."

Beside Wade, Missy's voice joined the others. He sang along. Today, he could think life was good and full of abundant promises. Promises he could trust.

He corrected that thought. He had faith in God's promises. It was his own resources and abilities he did not trust.

They sang three hymns, then Bertie stood to speak.

"I'm not a preacher, just an old cowboy who now helps make meals for you and sees you have a full stomach each day. But there's more to life than food and riding. And that's found in a loving God. This is the last day of the year, as my good wife said already. I want to tell you all that we can look forward to the New Year with its surprises and disappointments, knowing nothing that happens is out of God's good hands."

How could the man so easily say that? Had he not faced things that challenged that belief?

Bertie continued. "Many of you know that I was a prodigal son for many years, wasting my life in reckless living. I made some mistakes I sorely regret. I've seen some awful things. I'll spare your tender ears from hearing what they were. But believe me when I say I had good reason to think God might have given up on me. He didn't. I thought I had enough reason to give up on myself, but eventually a wonderful truth hit me. If God still cared about me, then maybe I should, too."

Murmurs of agreement came from many of those present. Wade, for his part, ached to believe instead of having reservations.

Bertie opened his Bible. "Go fearlessly into the New

Year knowing that God goes with you, before you and behind you. I want to read you a portion of scripture to encourage you. This is one of my favorite Psalms. Chapter 37." The man read in a strong, ringing voice.

The words washed over and through Wade.

"'The steps of a good man are ordered by the Lord: and he delighteth in his way. Though he fall, he shall not be utterly cast down: for the Lord upholdeth him with his hand.'"

Bertie continued to read, but Wade's thoughts stopped at those verses. Did God uphold a man such as him? Wade's chest filled with hope. With God at his side, perhaps he could face the uncertainties of the future.

Bertie closed the Bible and sat, and Cookie stood again.

"Many of you know the new song 'It Is Well with My Soul.' Those of you who don't, try and follow along. I think this hymn is an encouragement to all of us to trust God for the past and for the future, no matter what has come our way or what comes next."

Whatever my lot, Thou hast taught me to know, It is well, it is well, with my soul.

The words bit deep into Wade's soul. The events of the past had left him fighting the future, afraid to allow others to be part of his life, lest he fail them. He longed to change that, but he wasn't willing to risk repeating his failures. They loomed too big, too devastating to ignore. His inadequacies had led to Tomasina's death. He'd willingly admitted it even without the accusation of her parents.

He wrapped an arm about Annie on one side and leaned ever so slightly toward Missy on the other.

These two, and Joey, were far too precious for him to risk their happiness by letting them grow dependent on him. If he should fail them as he had Tomasina...

A cruel hand seemed to reach into his chest and squeeze the blood from his heart. He must surely have gasped with the pain, for Missy glanced sideways at him. Perhaps she saw more than he cared for her to see, for she laid her hand on his arm. He felt her touch all the way to his aching heart.

The service ended in a prayer of blessing, and slowly, mercifully, life returned to Wade's limbs.

The tables were pushed back into place and the adults crowded around them. Annie and Joey went to join the other youngsters, but Missy stayed at Wade's side, as if she thought he needed her comfort.

He wanted to deny it but he couldn't. Having her there was a joy. It made him feel bold and courageous. Almost enough for him to throw away all his caution and go boldly and fearlessly into the future, as Bertie said.

Almost but not quite.

Cookie served coffee and set out big plates of cinnamon rolls. She waited while Wade took his first bite. He realized she expected a comment.

"Umm. Best rolls I ever tasted." And he wasn't exaggerating.

Cookie beamed with pleasure.

He settled back, content to listen to the hum of conversation around him. But it was not to be.

Brand speared him with a question. "How was the courtin' hill?"

If Wade wasn't mistaken, every eye around the table looked at him. He dared not glance at Missy to see how

she reacted to the question. If she seemed offended by it, he would be hard-pressed to hide his disappointment. But if she blushed and looked embarrassed he would surely blurt out something stupid, such as an invitation for her to accompany him on a walk in that direction.

"We didn't go there," he managed to reply. At least not the time Brand meant.

How come everyone looked either disappointed or disbelieving? It wasn't as if he was courting Missy. Nothing could be further from his plans.

"Is that so?" Brand shook his head. "Sooner or later, I guess."

Sybil placed her hand over Brand's. "Don't you go turning into a matchmaker. Let them work out things for themselves."

At her word, thankfully, the conversation returned to general things.

Wade wanted to inform them all there was no need for a matchmaker. He and Missy both understood the limits on this friendship. It would come to an end as soon as he heard from the Bauers regarding the children.

He couldn't deny he welcomed the delay. It gave him time to spend with the children and to give them a special Christmas. Plus, he would never regret the joy of knowing Missy, even though he'd miss her terribly when he was gone.

Soon, one by one the cowboys drifted away from the table, but the others lingered until Linette said she must attend to the meal. Immediately everyone rose. Wade had expected the couples to each go to their own homes, but they followed the Gardiners up the hill.

"Everyone comes for Sunday dinner," Linette explained. "It's one of our traditions."

"Sounds like fun." But he couldn't decide if he welcomed the crowd, making private conversation with Missy impossible, or if he wished it could be otherwise. He would have liked to ask her what she thought of Bertie's talk. Had she been challenged to go after what she really wanted? Because Wade was certain being a secretary was only a means of running from the risk of following her heart.

He managed to repress a heavy sigh. Seemed they weren't all that different. Both were doing their best to avoid a repeat of past sorrows.

But she was young and attractive. She shouldn't deprive herself of the family she truly wanted.

Unless he was mistaken in his assessment of her.

Thankfully the men gathered in the sitting room, while the women helped with meal preparations. Wade turned his attention to the conversation around him, glad that for now he would ignore the questions and wishes in his heart.

Missy kept herself busy all afternoon. She helped prepare and serve a meal to the crowd, insisting that Linette should sit and enjoy visiting with her friends.

"Thank you. You're such a blessing." Linette's words fell like raindrops in Missy's heart. It was pleasant to realize she wasn't a burden to anyone here even if she'd landed uninvited on their doorstep, running from Vic. Thankfully, no one had mentioned the man today. Perhaps they accepted that he had been captured.

She helped with the dishes and then set about amus-

ing all the children. "Let's go upstairs where we won't bother the adults." She traipsed down the hall and, as she passed, glanced into the room where the grown-ups were gathered.

Her gaze connected with Wade's and her heart skipped a beat. He looked as if he wanted her to stay, to spend time with him. She knew it was only her imagination. Her own longing. Ever since the trip home from town yesterday she'd been wanting to ask him what he meant by his question, *Are you brave enough to step into a future that offers no guarantees, yet is full of hope?* Did he think her a coward simply because she meant to take steps to be self-sufficient? He'd surely understand if he considered for a moment. If she was self-reliant, no one would have to be responsible for her. No one would consider her a burden or be forced to find ways to make her feel useful.

Louise, to her credit, had done her best in that regard and Missy was grateful. Just as she was happy that Louise could now live her own life and not have to worry about her little sister-in-law.

But Missy would not dwell on regrets from the past. They were about to embark on a new year and she meant to make the most of it. She'd take the secretarial course and she'd take care of herself.

She spent a couple hours organizing games for the children. Neil and Daisy seemed a little bored with the activities, so she suggested they join the adults. After all, the two of them worked side by side with their parents on a daily basis.

"I should help watch the little ones," Daisy protested.

"Nonsense. I can manage. You deserve a little break today."

Daisy smiled in appreciation. "Thank you. You're a very kind lady. I hope…" She ducked her head.

"What is it? You can say what you want. I won't be offended."

Daisy slowly brought her head up again. "I hope you and Wade fall in love and get married and adopt Joey and Annie just like Cassie and Roper did for us." Her voice fell to a whisper. "I am so grateful they did."

For several seconds Missy couldn't find words. Why would Daisy wish for such a thing? "I don't think that's going to happen," she said gently. "But I pray the children will be happy in the future…as happy as you and your sister and brothers are."

The girl nodded. "I hope so, too." She left with a backward look at her little sister, who was playing happily with Annie, rocking her dolls.

Some time later the mothers came up to get their children. Cassie shepherded away her two younger ones. "Come on down now," she told Missy. "Linette says the party is about to begin."

Missy nodded. "I thought I heard wagons approach."

"Claude and Bonnie Morton came from town. People have arrived from the OK Ranch, as well as a few others from town."

Missy hurried down the stairs after Cassie. A New Year's party for the adults. How exciting.

She stepped into the room. Chairs crowded every corner and almost every chair had been filled. The only available one was next to Wade. Had he saved it especially for her or was it only happenstance?

Either way, she was glad enough to sit beside him,

though she was squeezed in so tightly she could barely move her arms. She sat back, and he leaned forward slightly so his bent arm half crossed in front of her. It gave her the most delicious feeling of being cared for.

It took a moment for the thought to register. Hadn't she determined she didn't want to be cared for? That it made her feel like a burden?

Only it could also make her feel valued. She'd almost forgotten that feeling. Perhaps she had even closed her mind to it after her parents' deaths and Gordie's constant complaining about being stuck with her.

Maybe tonight was a good time to remember the blessings of the past and forget, for the moment, the things that had caused her pain and regrets.

A party was a perfect place to do exactly that.

Linette had organized parlor games. With each, Missy grew more giddy, laughing for the slightest reason, which left her totally unfit to play the game Do As I Do. Louise was "it" and had to point at someone and say "do as I do." She would proceed to do something silly, such as sneeze or cough, and the person she indicated was supposed to repeat the motion without laughing.

Oh, please, Missy silently begged. *Don't pick me. I am almost out of control with the joy of the evening.* A joy, she freely admitted, that had a lot to do with Wade at her side.

Louise pointed at Eddie, who didn't show any emotion as he wiped his eyebrows. Then she pointed to Nate and gave a naughty wink. How Nate managed to return the wink without a hint of smile was beyond Missy, as she covered her mouth to hide her amusement.

Louise turned, spied Missy trying to tame her smile, and pointed at her. Louise poked her finger in her ear.

Missy sucked in air, managed to stifle a smile and poked her finger in her ear. And burst out laughing.

She was "it."

But she wouldn't pick Wade. Someone was sure to misinterpret such a move. So she pointed toward Daisy, who widened her eyes and, even before Missy had finished wiping her finger across her nose, laughed and traded places with her.

Missy sat down, but now she was several people to the right of Wade. She looked at him. He raised his eyebrows and gave a slanted glance toward the chair now occupied by Louise. Missy shrugged. There wasn't much she could do about the situation, but she missed being next to him.

Several games and much hilarity later, Linette had them count off from one to five around the circle to draw up teams for Charades.

Missy tried not to be disappointed when her number wasn't the same as Wade's.

Louise watched them glance at each other and smiled knowingly. She whispered something to Wade and he grinned and nodded. Quickly they traded places and he gave Missy a look of such victory that warmth rushed up her neck.

If she wasn't mistaken, he was flirting with her. And she was enjoying it.

They continued playing games for some time, then Linette clapped her hands and drew their attention.

"I've prepared refreshments. They're set out in the kitchen. Eddie will ask a blessing on our food and our gathering, then help yourselves."

Missy felt a pang of guilt. She'd been enjoying herself so much she hadn't noticed several of the ladies had slipped away to help Linette with the refreshments.

Her guilt was short-lived, though, as Wade caught her elbow.

"May I?" he asked, his voice deep and warm.

"You may indeed." She tucked her arm about his and he guided her into the kitchen.

He picked up two plates and handed one to her.

She smiled her thanks at him, and for the space of two heartbeats the others disappeared and she and Wade were alone, lost in each other's gaze. Someone jostled her and she jerked back to the present. She was simply giddy and imagining things, Missy told herself. Or was she? She stole a glance at him, but he was trying to choose between the chocolate brownies and the matrimonial squares.

"Take both." And she put one of each on his plate.

"You, too." Wade served her in turn.

"Thank you, kind sir." She grinned at him and he grinned back. They proceeded down the table, each choosing something for the other, each time smiling in a way that made her feel syrupy inside.

With their plates full, they returned to the sitting room, where he shepherded her into the farthest corner. Missy harbored a little hope that he'd done it purposely so they could be alone. As alone as they could be in such a crowd. Yet the way he turned toward her and smiled made her forget all the others.

Their arms brushed as they each lifted a bite to their mouth. With every touch, a little thrill raced through her. She knew it was only pretend, only for this one evening, but for this short time she wouldn't worry that

he was leaving, nor would she concern herself with the pain she'd have to deal with when he did. Even more, she would not think how sitting beside him dreaming of letting herself fall in love with him was totally in conflict with her plans.

Refreshments ended and the dishes were taken to the kitchen.

"Time is winding down," Eddie said.

His words startled Missy, as if he meant to remind her that Wade would soon be leaving. Then she realized he meant the countdown to the New Year.

The room grew so quiet they could hear the ticking of the clock on the wall. They all turned to watch the hands move. Wade shifted and draped his arm across the back of her chair. It seemed an innocent gesture, but her heart reacted with several racing beats.

"Ten, nine…" Eddie began the countdown and the others joined him.

"…three, two, one. Happy New Year!" Everyone came to their feet.

Wade caught Missy in his arms and pulled her in for a sweet, gentle kiss. At least it started that way, but then his lips lingered, his arms tightened about her. She planted her hands on either side of his waist and kissed him back.

A shuffling sound, as the others withdrew from their own embraces, reminded her they were not alone, and she stepped back reluctantly. She felt Wade's gaze lingering on her and turned away, her cheeks hot. Only when she saw that no one seemed interested in them did she relax.

The guests began to depart. Those with children gathered up their young ones, who had fallen asleep in

various rooms of the house. Joey and Annie had taken themselves to bed some time ago.

Wade stayed at Missy's side as she went through the motions of bidding goodbye to the guests. But her words were rote, her gestures wooden as she shook hands with the men and hugged the women.

Louise and Nate prepared to take the stairs to their room. She paused to hug Missy.

"Happy New Year, little sister." Before Missy could protest that Louise didn't need to consider her that any longer, her friend addressed her concern. "You will always be my little sister, and don't forget it."

"Yes, ma'am."

Louise chuckled. "I know you're not little anymore. You're all grown up. I'm so pleased to see you interested in grown-up things." Her gaze went deliberately to Wade. "You two make a lovely couple."

As Nate escorted Louise up the stairs, Missy stood openmouthed. She could not look at Wade. Surely he wouldn't think she had her eyes set on him.

Though the idea was more than a little tempting.

It was only because of the excitement of the party.

And his innocent New Year's Eve kiss.

"Happy New Year," she murmured, and fled down the hall to her room.

Wade stood at the foot of the stairs, too stunned by the events of the last two minutes to move. *You two make a lovely couple.* He wished it could be true.

He should not have kissed her, even though he'd meant it only as the customary New Year's tradition. But it had changed something. And try as he might, he couldn't undo that.

It was only because he was tired. Tomorrow he would sort things out.

He made his way to his room, checked on the children. They were both sound asleep. A few minutes later he lay stretched out under the covers, his hands folded under his head as he stared at the dark ceiling. He didn't need light to see the things racing through his head, mostly images of Missy laughing with abandon. He smiled with renewed pleasure. My, he enjoyed hearing her laugh. Almost as much as he enjoyed seeing her have a good time. But not nearly as much as he enjoyed having her sit so close to his side that he could feel her every inhalation and note the summery scent that wafted to him when either of them moved.

He replayed many of the scenes from the party, but each one led directly to the kiss. He could do nothing but stare into the dark and grin.

Wade woke with the same smile the next morning when the children tiptoed into the room.

"Can we get up?" Joey whispered. "We'll be very quiet so we don't wake up the others."

"I'll tell you what. If you can get dressed without making a sound, I'll take you outside."

They slipped from the room on silent feet and, suspecting they'd hurry back, leaving him no opportunity to lie about remembering the night before, Wade hurriedly dressed. Just in time, as the pair returned.

"Did you hear us?" Annie asked.

"Nope. You did good." Now to make it down the stairs without waking the household.

He held his finger to his lips as they eased down each step. He paused at the bottom and listened. Not

a sound. Good. He cracked the door open and they slipped outside. "No noise until we are away from the house." He glanced about. There were cabins and houses everywhere. "I guess no noise until we get away from the ranch."

The door whispered open.

"May I join you?"

His heart skipped with joy at Missy's softly spoken question and he turned to smile in welcome. He crooked his elbow, inviting her to put her hand on his arm. She did and his smile came clear from the deepest part of his heart.

"We're trying to be quiet so we don't wake up anyone," he explained, as the children tiptoed across the frozen ground.

"Good idea." Missy's words were laced with amusement. "Where are you going?"

"Away from the buildings." His gaze followed the path across the bridge and past the pens to the courting hill. It could hardly be seen as that with two children in attendance.

But no matter. The sun was bright in a cloudless sky. The air was clear and pure. And Missy walked at his side.

They passed the cookhouse and the little cabin where Seth and Jayne lived. They would have to leave the yard behind before the children could be allowed to play, so he indicated they should head down the path toward the Jones house.

As they approached it, the door flew open and Billy peeked his head out. "Can Joey and Annie come in and play with us?"

Cassie poked her head out above her son's. "You're welcome to come in."

Wade turned to Missy. "Do you want to visit with Cassie and Roper or go for a walk?"

She ducked so he couldn't see her expression, but not before he saw a flash of delight in her eyes, and Wade tucked the knowledge into his happy heart.

"It's a beautiful morning," she murmured. "I'd very much enjoy a walk in the fresh air."

His smile came from the depths of his heart. "Me, too." He turned to Cassie and called, "Do you mind watching the children while we go for a walk?"

"Not in the least. Enjoy yourselves." She ushered the two inside and closed the door.

Missy's hand was still tucked around Wade's arm and he pressed it close to his side as, with a heart full of promise, he turned toward the bridge.

They took their time crossing the river, as if they had no destination in mind and were simply following the path. They sauntered past the pigpen, past the wintering corrals, pausing often to watch the animals and to comment on this and that. The noise the pigs made. The way the cows all lifted their heads and watched with bovine expressions. The chill in the air as they left the shelter of the pens and stepped past a clearing toward the tree-lined path that led up the hill.

Wade didn't point out that the direction they chose would take them to the courting hill, as Brand called it. But if he wasn't mistaken, Missy understood that fact.

They continued to take their time, pausing to look for the snowy owl.

"I wish we'd see him again," she murmured.

Wade pressed her hand closer to his side. Was she

mostly wanting to see the beautiful bird once more or was she recalling the way she'd practically fallen into his arms the last time? He thought only of the latter.

They reached the top of the hill, where a half circle of trees stood, bare limbs outstretched, welcoming them into their shelter. Wade led Missy into it, turning so they faced outward. The landscape dipped toward the snow-covered pasture below and then rose in hill after hill dotted with pine and spruce trees, clear on to the mountains, which reflected the pink of the sunrise to the east.

He glanced at her to see if she was enjoying the scenery, and caught her turning her head away. She'd been looking at him, not the mountains or the trees. But now she studiously kept her gaze on the majestic scene before them.

Wade waited several seconds for her to look at him, but she didn't. He wondered why. Was she upset at him about their New Year's kiss?

"About last night—" he began.

She turned back to him so fast it must have hurt her neck. "Don't say it was a mistake." Her voice rang out clearly, but her eyes revealed distress.

He caught her by the shoulders and turned her to face him. He took his time studying her, the flyaway strands of sunlit hair escaping her hat, her pure skin, full lips and blue-green, challenging eyes.

"Does this seem like I think it's a mistake?" And he claimed her sweet mouth.

She sighed and leaned into him, obviously wanting this as much as he.

When he pulled back, he saw her eyes had a dreamy

look to them, and he glowed inside with the satisfaction that he'd put it there.

She shifted to gaze at the scenery again. "What did you think of Bertie's sermon yesterday?"

Wrapped up in her kiss, Wade could barely recall it, but he dragged up something from his distant memory. "I liked how he thought we should go boldly into the future." That was what Bertie had said, wasn't it? Wade couldn't be certain now.

Missy nodded. "Me, too." She slipped away, just far enough that he could feel the cool air drift between them.

He thought of pulling her back, but she seemed to be considering something so he waited.

She began to speak slowly, softly. "The New Year is a time for new beginnings. A time to start over. A time to put old things aside and reach out for new things."

His breath stalled halfway up his throat. Was she about to make major changes in her plans? He tried to guess what that would mean. Maybe she'd want to—

But he couldn't, wouldn't even think what it might be. Nor what he might wish it to be.

Her eyes flashed. "Wouldn't now be a good time for you to put aside whatever is in your past? Whatever you think prevents you from making a home for the children. I know it's more than the fact you're a cowboy. That's something you can work out. I see how much you love the children and they love you. Face the future boldly. Give them a home." Missy lapsed into silence, but her eyes challenged him.

He stepped back as if she'd physically dealt him a blow. Oh, she'd dealt a terrible one, but not with her fists. "I love them, it's true. But love isn't enough."

At the surprise on her face he knew he had to explain. "I loved my wife and Tomasina loved me, but it wasn't enough to stop her from taking her own life."

Missy lifted a hand as if to comfort him, then lowered it. Her eyes were wide and dark.

She was as shocked and dismayed by the knowledge as he was burdened with it.

He should not have told her. Now she would see him for who he truly was…a man unable to care for those he loved. His whole being hurt at the prospect.

New beginnings were not possible for men like him.

Chapter Thirteen

Missy's arms grew numb. The feeling spread throughout her body, leaving her unable to move, barely able to get air into her lungs. She must fight the sensation, say something or do something as Wade stared at her, his eyes hard as the frozen ground they'd recently crossed.

Only one word came to mind. "Why?"

He averted his gaze and turned from her in one swift movement that left her aching inside.

She waited, any words she might have spoken sucked away by wave after wave of shock.

"It was my fault." He managed to squeak out the words.

At the agony in his voice, the dam stopping her from speaking broke. She wanted to touch him, comfort him, but he was so brittle she feared that he'd shatter if she did. "Tell me what happened."

He stared out at the mountains, but she knew he didn't see them. He saw something so horrible, so unforgettable, that he shuddered. Missy wondered if he heard her request, and if so, if he meant to answer it.

"I found her."

A groan ripped from Missy's heart.

He continued, his voice a deep monotone. "She was in bed. At first I thought she might have hurt herself fatally, but I could see no sign of injury, and then I spied the lye bottle beside the bed." He shuddered clear to his toes.

Missy wanted to ask why. Why would a woman do such a dreadful thing? But she dared not ask. Not with Wade looking as if the blood had drained from his body.

She edged closer, wondering if he would collapse, but then he sucked in air and released it in a whoosh.

Slowly, he continued. "I didn't even know she was unhappy. Yes, I knew she was disappointed we hadn't had children, as was I. But I said it was okay. We could be happy without them. I thought she *was* happy. I was so blind. I didn't see that she was so desperate."

Missy rubbed a hand along his sleeve. What did one say in the face of such a terrible thing?

Wade came about to face her, and at the desperation in his eyes her throat clamped shut. "I failed her." The words rasped from him.

Stung by the depths of his emotions, she silently asked God to guide her words. "You can't blame yourself."

"But I can and I do. I should have seen her need. I should have done something to help her."

"Wade, you aren't responsible for the choices and actions of another. I think Tomasina had some serious problems. She must have been very unhappy to do such a thing. Sometimes…" The words came slowly, hesitantly. Missy did not want to offer an easy answer, nor make light of how devastating it must have been to find

his wife dead. "Sometimes a person needs more than any other individual can give them. The fault then is with that person. It does not indicate a failure on the part of those around him or her."

Wade clung to Missy's gaze, searching beyond her words. Perhaps seeking understanding both from her and his own heart.

Then his eyes darkened and she knew before he spoke that he didn't believe her.

He shook his head. "It was my job to take care of her and I didn't do it."

Understanding came in a flash. "It's why you won't keep the children. You think you'll fail them."

He didn't nod, didn't say a thing, but Missy knew from the way he hunched his shoulders that she was correct.

"Oh, Wade." She cupped her mittened hands on either side of his neck. "What a heavy burden you carry."

He groaned ever so softly.

"You can't control everything and everyone. Not even those you love. But you can love them. Love covers a multitude of sins."

"I wish I could believe love is enough." His voice was harsh. "I really do."

She pulled his head closer and whispered, "It's the best we can offer, even if it's not perfect." She lifted her lips to his and kissed him gently, encouragingly.

He wrapped his arms around her and pulled her close and kissed her back.

She pressed one hand to the back of his head and held him, her heart about to burst with sorrow and love all laced together in one sweet uncertainty.

They broke apart. Unwilling to leave the shelter of

his arms, she rested her cheek on his shoulder. He lowered his head to hers and they remained in the embrace.

He released a pent-up sigh. "I couldn't bear to think I might not understand the children's needs and fail them as awfully as I failed Tomasina."

Missy wrapped her arms about his waist and held on tight so he couldn't break away. "Wade, the biggest failure might be in giving them away. Have you ever considered that?"

"It could be the best thing for them."

She was unable to tell if he thought so or if he was trying to convince himself. "You only believe that because you are afraid of the risks. Life doesn't come with guarantees. Only with promises—God's promises. That should be all we need."

He nodded.

She smiled a tiny bit. If he would begin to understand that, then perhaps he would find a way to keep the children.

He caught her chin with his gloved fingertip and lifted it so they looked into each other's eyes. At the growing confidence she saw there, she slipped off her mitten and touched her bare fingers to his cold cheek, enjoying the feel of the stubble on his face. She trailed her finger to the corner of his mouth.

He caught her hand in his and dipped his head to kiss her palm, sending sweetness throughout her being. Then he captured her lips in a gentle kiss that she wished could go on forever. He sighed and looked out at the scene before them. "I thought life would be easier than this."

She turned as well, to look at the distant mountains. "Me, too. But God is our refuge and strength." Guilt

stirred within her. She said the words and she wanted Wade to believe them. But did she apply them to her own life? What would she do differently if she did?

Wade lingered on the hilltop for another ten minutes with Missy in his arms. She'd given him much to think about. Had Tomasina needed more than he could give her? More than was humanly possible to give? If he chose to believe that now, could he find the courage to keep the children and somehow make a home for them? He liked to think of it being a possibility, but there remained the risk of failure. Even with God's help he could fail completely and utterly, and the children would pay the price. Was he willing to take the risk? Was he being selfish in thinking he could?

"If only God would send a sign," he murmured.

"Perhaps He will."

"That would be nice." The day had fully dawned and the children would no doubt be looking for breakfast. "They might worry where we've disappeared to." Wade meant those in the house, as well as Joey and Annie.

Missy stepped from his arms and pulled on her mitten. "Goodness, I didn't think about that. We need to hurry. Louise will think the worst."

At the reminder of potential danger, Wade jammed his palm to his forehead. "I forgot all about Vic. It just goes to prove—"

Missy grabbed his hand. "It proves nothing except confidence the Mounties have lived up to their reputation and gotten their man. Besides…" She ducked her head and her voice fell to a whisper. "I was perfectly

safe with you. Vic would not bother me if he thought he'd have to confront someone equal in size."

Thrilled at her trust in him, Wade hugged her. Then they hurried down the hill, stopped to collect the children and continued to the big house. They burst in the door, only to be met by Nate, who was dressed to go outdoors.

"Louise wanted me to go looking for you. She worried Vic had come. I told her Missy was safe with you."

Missy rushed to her friend. "I'm sorry for causing you worry. We simply went for a walk. It's a very lovely morning."

Louise hugged her. "No harm done, it seems. But I won't be able to relax until we get news that Vic has been captured."

Wade nodded. "My sentiments exactly. Believe me, I won't be letting Missy venture out alone until we know that man is behind bars."

They joined the others for a leisurely breakfast. Wade noted the many times the children turned to him for assurance and guidance, how they both pressed to his side after the meal. If only he could believe he could keep them forever and care for them in the way they deserved.

He left them in Missy's care and went with Eddie and Nate to handle the chores.

"Just the essentials today," Eddie said, and neither of the others raised a protest.

Wade, for his part, wanted to be with the children today and think about their future. Thoughts of them were his constant companions throughout the day.

After dinner, Louise and Nate and baby Chloe, Eddie and Linette and little Jonathan, retired to their

rooms for a rest. Grady, Joey and Annie stayed behind, with Wade and Missy to supervise.

He'd hoped they'd play quietly, allowing him time to talk to Missy. He wanted to hear her say again that he didn't need to blame himself for Tomasina's death.

He sat in one of the wingback chairs that gave a view of the ranch. Missy sat in the other. He couldn't help but think how right this felt. It was a thought he'd previously had only in his dreams.

He relaxed, ready to enjoy a quiet spell, but Annie stood before them.

"I counted. This is the eighth day of Christmas."

He tried to think what the child meant.

Missy laughed. "So it is." She turned to Wade and gave him a special smile. "I thought they might forget about the twelve days of Christmas."

Annie shook her head. "We didn't forget."

Two little boys hovered nearby.

"Hmm." Missy looked thoughtful. "I wonder what we can do. The babies are sleeping so we'll have to do something quiet. Would you like to help me make up a story?"

Annie nodded, but Wade thought the boys looked doubtful.

"It will be fun," Missy assured them. "Wait while I get paper and pencil." She bustled away and returned with the supplies, then sat down and started writing. Over her shoulder Wade saw she was leaving blanks in the story.

"Okay, I'm ready." She asked the children questions such as who was their best friend, their favorite animal, what they liked to eat, and then used the answers to fill in the blanks of the story. Finally she read it aloud

and the children rolled on the floor at the silliness of a tale that began, "Once upon a time, a red apple found a piece of candy…"

Wade grinned. She was so good with the children, so creative and full of fun.

A scene flashed through his mind. Sharing many days like this with her…the children nearby, a feeling of peace in the room and a sense of unity and rightness filling his heart.

Was such a future possible? Even with God's help? If only he could be sure.

A noise drew his attention to the window. He turned to look out and saw a covered wagon approaching. Odd, he thought, as it was cold to be traveling about like that. As it came closer, he could make out a man and a woman atop the bench.

A shiver crossed Wade's shoulders though he didn't know why.

Chapter Fourteen

Even though they didn't touch, Missy felt Wade's sudden stiffening, and lifted her head from reading the story. She followed his gaze out the window to an approaching wagon. A man and woman passing through, traveling in the dead of winter. They must be lost or looking for a place to settle. Maybe Linette would prevail upon them to spend the rest of the winter on the ranch. But why Wade should furrow his brow over their arrival baffled Missy.

Eddie must have heard them approach, as well, for he came down the stairs and waited for the wagon to pull up to the house and the pair to descend. Then he opened the door.

"Happy New Year to you. Come on in. This is the Eden Valley Ranch. I'm the owner, Eddie Gardiner." He continued to speak as the pair stepped inside and shivered.

The man held out a hand. "I'm Fred Bauer. This is my wife, Mabel."

The bottom dropped out of Missy's heart. This was the couple with whom Wade had corresponded about

adopting the children. She reached for Joey and Annie and drew them close.

As Eddie hung their coats, Linette descended. "You must be cold. Come in and have tea with us."

They led the couple into the room. "May we introduce Missy Porter and Wade Snyder. And the children are—"

Wade was on his feet before she could finish. He caught Joey and Annie by the shoulders. "Go upstairs and stay there until I call you," he told them.

Joey grabbed Annie's hand as if sensing his uncle's seriousness, and the pair passed the Bauers, whose eyes followed their every move.

"Grady, you go with them," Linette said. She waited until the children were gone, then turned to the adults. "Let's go to the kitchen and then someone can tell me what's going on."

Missy waited until the Bauers were seated, before she settled across the table and tugged Wade's hand to get him to sit beside her. He was so stiff his bottom barely touched the chair.

Linette made tea and set out cookies. Eddie made polite conversation about the weather, but responses to his questions were short. The tension around the table was thick enough to cut with a knife and spread on fresh bread.

Linette poured the tea, then sat down. She turned to the Bauers. "You are more than welcome, but we need to know your intentions."

"I'll answer that," Wade said. "These are the people who want to adopt Joey and Annie."

Mr. Bauer leaned forward, earnest and eager. "We couldn't wait until the stagecoach ran again, or until

spring, when travel would be easier. So we left shortly after Christmas. We're that anxious to meet the children and take them home with us." He held up a hand as if fearing protests. "We have the wagon outfitted to keep us warm, and will stop at a way station should a storm blow in."

"Storms don't always send out advance notice," Wade said, his voice deep, as if he'd pulled it from the depths of a dark well.

"We won't be taking any risks. Might even stay in Edendale if there's a place available." Mr. Bauer seemed willing to make whatever concessions he deemed necessary.

"Can we meet the children?" Mrs. Bauer spoke for the first time. Her voice was surprisingly guttural.

All eyes turned toward Wade.

Missy wanted to grab his hand and hold on, whether to encourage him or comfort herself, or perhaps to do both, she didn't know.

Wade jerked to his feet, sending the chair skidding away. "I'll get them." He strode from the room without once looking at Missy.

A vise squeezed her chest, so tight she couldn't draw in a satisfying breath. Her heart struggled to pump out blood. She wanted to rush after him and demand he send the Bauers away, but her papa's saying once again rang in her head and stopped her. *A man convinced against his will is of the same opinion still.* Nothing she said would change Wade's mind. He must be persuaded in his own heart what was best for the children.

At least the Bauers seemed like decent people, she

thought, even if Mrs. Bauer had a rather unpleasant voice. That was no reason to judge her harshly.

Wade's boots sounded on the steps as he descended, as did the patter of smaller feet.

"We gonna have cookies?" Annie's childish voice rang with pleasure. She might not have been quite so excited if she knew what lay before her.

Wondering what the Bauers thought, Missy shifted enough to see them without appearing to watch them. Mrs. Bauer pursed her lips.

Was she disapproving of something, Missy wondered, or only trying to control her emotions?

The three children rushed into the room.

Linette called Grady to her side and Wade clamped his hands on the shoulders of the other two. "Mr. and Mrs. Bauer, these are my niece and nephew, Annabelle and Joseph. We call them Annie and Joey."

The children politely said how do you do.

Annie squirmed under Mrs. Bauer's scrutiny, until Linette had the three children join them at the table. She gave them each two cookies, which they ate hurriedly. Joey darted glances at the Bauers, wondering, no doubt, why he was the subject of their blatant interest.

"You may be excused," Linette said, when the children finished.

"I'll take them upstairs." Missy led them to Nate and Louise's room so they wouldn't overhear anything said in the kitchen. Nate was rocking Chloe while Louise folded baby clothes, so Missy pulled her friend aside and explained the situation.

Louise nodded. "I'll keep them amused here."

Missy hurried back to the kitchen, not wanting to miss anything that was said.

"We'd like to spend some time alone with them," Mr. Bauer was saying as she entered.

"I'm sure that can be arranged." Wade looked to Linette. "Perhaps they could use the office."

"By all means." Linette managed to look as if this was a normal course of events, but Missy wondered if that's how she felt.

For her part, Missy wanted to grab Wade by the shoulders and shake him until he came to his senses.

"We'd like to conduct this business as quickly as possible," Mr. Bauer added.

"The children need time to get used to you." Missy didn't care that it was not her responsibly. When it came to seeing Joey and Annie were given proper consideration, she made it her business.

Mrs. Bauer pursed her lips, yet somehow managed to speak. "And who are you?"

Wade answered before Missy could get a word out. "I hired Miss Porter to take care of the children until you came."

Hired! Until she could be replaced! The thought burned through Missy's brain. Was that all she was? Paid for and replaceable? Why had she let herself think otherwise?

But then an image of Annie and Joey flashed through her mind and her anger fled as quickly as it came. This wasn't about her. It was about the children and what they needed.

For some reason, she did not like the Bauers. Yes, she admitted it might be only because they wanted to

adopt the children, and Missy loved them too much to see them go.

But it was more than that, though she was at a loss to say what bothered her about them.

Wade fought to remind himself that this was what was best for the children—both a mother and a father. A permanent home. But didn't like the Bauers. Plain and simple, for no other reason than they'd shown up on New Year's Day just when he was thinking he might be ready to reconsider his future.

But he'd asked for a sign from God and this was it.

It wasn't fair to Mrs. Bauer to compare her to Missy, and yet he did. She had a husky voice and looked to be near thirty. From the darkness of her skin, she must work outdoors with her husband.

The idea nudged something inside him, but he couldn't pinpoint exactly what it was. Perhaps just the thought of a woman working like a man. He knew of some women who actually were forced to pull a plow. Which, to his way of thinking, was no way for man to treat his wife.

He appreciated Missy's concern that the children be given time to get to know the Bauers. "I won't be agreeing to them leaving with you until they're ready."

Mr. Bauer's expression hardened. "They'll get used to us on the road." His voice softened measurably. "But of course I understand your concern."

Almost satisfied they had an understanding, Wade agreed to bring the children to the office and let the Bauers have a little time with them.

Missy followed him from the room. "What are you going to tell them?"

"Tell who?" He could barely get a coherent thought from his brain, so didn't know what she meant.

"The children. Aren't they going to wonder why they are to spend time alone with perfect strangers? Though I'm not sure they're perfect by any means."

Wade stopped so suddenly she bumped into him.

"I haven't thought what I'd say to them." He scrubbed a hand on the back of his neck. "I guess I'll tell them the truth. The Bauers are going to adopt them."

Missy grabbed his elbow and shook it. "You've made up your mind a few minutes after meeting them?"

His head hurt. He couldn't think. Hadn't he already reasoned this all out when he'd let it be known the children were available for adoption? Hadn't he thought the Bauers sounded ideal when they'd contacted him? "I made up my mind before I met them." The pounding inside his head grew louder. He felt as if there were little people in his skull attacking it with sledgehammers.

"I'm sorry, but you simply can't make this kind of decision without proper consideration." Missy crossed her arms and faced him in silent challenge.

He made to edge around her, but she wouldn't budge. "Fine. I'll reserve my decision until I get to know them better."

"So what do you plan to tell Joey and Annie?"

The way Missy stuck out her chin, he understood she wasn't letting him pass without an answer that satisfied her.

He tossed his hands up in frustration. "What do you suggest I tell them?"

"Do you really care what I suggest?" Her nostrils flared.

"Of course I do." He caught her hand and stopped it fluttering. "Tell me."

She drew in a deep breath. "I think you should tell the Bauers to leave, and then figure out how you can keep the children." Missy must have seen the protest in his eyes. "See, you're not going to do that, are you? But if you insist on giving them to the Bauers—" Tears filled her eyes and she couldn't go on.

He wiped the droplets from her cheeks with the pad of his thumb. He didn't like being the cause of her unhappiness, but what could he do? He'd already made arrangements with the Bauers and his reasons hadn't changed.

A tiny thought forced its way through his confusion. Maybe *he* had changed.

Before he could contemplate that idea further, Missy drew his attention.

"Why not tell Joey and Annie the Bauers want to know what it would be like to have two children just like them?"

Wade accepted her suggestion and they continued up the stairs. She stood at his side as he squatted to eye level to talk to the children.

Annie eagerly agreed. "They'd like having two children, wouldn't they?"

Joey wasn't as easily convinced. "Where would they get two children?" The fierce, defiant look he gave Wade informed him that Joey suspected this might be what Wade had in mind for them. *Oh, please, Joey, don't do something crazy.*

Nevertheless his nephew obediently accompanied Wade and Annie down the stairs, with Missy at their heels.

The Bauers waited in the office and Wade ushered the children in. He paused to see what would happen.

Mr. Bauer asked the children to step forward, and looked Joey up and down as if measuring him. "Let's see you make a muscle."

Joey did.

Mr. Bauer smiled. "You're a strong lad, aren't you?"

Mrs. Bauer ran her gaze up and down Annie. "You say you're five?"

She nodded.

Mrs. Bauer appeared troubled. "I thought you'd be bigger."

Annie drew herself up tall. "I am bigger."

Mr. Bauer saw Wade hovering in the doorway. "We'll be fine. You can leave."

They might be, but Wade would never be fine again.

Missy watched from the kitchen doorway and seemed to sense his condition. She took his hand, led him to the table and pushed him into a chair. She poured coffee and set it before him.

He stared at the cup without understanding what he should do.

"Drink. It will make you feel better."

He drank, though he knew nothing in a cup had the power to make him feel better.

He couldn't say how long the children were in the office with the Bauers. None of them said a word as they returned, the Bauers to the kitchen, the children upstairs to join Grady.

The Bauers gave no indication of what they thought. But then, why should they? Their decision had been made weeks ago.

Somehow Wade made it through the rest of the day.

Somehow he managed to answer questions and respond to the conversation around him as the Bauers joined them at the table for supper. But he couldn't have told anyone what was said. Bedtime arrived and he was only too glad to go upstairs with the children. He had no intention of rejoining the adults when the children were tucked in bed.

As he helped them prepare for the night, Joey's eyes followed Wade's every move, accusing and condemning. But no doubt the boy understood that he couldn't say anything in front of Annie lest he upset her.

Wade tucked them in, heard their prayers, then retired to his own room. He would read awhile, he decided, and crawled into bed with a book. Unfortunately, the story did not hold his attention. He was about ready to turn out the lamp and stare into the darkness when Joey tiptoed into the room.

He glowered at Wade.

"You're going to make us go with those people, aren't you?"

Wade stared at the boy, uncertain what he should say. "Joey, I promised your mama I would make sure you got a good family to live with."

"I don't like them."

"Why not?" Joey hadn't had time to form such a definite opinion.

"I just don't. And I'm not going with them." He crossed his arms and slammed them to his chest.

Wade closed his eyes and tried to find a reasonable argument. He simply couldn't. "Joey, sometimes in life we don't get to do what we want."

Joey gave him a look of pure disbelief, then stomped back to his room.

Wade stared at the ceiling. The Bauers were a nice couple. Hardworking. Obviously dedicated, to come all this way in the dead of winter. They'd be an ideal family for Joey and Annie.

Was he looking for a way to convince Joey…or himself?

The next morning, the Bauers suggested Joey and Annie show them around the ranch.

Annie smiled. "That will be fun."

Joey scowled, but donned his coat.

Wade figured the boy went along simply to protect his little sister. Wade would have liked to follow the four of them, to guard the children. Instead, he stood before the window watching them. Joey scuffed along behind the Bauers and Annie raced ahead, turning often to point out something.

Missy joined him at the window. "Joey understands what this is all about, doesn't he?"

"Uh-huh."

"He's none too pleased."

"It means another big change in his life, but the sooner he gets settled permanently, the better for him." Wade hoped she wouldn't badger him about keeping them. He didn't know how he would answer her without revealing the depth of his despair over what he must do. Of course, she'd suggest he could choose to do otherwise. He wished he could believe it was possible.

Thankfully she said nothing, but continued to watch the foursome outside. Not that any words were needed to communicate her unhappiness. Her feelings were very evident.

The tour ended back at the house and the children escaped upstairs.

Mr. and Mrs. Bauer took their time about shedding their winter coats. Finally, they stepped into the room and glanced around. Only Wade and Missy were there.

"We need to talk," Mr. Bauer said, as he and his wife sat side by side in wooden chairs.

Wade grabbed two more chairs and placed them across the room from the Bauers. He indicated he wanted Missy to sit beside him. Despite her disapproval, he didn't want to face the final plans on his own, and knew she'd offer him comfort even if she didn't agree with his decision.

Mr. Bauer cleared his throat. "We've decided we'd like to take the boy, but the girl is smaller than we thought."

Smaller? What did that have to do with anything? Wade wondered. She was bright and cheerful, the kind of child to brighten any home.

"It would be several years before she's of any use," Mrs. Bauer growled.

Missy gasped. "You only want them to work."

The truth of her observation slammed through Wade's heart. And the Bauers didn't even look guilty about it. He'd almost made the most colossal mistake of his life.

Wade rose to his feet. "I'm not prepared to sell my nephew as a slave. I'm sorry. The children are no longer available for adoption."

Mr. Bauer pushed to his feet, his hands hanging at his sides. "I thought we had an understanding."

"I obviously misunderstood your intentions. Neither of them will be going with you." He grabbed

Missy's arm and hustled her out of the room and up the stairs. He had no idea where he meant to take her, but he didn't slow his steps until he reached the end of the hall.

The children heard their footfalls and peeked out of Grady's room, their expressions revealing both concern and curiosity.

Wade turned his back to them, not wanting them to see his anger.

He looked into Missy's face. "Now what?"

She smiled and smoothed her hand along his arm. The touch went clear to his heart and wiped away the tension. "You'll think of something and it will be better by far than the Bauers."

"I don't know what."

Her eyes flashed. But he cut her off before she could again tell him he must keep the children. "I would if I could. But I'm nothing but a homeless cowboy."

I could help you. Missy almost blurted out the words, but caught herself in time. He'd want someone older, more mature. Someone willing to care for the children while he did his cowboying. Someone convenient. She loved the children and would gladly devote her life to caring for them, but she wanted to be so much more than a convenience. That was almost as bad as being a necessary nuisance.

"You could rent a house in town, find a housekeeper and pay her to care for them." The words seared Missy's throat. It wasn't ideal. The children would be heartbroken. "Of course, you'd need to check in on them often and make sure they were doing okay."

"I suppose so." He turned away.

He didn't like the suggestion? Good. Maybe he'd realize he needed to be the one who cared for the children. They deserved love more than they needed a good home and two parents. Even as she thought it Missy knew he couldn't manage on his own. *I'll help you.* Again the words almost escaped.

There came a noise from downstairs and they hustled to the landing to peer down. The Bauers had donned their coats and were thanking Linette for her hospitality.

"We have no further need to delay our return." Mr. Bauer's gaze met Wade's and he gave him a look of accusation.

Linette bade them goodbye and watched in silence as they climbed aboard their wagon and departed. Then Wade and Missy went down the steps to watch out the window as the Bauers trundled down the road and out of sight.

"Anyone care to tell me what happened?" Linette asked. Eddie had joined her, and Louise and Nate stood nearby. Missy could feel their concern. They all knew Wade had planned to let the Bauers adopt the children, just as they knew he was expected to take over a ranch for his friend and would have to leave soon.

He scrubbed at his neck. "They only wanted Joey because they deemed him big enough to work." His voice hardened. "The children need a home. Does anyone know of a woman willing to be a housekeeper? I could set her up to take care of the children."

So he was planning to give her suggestion a try. Missy felt no satisfaction, only disappointment.

She looked up to find Louise giving her a considering look. Her sister-in-law raised her eyebrows as if

to ask why Missy hadn't volunteered. But the question she should be asking was why hadn't Wade asked Missy?

And what would she say if he did?

Chapter Fifteen

Missy didn't have to come up with an answer to her question, because Wade never asked. Eddie said he knew of a woman who had recently joined her sister and brother-in-law in town, and made it known she would welcome a position.

"Is there a house available in town?" Wade asked.

"I believe there is," Eddie said. "Shall we go in tomorrow and look into it?"

Wade nodded, a thoughtful expression on his face.

Missy went to the kitchen and started cooking up enough food to feed them three times over. She had to keep busy. It was the only way she could keep from speaking her mind. The children didn't need a housekeeper. They needed a family. A mother and a father who loved them. A picture flew into her mind of a loving family. She gasped as the picture sharpened and the truth of her heart revealed Wade as the father and herself as the mother.

Her hands grew idle, her breathing rapid as the truth grew clearer. That's what she wanted. Had perhaps wanted from the beginning. She loved the chil-

dren, but she loved Wade just as much…his sacrificial,
soul-deep loving; his gentleness and his…everything
about him. Her joy at acknowledging how much she
cared rushed through her until she had to clamp her
teeth to keep from shouting and laughing. She would
marry him in a heartbeat if he would only ask. She
would spend the rest of her life making him and the
children happy.

But she wouldn't settle for being a housekeeper. Nor
would she settle for a marriage of convenience. She
wanted it all—love and marriage, husband and children, and a love to live for.

She busied herself in the kitchen the rest of the afternoon, pausing from her labors only long enough
to eat. At all costs she would avoid being alone with
Wade. Her heart was too fragile at the moment.

It was easy to keep away from Wade the next day,
as he left for town early, in Eddie's company. She continued to create a flurry of work in the kitchen.

It turned out Louise was the one she needed to
avoid.

"Missy, are you going to stand aside and let him put
the children in the care of a stranger? Someone paid
to look after them?"

Missy pretended a great deal of interest in shaping
cookies, and refused to look at Louise. "I fail to see
how I can stop him."

"You can tell him how you feel."

That brought Missy's attention to her sister-in-law.
"What are you suggesting?"

"I'm saying tell the man you love him. Tell him
you're—"

Missy shook her head hard. "I've spent enough of my life being a nuisance. I won't settle for being a convenience. Once the children leave the ranch I'll go to town and tell Macpherson I'm ready to take the job he offered. By March I'll have enough money to start my course." She clamped her teeth together and turned back to the cookies.

Louise shook her head. "I can't believe this is what you want."

Sometimes a person couldn't have what she wanted. Hadn't Missy learned that when her parents had died? When Gordie was killed? And in hundreds of little things along the way?

Wade and Eddie returned late in the day.

"Well, it's done." Wade sounded weary. "The housekeeper is putting the final touches on the place and I take the children in tomorrow."

Missy had vowed to keep silent, but found she had to speak up on behalf of the children. "I hope you mean to spend some time with them and not just toss them in with a stranger."

"I plan to stay a few days." He certainly did not sound enthused about it.

"Do you mind if I go with you tomorrow?"

"You're going to make sure everything is as it should be?"

"I'd like to see where they'll be living. But since my job here with the children is done, I, too, am moving on to something new. Macpherson is expecting me to run the store for him so he can go visit his daughter."

Somehow that assignment didn't inspire as much excitement in her as it first had. But at least she'd be in the same vicinity as the children and would get to see them occasionally.

* * *

The children sat between Missy and Wade on the way to town. Missy's entire body felt brittle, ready to shatter into dull, lifeless fragments.

"Is she a nice woman?" Annie asked, her little voice thin with worry.

"She seemed nice enough," Wade answered. He looked to Missy, but if he expected her to offer encouragement, he would have to look elsewhere. She'd done her best last night to prepare the children, pointing out how it meant Uncle Wade would be their guardian and spend lots of time with them when he came back from spending the winter at the ranch.

It about broke her heart when Joey had asked, "Why can't you be the one to care for us?"

She hadn't said because Wade hadn't asked. If he had, even knowing she wanted so much more, she wasn't sure she would have said no.

Now Joey sat in the wagon with a wooden look on his face, knowing he didn't have any choice about the way things were turning out. Oh, how well she knew that feeling. She squeezed his shoulder and gave him a smile of encouragement. At least she'd been able to reassure the children that she'd be in town and nearby for a few weeks. If they needed anything, they could come to her.

They reached town and pulled up a side street to a small house. Smoke came from the chimney and crisp white curtains hung at the windows. Had the woman made the curtains already or did she have some prepared just in case?

Wade helped them all down and escorted them in-

side. "Mrs. Williams, these are the children. And this is Missy Porter, who has been caring for them."

The older woman, somewhat stout with her hair in a tight, gray bun greeted Missy cordially enough, then reached for the children's bags. "Let's get you two settled."

The children obediently, if somewhat guardedly, followed Mrs. Williams across the room. She pointed to the bedroom and they dropped their belongings on the bed, then hovered at the doorway, misery and sadness twisting their faces.

Missy scrubbed her lips together and held back tears. This was Wade's decision and she could do nothing about it except wish and pray he'd change his mind.

She looked around. Everything looked neat and if it felt somewhat sterile that would soon be changed by the presence of two little people. Mrs. Williams smiled and nodded at the children who stared at her uncertainly before they glanced at Missy. She gripped her hands together to keep from rushing to them and holding them tight. There was nothing for Missy to do here. "I'll go tell Macpherson I'm here to work."

"You'll be back?" Wade asked.

She almost felt sorry for him, he looked so miserable. "Sure. I'd like to speak to the children after they're settled. Will you be here?"

He nodded. "I told you. I'm going to stay with them for a few days."

"I'll see you later then." She reached out and squeezed his hand. She couldn't help herself. "I'm glad you're not giving them away, at least." Before he could respond, and before she broke into tears, she hurried out the door.

She didn't slow down until she was out of sight of the house, then she paused to catch her breath and sort her thoughts. He'd be in town a few days. She'd be in town. Surely they'd see each other. And if God answered her prayers, Wade would start to see that the children needed a family and—

She'd almost convinced herself she'd marry him if he asked, even if it wasn't for love, but only to provide a home for the children. She could learn to be happy without having the love her heart yearned for.

As she made her way to the store, she wondered if she would eventually regret settling. Or—hope flared in her heart—perhaps Wade would learn to love her.

She reached the store and stepped inside.

"Morning, Mr. Macpherson."

"People just call me Macpherson."

"Okay. I told you I'd come back when I was no longer needed to care for the children. I'm here and I'm ready to take over so you can go see your daughter."

Macpherson stared at her. "I guess I should have let you know."

She waited, her heart flopping like a fish out of water. "Let me know what?" she asked after several seconds of silence.

Instead of answering he went to the door leading to his living quarters. "Becca, come here."

A blue-eyed young woman stepped into the store, a boy and girl at her side. Dark-eyed little children that reminded Missy of Joey and Annie.

Macpherson drew the trio closer. "This is my daughter, Becca, and her children, Marie and Little Joe. They've come to visit so I don't need to leave."

Missy couldn't think what to do. She felt as if she'd been struck by a runaway wagon.

"I'm not leaving so I don't need your help. I'm very sorry."

"I understand." She stumbled from the store and hurried around to the back, out of sight of any passersby. She leaned against the corner of the building and struggled to pull in enough air to satisfy her tight lungs. Now what? She had nothing. No place to go. No future. Yes, she could return to the ranch. Linette said she was welcome anytime. She planned to visit regularly. But she'd hoped to board in town and work at the store. How was she to earn money to go to the secretary school with no job?

A wagon drew up to the back of the store and she hurried on, making her way toward the trees along the river, where she might find solitude and be able to figure out what to do next.

Was there somewhere else in town she might find employment? Or on one of the nearby farms? Perhaps the OK Ranch. But she didn't want to leave town. Not with the children living there. Not while Wade was still in the area.

Oh, how tangled were her thoughts. She bowed her head. *Lord, I feel like I'm in a deep pit. Please help me.* It was a prayer of desperation, but she had no one else to turn to. *I need—*

Her prayer was cut off when a pair of arms came around her.

She struggled to pull away, but was imprisoned by heavy arms covered in a dark, odorous coat. A scream rose to her mouth, but before she got more than a squeak out, a large gloved hand covered her lips.

"Did you think you could get away?"

She recognized the voice. Even without looking at his face she knew who it was. Vic. The fear that threatened to turn her muscles to pudding would not be allowed to control her. She kicked every which way. She twisted and turned, determined to escape.

He squeezed hard until her lungs fought to work as he dragged her into the trees, where no one would see them. "You can fight all you want, but I've waited too many years to let you go."

Weak from lack of air, she grew limp in his arms. Certain he had conquered her, he relaxed his grip. She gasped in strengthening air and with a mighty shove escaped his grasp.

He lunged after her, caught her coattail and stopped her flight.

She turned, faced him, poised for an opening, but every time she moved he dodged to prevent her escape.

"You're mine now. All mine. I wanted Louise, too, and had a sale for that baby of hers, but all I've ever wanted is you."

"I'm not yours and never will be." She'd fight to the death. His death, if need be. She'd been at the mercy of others far too many years and wasn't about to become so again. And certainly not at the mercy of this vile creature.

Wade carried in the boxes containing the children's belongings. The house was pleasant enough and certainly roomy. A married man with four or five children—no one seemed to know how many for certain—had built it only a few months ago, and lived in it until recently, when his wife took ill and he'd

moved his family closer to medical help. The curtains had been left at the windows, along with the basic essentials and furniture. What else Wade needed came from Macpherson's store or from extras at the Eden Valley Ranch.

Yesterday, he'd set up beds in the three bedrooms. Now he took his own things into the one he'd chosen and sat on the edge of the mattress.

He was now owner of a house. One step closer to what he had vowed he would never again allow himself. Two steps, counting the children. All that remained to fulfill his long-denied and dashed dreams was a woman who loved him. One who was strong enough to deal with his failures and the disappointments of life in general.

He didn't even try to push away the picture that came to mind. Of Missy flying about the kitchen, bending over one of the children, to listen or give instructions. Longing pinched the back of his heart as he thought of her comforting touch, of the times he'd felt they agreed on things, of her kisses. He'd never be able to forget them.

He'd never be able to forget *her*.

She owned a large portion of his heart. He would forever cherish her. Several times in the past day he'd considered asking her to forsake her plans to become a secretary, but how could he? She had good reason for wanting to be on her own, to feel as if she wasn't anyone's duty.

Being his wife would make her his responsibility. One he feared he'd fail at. But he was more than half willing to take the risk for the pleasures being married to Missy would bring.

He pushed himself to his feet and went to see what else needed to be done in the house. He'd have firewood delivered, but in the meantime he had to provide enough to keep them warm, and went out back to chop wood.

A little later he returned to the house. The children were sitting at the table, pieces of brown store paper before them.

Joey sent him an accusing look. Annie chewed on her bottom lip.

Wade peered over their shoulders and saw Joey had a row of arithmetic problems before him and Annie had letters to copy.

Mrs. Williams bent over the oven, removing a tray of biscuits.

It was on the tip of Wade's tongue to say the children could be allowed a few more days of enjoying Christmas. After all, he and Missy had promised them twelve days of Christmas and this would only be day ten, but perhaps it was best for them to get into a routine.

Christmas was over and all that remained were the memories. Memories that left a hollow ache in his gut.

"Will your friend be joining us for dinner?" Mrs. Williams asked.

"Missy? I expect so."

"I hope she comes soon. The meal is almost ready."

Realizing the late hour, he said, "She should have been back by now." He headed for the door. "I'll go check on her." Perhaps Macpherson had been ready to leave at a moment's notice and Missy was in charge. Wade grinned at the idea of going into the store and

lingering over the candy counter as Missy hovered nearby.

When he clattered up the steps into the store, Macpherson stood behind the counter. Wade told himself he wasn't disappointed to see the man.

"What can I do for you?" Macpherson asked.

"I came for Miss Porter. She'll be joining us for dinner."

"She left some time ago. I'm not sure where she went. She was a tad disappointed that I didn't need her to help at the store anymore."

Though he wanted to ask why, Wade turned about, intent on finding Missy. Perhaps she'd gone to visit the Mortons. In which case, he would have missed her as she returned to the house. But the way the back of his neck prickled, he knew there was something wrong. He needed to find her.

"Say, you know you're the second fella to ask after her this morning."

At Macpherson's statement Wade stopped midstride and slowly brought himself around to face the shopkeeper again. "Someone else asked after her? Did you get his name?"

"Didn't ask. I've learned a lot of people don't care for questions."

Fear scampered up his spine. Could it have been Vic?

"I didn't much care for the look of that other fella. I consider myself a pretty good judge of character and I'd say he was not an upstanding citizen, if you know what I mean."

Wade knew all too well. He was out the door so fast he probably left boot marks on the floor, but once

outside, he hesitated. Where would she go? If Vic had found her, he'd drag her to a place where he could hope to avoid detection. His heart hammering against his ribs hard enough to break them, Wade dashed toward the river. As he neared, he slowed his steps. Surprise would be his greatest weapon, so he must approach quietly.

He paused to listen for a telltale sound. A crackling came from his right and he made his silent way in that direction. He saw that the snow had been trampled before him and he prayed it was her trail he was tracking.

Wade ducked under some overhanging branches. A stand of spruce provided perfect cover for anyone hiding, so he skirted the trees as quietly as possible. A small clearing came into view and that was when he saw them: Missy and a man he knew had to be Vic circling each other like boxers looking for an opening. Wade's breath froze and his heart refused to beat.

He had to save her. This time he would not fail. He would not be absent when the woman he loved needed him.

He had come without weapons or he'd shoot the man on the spot. Instead, he had to choose a weapon from what lay at hand and he looked about for something suitable.

But before he located anything, Missy lurched to one side and Vic went after her.

Wade's heart clambered up his throat and stayed there, quivering with fear. He crouched, ready to spring to her defense, but before he could move, Missy grabbed a hefty looking branch from the snow and swung it with all her might, landing a blow to Vic's

head. The man went down, falling into the snow so quietly Wade could hardly believe it was real.

Missy stood over her fallen opponent, the branch lifted, ready to protect herself further. But Vic didn't move. She nudged him with her foot. "Did I kill you?" Her voice quavered, whether from fear she might have killed him or fear she hadn't, Wade couldn't guess. Perhaps a bit of both.

Without a second of delay, he bashed his way through the snow and underbrush, and swept her into his arms.

Realizing it was him, she came readily, shaking and crying. "Is he dead?"

Wade kept his eye on the man while comforting Missy, but detected no movement. He held her in one arm, not wanting to ever let her go again, and bent to feel the body for a pulse. "It's Vic, isn't it?"

She let out a breath that sounded more like a sob. "Wade Snyder, meet Vic Hector. Is he dead?"

Wade felt a pulse in the man's throat. "Nope. Very much alive. We need to take him to the Mountie."

She snorted. "How are we going to do that?"

Vic moaned and grabbed his head. He was coming to and no doubt he'd be good and angry.

"Here, get on your feet." Wade grabbed the man and dragged him upward. Vic swayed so badly Wade needed both hands to keep him upright. "Better bring along that branch in case you need it again," he told Missy.

"You can count on it." She followed close at Wade's heels as he and Vic staggered from the trees toward the Mountie's office and jail. All the way, she carried the branch before her, ready to defend herself.

Something about that thought circled in Wade's brain, but he didn't have time to dwell on it.

The Mountie must have been looking out the window, for he met them before they reached the place. "Constable Allen here, at your service. What do we have here?"

"Vic Hector," Wade grunted.

"We've been looking for him." The lawman grabbed one of Vic's arms. "You are under arrest for kidnapping and various other crimes."

Wade helped get the man into jail. "Does he need a doctor?"

"There is no local doc. He'll have to make do with me." The Mountie took a statement from both Wade and Missy. Satisfied at last, he told them they could go, promising Vic would never again be a threat to them or anyone else.

Vic shouted his displeasure from the cell. Not until they reached the street again did Wade let the full impact of Missy's danger hit him. She might have been killed. He would have missed the opportunity to tell her he loved her.

He didn't mean to miss another opportunity.

"Thank you for coming for me and for helping get Vic to jail." Her voice shook just enough to inform him how frightened she'd been.

He wrapped one arm about her shoulders and pulled her close. If they weren't in the middle of the main street of Edendale he would have kissed her.

"How did you know to come?" He couldn't tell if she sounded relieved or just plain curious.

"I knew when you didn't return to the house in a timely manner, and when you weren't at the store, that

there was something wrong." The truth of his words hit him like a blow to the head. He'd known she needed him. He'd seen what she needed. Was it possible he had changed? That he now could trust himself to love and take care of someone when necessary?

He recalled her standing there hefting the tree branch. "Truth is you didn't need me to take care of you. You can take care of yourself."

She stared at him. "I believe you're right. At least in this instance." A smile tugged at her lips.

"Come on. Let's go home before the children begin to worry."

Home. The word echoed through him. Was it possible he could do more now than simply dream of a home?

Chapter Sixteen

Missy vibrated to the core of her being with a mixture of fear and victory. She'd taken care of herself in a dangerous situation. Whether she became a secretary or not, she would carry that knowledge with her. She need never again feel she was a burden to anyone. From now on, she knew she could take care of herself.

But as they continued on to the house Wade now owned, the sense of victory began to feel a little unsatisfying. Why wasn't it enough? Yes, it proved she was strong. That she could survive on her own. But that now seemed such a lonely thought.

They reached the house.

At the sound coming from within, she grabbed Wade's arm. "I hear yelling. And not in play."

Wade's expression darkened. "I know." He took her hand as he threw open the door.

The sight before them made Missy gasp. Mrs. Williams bent over Joey, her voice raised in harsh tones as she threatened to whip him if he didn't finish his work.

Annie crouched in the corner, her eyes filled with fear.

Wade stepped to Mrs. Williams. "What's going on here?"

Joey skittered away, huddling behind the rocking chair.

Missy scooped Annie into her arms and fled to the rocking chair to hold her tight, one hand pulling Joey to her side.

Mrs. Williams smoothed the front of her dress and faced Wade, her expression tight. "The boy defied me. Said he wasn't going to do the arithmetic. Said his uncle wouldn't make him. I intend to show him that while I'm caring for him, I am boss. He will do what I say." She shifted about as if trying to ease the strain on her corset. "It's necessary to establish one's authority from the onset."

"That is not the way to do it. You're being a bully. My niece and nephew don't need your methods. You have ten minutes to collect your things and leave."

With a mighty huff, Mrs. Williams headed for her room. "I'll not be staying where my authority is challenged."

"You'll not be staying at all. That's already been decided."

The children shivered in Missy's arms as Wade stood at the door, waiting for Mrs. Williams to leave. She took but half of her allotted time and stormed past Wade and out into the cold without so much as a goodbye.

He closed the door quietly behind her and let out his breath with a whoosh, then studied the frightened children. With a muffled groan he crossed the floor and squatted before Missy and her lapful of children.

"I am so sorry that happened. It's my fault. Can you ever forgive me?"

Annie threw herself into his arms, sobbing against his neck.

He held out an inviting hand to Joey who stiffened in Missy's arms a moment, then leaned forward into Wade's embrace. He held them both and lifted his eyes to Missy.

Seeing the misery and sorrow written in his gaze, she pressed her hand to his cheek. He closed his eyes and held the children until they grew restless.

Now was her chance to do something for him. To make him see what a good man he was.

"Children, would you please go play in your bedroom while your uncle and I talk?"

Joey took Annie's hand and led her away. He paused at the door to look back.

Sensing his fragile state of mind, Missy smiled. "It's okay. You're safe now."

Wade rose as the children left. He scrubbed at his neck. "I made rather a mess of that, didn't I?"

"On the contrary. I'd say you prevented a disaster."

His eyes sought an explanation.

"You could have let Mrs. Williams continue to use her methods."

He shook his head. "Her methods are far too severe. The children only need a gentle word to guide them."

"That's right." Missy smiled. "Did you hear what you said?"

"I said her methods are too severe."

"You said more than that. You said they only need a gentle word. Don't you see? You know what they need and you give it to them."

Realization dawned. "I guess I do." His shoulders sagged again. "But I can't look after them by myself. What am I going to do now?"

"You'll figure it out. You know what they need. You simply have to listen to your heart."

As he considered her advice, a slow smile came to his mouth. He pulled her into his arms. "If I were to follow my heart I would ask you to stay and take care of them. Will you?"

She loved the children and it was on the tip of her tongue to say yes, but she wanted so much more. "I want to be more than a temporary housekeeper."

He dropped his arms and stepped back. "You want to be a secretary."

"Not necessarily. Secretarial school is only a place where I hoped I'd find some value. Where I could do something that would make me feel independent." She now understood what she truly wanted was to be needed.

"You're needed here."

Yes, it was true, and she was sorely tempted to accept the position of housekeeper simply so she could stay with Wade and the children. But too often in the past she had been a convenience at best, a nuisance at worst. "I need to be more than a convenience."

He laughed, though she couldn't imagine what he saw as funny in her statement.

"You've pushed and prodded me since I saw you in town before Christmas," he finally said. "You've made me uncomfortable at times. But you've also given me something I haven't had in a long time—hope that the future was worth pursuing."

"I'm glad." And she truly was. But was he preparing

to pursue his future without her? What did she have to do or say in order to get him to confess he loved her?

She hesitated. Was she so certain he did? Yes. Her heart threatened to beat right out of her chest. Yes, she knew he loved her. The question was, did he know it?

"Missy, I realized something when I saw you and Vic. When I thought he was going to hurt you." Wade chuckled softly. "You turned the tables on him rather quickly." He sobered again. "At that moment, I realized I don't have to take care of you. You can take care of yourself."

A protest pressed against her teeth. True, she had defended herself, but… "It doesn't mean I don't need anyone."

"It doesn't?" He pulled her closer and trailed a finger along her cheek.

Wrought wordless by his touch, she could only shake her head.

"I'm looking to the future more and more now," he said.

She nodded. When had she ever been struck speechless before? And now, when she wanted so badly to say the things filling her heart, her tongue refused to work.

Wade's smile was gentle. "Which is not to say I might not make mistakes in the future. I might fail those I love."

A protest escaped her frozen tongue. "But not on purpose."

"Never on purpose." He continued his distracting way of stroking her face, when all she wanted was to hear him confess he loved her. "So you're not set on going to secretarial school?"

She grabbed him by his upper arms, momentarily

sidetracked by the strength beneath her palms. If she got her way, she'd get plenty of opportunity to admire his muscles in the future.

"Wade Snyder, I love you. Why would I want to go to secretarial school?"

His eyes widened, then a slow, bright-as-the-sun, sweet-as-the-moon smile lit his features. "What did you say?"

She gave him a bold look. "You heard me. Now what are you going to do about it?" Never in her life had she been so forward. Nor so sure of herself.

He tipped his head back and laughed. Then, still grinning, he pulled her to his chest. "This is what I'm going to do about it." He kissed her.

With all her heart and soul, she wanted to respond. But there was one thing she wanted even more, and she broke off the kiss.

"What's wrong?" he asked, his gaze lingering on her mouth.

"Haven't you forgotten something?"

"I don't think so. The woman I love has just said she loves me. What else is there to remember?"

Her heart overflowing, she chuckled. "You forgot to tell me you love me."

For a moment he looked confused. "Why, so I did. Missy Porter, I love you to the moon and back. I love you deeper, wider, farther than I thought was possible." He fell to one knee and took her hand. "Will you do me the favor of becoming my wife?"

"Let me think about it a moment." She pretended to give it serious contemplation while he waited on his knee. But she couldn't contain her joy. "Yes, I'll marry you. A thousand times over." She pulled him

to his feet, threw her arms around him and lifted her face for a kiss.

The look he gave her made her glow inside, and then she forgot everything as he kissed her. She'd come home. Back to love and belonging. She vowed she would do her best to provide the same for those in her home.

Wade could never have guessed at the whoops and hollers, the flurry of activity and the heap of comments that would ensue after his announcement that he and Missy meant to marry.

"We have decided to get married right away," he said when things quieted down. "There's the children to consider. They need a settled home."

"But Missy deserves a church wedding," Louise said. "It's what her parents would have wanted."

As soon as she said that, Wade knew he had lost any argument he might have before he launched it. "How long does it take to do a church wedding?" He foresaw months of preparation to perfect a thousand things he knew in the back of his mind must be done. "There isn't even a preacher here." And barely a church. The outside was done, the pews made, but he wasn't even sure what else needed doing.

Eddie held up his hand. "Constable Allen is able to perform marriages and he's in town for a day or two."

"How long would it take to find a suitable dress for Missy?" Wade pressed.

"I have something that will do, I believe," Linette said. "Unless she's got her heart set on something fancy. In that case we have to order yard goods and make the dress. That would take, oh, probably most

of the winter, unless we can persuade Petey to make a special trip for us."

Wade sensed she was teasing but he wasn't certain.

Missy shook her head vigorously. "I don't want a fancy dress. I just want to get married." She sat next to Wade, gripping his hand hard enough to make his fingers tingle. Or was that simply from the knowledge they would soon be married? His heart picked up its pace at the thought. He could hardly wait to share the rest of his life with Missy and the children. Perhaps many more children if God saw fit to allow it.

Eddie slapped his knee. "Then what's wrong with Saturday?"

Wade could not stop a grin from spreading clear across his face. "Saturday sounds ideal." Missy agreed before the words were out of his mouth.

The next day was a flurry of activity as the women baked up a storm in the kitchen, then disappeared upstairs to fit a dress for Missy.

Eddie took Wade to town to help prepare the church and speak to Constable Allen.

Cassie kindly offered to take care of the children for the day.

It wasn't until evening that Wade got a chance to speak to Missy alone. "Are we going to survive this?"

She laughed. "We certainly are, and we'll look back on our wedding day as a celebration shared by our friends." She grew pensive. "I only wish Mama and Papa could be here."

"And I wish my sister and her husband could be, too." He considered that for a moment. "But I suppose if they were here, we might never have met." It was a strange thought.

"Things have worked out in surprising ways," Missy concurred. "Perhaps if it wasn't for Vic, Louise and I might still be back in Montana. And I might still think I was a bother to everyone."

Wade pulled her into the circle of his arms. "I hope you never think that again. You are dearer than life to me. I expect as we spend our years together, our love will continue to grow, though at the moment, it hardly seems it could get any bigger."

She hugged him. "I might need to be reminded from time to time."

He smiled down at her in the moonlight. "I will spend the rest of my life looking for ways to remind you. But for now, will this do?" And he claimed her lips.

Epilogue

The children had stayed with Linette for two days
after the wedding, allowing Missy and Wade time to
be alone in the house in town. She would carry the
memory of those two days with her the rest of her life.
Wade had said their love would grow and grow with
time. She hadn't seen how that was possible when he
said it, but the past two days had proved it. She loved
him so much she wondered how she could contain it.
But she'd discovered a little secret. The best way to
deal with the overflow of her heart was to pour it into
loving acts and words to Wade. And once the children
returned, she'd share it with them.

She stood at the window, watching for Wade to arrive
with them. He'd left a while ago to fetch them home.
Home. She hugged herself. Home sweet home. That
gave her an idea. One of the first projects she'd tackle
would be to embroider a wall hanging with those words.

Though she wasn't sure which home she'd hang
it in.

A few days ago Wade had sent a messenger to tell

his friend that they would journey to the ranch in a few weeks.

"We'll take one step at a time," he'd told her then. "But if you and the children like the ranch, I'll accept Stuart's offer and become his partner."

She'd assured him she would be quite happy living in Edendale or on the ranch or wherever suited him, but she knew he needed to be able to ride his horse and herd his cows. "Ranch living will suit me just fine, and I know it will suit the children, too. All that matters to them is that we're together."

Right on cue, the wagon approached the house. She had the door open and was running to greet the children before the wheels stopped turning.

They raced from the wagon and straight into her arms.

"I've missed you two," she said as she hugged them and breathed in their familiar scent.

"We missed you, too," Annie assured her, and Joey hugged Missy about the neck.

The four of them entered the house together and let out a collective sigh of satisfaction.

Annie spoke for all of them. "This is better than twelve days of Christmas."

Missy pulled Wade to her side and gathered the children to them. "This is better than anything I ever dreamed." She kissed the tops of Annie's and Joey's heads, then turned to receive Wade's adoring kiss.

Her heart had found what it wanted and she couldn't be happier.

* * * * *

Dear Reader,

I loved writing this story of children finding a forever home at Christmas. I pray it will provide a healing touch to my readers.

Christmas is a special time for families, and ours is no different. Like many of you, I have struggled to balance the consumerism all about me and turn the focus to the true meaning of Jesus coming. Every year, I try and tell the Christmas story in some way to my family, and now especially to my grandchildren. I do the same at Easter and was encouraged when the little grandchildren remembered the Christmas story we had done and understood that Christmas baby was the same person who died on the cross. Without the Christmas baby there would be no Easter. Without Easter the Christmas story would have no meaning.

May God dwell richly in your hearts this season.

I love to hear from my readers. You can contact me at www.lindaford.org, where you'll find my email address and where you can find out more about me and my books.

Blessings,

Linda Ford

COMING NEXT MONTH FROM
Love Inspired® Historical

Available January 5, 2016

INSTANT FRONTIER FAMILY
Frontier Bachelors
by Regina Scott

Maddie O'Rourke is in for a surprise when handsome Michael Haggerty replaces the woman she hired to escort her orphaned siblings to Seattle—and insists on helping her care for the children he adores.

THE BOUNTY HUNTER'S REDEMPTION
by Janet Dean

When bounty hunter Nate Sergeant shows up and claims her shop belongs to his sister, widowed seamstress Carly Richards never expects a newfound love—or a father figure for her son.

THE TEXAS RANGER'S SECRET
by DeWanna Pace

Advice columnist Willow McMurtry needs to learn to shoot, ride and lasso for her fictional persona, and undercover Texas Ranger Gage Newcomb agrees to teach her. But as the cowboy lessons draw them closer, will they trust each other with their secrets?

THE BABY BARTER
by Patty Smith Hall

With their hearts set on adopting the same baby, can sheriff Mack Worthington and army nurse Thea Miller agree to a marriage of convenience to give the little girl both a mommy and a daddy?

LOOK FOR THESE AND OTHER LOVE INSPIRED BOOKS WHEREVER BOOKS ARE SOLD, INCLUDING MOST BOOKSTORES, SUPERMARKETS, DISCOUNT STORES AND DRUGSTORES.

LIHCNM1215

REQUEST YOUR FREE BOOKS!

2 FREE INSPIRATIONAL NOVELS
PLUS 2 *FREE* MYSTERY GIFTS

Love Inspired HISTORICAL

YES! Please send me 2 FREE Love Inspired® Historical novels and my 2 FREE mystery gifts (gifts are worth about $10). After receiving them, if I don't wish to receive any more books, I can return the shipping statement marked "cancel." If I don't cancel, I will receive 4 brand-new novels every month and be billed just $4.99 per book in the U.S. or $5.49 per book in Canada. That's a saving of at least 17% off the cover price. It's quite a bargain! Shipping and handling is just 50¢ per book in the U.S. and 75¢ per book in Canada.* I understand that accepting the 2 free books and gifts places me under no obligation to buy anything. I can always return a shipment and cancel at any time. Even if I never buy another book, the two free books and gifts are mine to keep forever.

102/302 IDN GH6Z

Name	(PLEASE PRINT)	
Address		Apt. #
City	State/Prov.	Zip/Postal Code

Signature (if under 18, a parent or guardian must sign)

Mail to the **Reader Service:**
IN U.S.A.: P.O. Box 1867, Buffalo, NY 14240-1867
IN CANADA: P.O. Box 609, Fort Erie, Ontario L2A 5X3

Want to try two free books from another series?
Call 1-800-873-8635 or visit www.ReaderService.com.

* Terms and prices subject to change without notice. Prices do not include applicable taxes. Sales tax applicable in N.Y. Canadian residents will be charged applicable taxes. Offer not valid in Quebec. This offer is limited to one order per household. Not valid for current subscribers to Love Inspired Historical books. All orders subject to credit approval. Credit or debit balances in a customer's account(s) may be offset by any other outstanding balance owed by or to the customer. Please allow 4 to 6 weeks for delivery. Offer available while quantities last.

Your Privacy—The Reader Service is committed to protecting your privacy. Our Privacy Policy is available online at www.ReaderService.com or upon request from the Reader Service.

We make a portion of our mailing list available to reputable third parties that offer products we believe may interest you. If you prefer that we not exchange your name with third parties, or if you wish to clarify or modify your communication preferences, please visit us at www.ReaderService.com/consumerschoice or write to us at Reader Service Preference Service, P.O. Box 9062, Buffalo, NY 14240-9062. Include your complete name and address.

LIHI5

SPECIAL EXCERPT FROM

Love Inspired HISTORICAL

Maddie O'Rourke is in for a surprise when handsome Michael Haggerty replaces the woman she hired to escort her orphaned siblings to Seattle—and insists on helping her care for the children he adores.

Read on for a sneak preview of
INSTANT FRONTIER FAMILY by **Regina Scott**,
available in January 2016 from Love Inspired Historical!

The children streamed past her into the school.

Maddie heaved a sigh.

Michael put a hand on her shoulder. "They'll be fine."

"They will," she said with conviction. By the height of her head, Michael thought one part of her burden had lifted. For some reason, so did his.

Thank You, Lord. The Good Word says You've a soft spot for widows and orphans. I know You'll watch over Ciara and Aiden today, and Maddie, too. Show me how I fit into this new picture You're painting.

"I'll keep looking for employment today," he told Maddie as they walked back to the bakery. "And I'll be working at Kelloggs' tonight. With the robbery yesterday, I hate to ask you to leave the door unlocked."

"I'll likely be up anyway," she said.

Most likely she would, because he had come to Seattle instead of the woman who was to help her. He still wondered how she could keep up this pace.

You could stay here, work beside her.

As soon as the thought entered his mind he dismissed it. She'd made it plain she saw his help as interference. Besides, though his friend Patrick might tease him about being a laundress, Michael felt as if he was meant for something more than hard, unthinking work. Maddie baked; the results of her work fed people, satisfied a need. She made a difference in people's lives whether she knew it or not. That was what he wanted for himself. There had to be work in Seattle that applied.

Yet something told him he'd already found the work most important to him—making Maddie, Ciara and Aiden his family.

Don't miss
INSTANT FRONTIER FAMILY
by Regina Scott,
available January 2016 wherever
Love Inspired® Historical books and ebooks are sold.

Copyright © 2016 by Harlequin Books, S.A.

LIHEXP1215R